PRAISE FOR GRANVILLE STREET

"Lamoureux's ability to help us understand the experiences a person who struggles with addiction goes through is as real as it gets."

Jim Scarpace, Executive Director,
Gateway Foundation

"You are quickly drawn into the personality of the characters and the complexity of their lives. The storyline is fascinating, nuanced, and believable."

Roger Stefani, PhD, Clinical Psychologist; President,
Hope for Healing Foundation

"No one steals a fifty inch television from Walmart because they want to watch Netflix at home. No one prostitutes themselves because they enjoy the sex. They do it to get money for narcotics. This novel depicts their struggles and their victories brilliantly."

Mark Lightfoot, Retired Staff Sergeant
Niagara Regional Police

"Lamoureux creatively plumbs the depths of the multiple layers of his characters' lives. An exciting must-read for parents, siblings, congregations, pastors, those in recovery, those incarcerated, and those simply wanting to understand the journey of people who struggle with this thorn in the flesh."

Jon E. McCoy, MDiv, PhD—Pastor,
North Northfield United Methodist Church

arris Clark

LOUIS LAMOUREUX

GRANVILLE STREET

— A NOVEL —

Published by Third Digital Inc.

ISBN: 978-0-9984071-1-1

Editor: Drew Weissman

Cover painting:
John Hawkins / johnhawkinsart.com

Cover design and interior formatting:
Mark Thomas / Coverness.com

To Paul,
and to all who suffer
from substance use disorder,
and to their loved ones

TUESDAY

CHAPTER ONE

Adam couldn't tell if the woman was alive or dead. He had to know, and if he could, he had to help.

A few minutes earlier, he'd been in the Starbucks on Granville Street enjoying a caramel frap, a treat he hadn't had for a while. He'd been mentally preparing for his first evening back at work, reading news on his phone about the Clinton/Trump election, and occasionally sharing smiles with the young women coming and going. His father had dropped him off and had lent him eight dollars. He'd walked only a block from Starbucks when he noticed her.

She was face-down on the sidewalk with her knees under her chest. He nudged her shoulder. "You okay?" No reaction. "Yo!" He pushed her more vigorously. Still no response. Turning her over, he saw a syringe pinned into her forearm. He removed it and placed it beside her. He shook her shoulders more, hoping for a response.

He yanked his phone from his front pocket to call 911 but stopped. The call would bring not only paramedics but also police, who might arrest her. He didn't wish that on anyone, even a stranger. Interaction with police wouldn't be good for him either, especially with his fingerprints now on the syringe. He listened to see if she was breathing. She seemed to be, but there was no other sign of life. She might get through it and wake up. She could also just stop breathing. Forever.

He stood up to think. Well-dressed people were walking by with accusing glances. He resented their judgement and dialed.

"911 operator. What's your emergency?"

"There's a woman unconscious on the street."

"Is she breathing?"

"I think so."

"Check again. Put your ear near her mouth and look at her chest."

Adam followed the instruction and this time couldn't detect anything. "I think she stopped breathing!"

"Where are you?"

He scanned for a landmark and an address. "Near the Harris Clark building. 551 Granville Street."

"Paramedics are on their way. Is there anything in her mouth?"

Adam put his phone on speaker, placed it on the ground, and squeezed her mouth open. "No, nothing."

"Okay. Tilt her head back, hold her nostrils closed, seal her mouth with yours, and blow two strong breaths into her."

He felt squeamish about the task but went ahead. Blow. Blow. Nothing. He tried again and again until he heard sirens and wondered if they were from police or paramedics. His hands became unsteady.

The sirens were now so loud, they hurt his ears. Adam sighed relief at the sight of the ambulance and the exiting paramedics. He told them the situation as one of them checked the woman's vitals and confirmed that she wasn't breathing. Adam heard the second set of sirens in the distance and knew what they entailed. He wanted to leave before police arrived but also wanted to stay in case he could help.

"Narcan," said the attending paramedic to her partner, who was already holding the small white container that looked like a bottle of nose spray.

Police arrived. Adam continued looking at the woman.

The paramedic inserted the nozzle of the container into the woman's right nostril and pushed the plunger. She placed a mask over the woman's mouth and pumped oxygen into her lungs. Adam was relieved to see the patient start to breathe. The paramedics had another Narcan container ready but didn't need it.

The woman opened her eyes, laid there for a few seconds, then tried to sit up. The paramedic put her hand behind the woman's back and helped her to a sitting position.

"What's your name, honey?" she asked.

"What?" The middle-aged woman looked around.

"What's your name?"

"Uh … Gabby. What's … what's going on?"

"You overdosed, and you stopped breathing. But you're okay now."

"Who are you?"

"I'm a paramedic. Just relax. There's a bad batch of heroin making the rounds. Looks like you got some. Fourteen people died in Chicagoland yesterday – more than normal."

The rescuer glanced at Adam, who was now answering questions from the police as he shifted his weight from one foot to the other. "This young man saved your life," she said, nodding her head toward him.

Gabby looked at the ambulance and all the equipment. "My insurance doesn't cover this."

"Don't worry about that right now. By the way, the police are here.

They want to talk to you. Then we need to take you to the hospital. They might accompany us."

Gabby remained sitting. "I don't need to go. I feel okay."

"It's procedure to take you to a hospital so they can monitor you for an hour or so."

"No, I'm really okay. I don't want *two* ambulance bills chasing me."

The paramedics had her sign a waiver, collected their things, and left. A few people had stopped to watch, and they also departed.

Adam relaxed as the two officers walked away from him, apparently believing his statement that he didn't know her and was not involved until she was unconscious. They approached Gabby. "We need to search you and ask you a few questions," said one of them.

Gabby looked at Adam and said, "Don't leave. I'd like to talk to you."

The officer continued. "What's your full name?"

"Gabrielle Jones."

"We need to look in your pockets."

"Fine." Gabby looked forward and raised her arms like people do for airport security.

He searched her bag and her pockets and found a couple of paperback novels, a library card, and a baggie with what appeared to be heroin residue. He held up the baggie. "Where'd you buy this?"

"I don't know."

"I bet you *do* know. If you cooperate with us, you may avoid going to jail tonight. Where'd you buy it?"

"Some guy … I never purchased from him before."

"What's his name?"

Gabby frowned, and her voice developed an attitude. "No idea. I wasn't planning to fraternize with him."

The questions and answers went back and forth until the radio on the other officer's belt squawked. "What's the location?" he said into the radio. "We're on our way." He looked back at Gabby. "We have an emergency to deal with, so we won't be arresting you today."

Before they left, the officer gave Gabby a card with his phone number. "Call us if you see the guy you bought from."

Gabby and Adam watched the police drive off. "They think I have a phone!" she blurted.

"You're lucky to be alive," he replied.

Now that she was conscious, Adam took a moment to examine her. She was wearing a blue jacket, jeans, and running shoes – everything a little soiled. She had shoulder-length straight dark hair that looked surprisingly well-combed. She was thin but not bony. Adam tried to guess her age. She *looked* around fifty but was probably in her early forties – a sign of her disease.

"I'm even luckier that I'm not in a police car on my way to jail. What's your name?"

"Adam." He still had some time before his meeting and wondered how she'd be, after receiving Narcan.

"Thanks for saving my life."

"The paramedics saved your life. How you feelin'?"

"I'm not feeling high anymore, I can tell you that. I've heard of Narcan, but I've never had it administered."

Adam was surprised at how well she spoke, and he detected spunk even though she had just come out of an overdose.

"You did save my life. I wish I could repay you in some way," she said.

Adam thought about the paramedics saying she should be watched for a while. "Do you feel good enough to walk? I have to go somewhere before I head to work later. Maybe you could walk with me for a bit. I could use the company."

"I'm certain you can find better company, but sure. Thanks."

Adam's destination was a few blocks east, so they sauntered in that direction. Late afternoon was giving way to early evening, and the sidewalks were becoming busy with business professionals on their way to the Terrace East train station to go home in other, smaller suburbs, or maybe to Chicago, doing the reverse commute thing. Maybe some were walking to one of the fancy apartments on or near Granville Street.

Terrace was a large suburban city about twenty-five miles outside Chicago. It had a population of 210,000 and had a busy downtown area that was centered on Granville Street and attracted not only Terrace's population, but also people from nearby towns. Bordering Terrace was Adam's hometown of Parkdale with a population of seventeen thousand. Parkdale was home to high-achieving residents and a competitive high school, from which Adam had graduated five years earlier.

They walked past the Cosmos Hotel, where two uniformed doormen stood under an awning, mentally tagging anyone who walked into the fancy establishment as either a guest or an undesirable. The Cosmos had a restaurant at the front, and in the summer, its tables sprawled out onto the sidewalk. Several outside tables were already occupied with people enjoying cocktails, probably to celebrate the end of the workday. Even on a Tuesday, these tables got taken early.

Two well-dressed women, their arms weighed down by shopping bags, walked past Gabby and Adam, looking eager to get to their next boutique or to one of the upscale restaurants. A disheveled teenager sat on a blanket behind an empty plastic container and a sign saying,

"Any Help Appreciated." Two tourist-looking twenty-something guys hauling backpacks examined a map on one of their phones. Probably a tourist guidebook had told them that a trip to Chicago must include a one-day venture to downtown Terrace.

Adam enjoyed hearing the familiar yet fresh sounds of cars, horns, large buses, pigeons, and whatever musical busker was at work. Gabby seemed to be walking okay, but he wondered if the late summer heat might be getting to her.

"How you feelin'?" he asked.

"I'm okay. I'm kind of overheated, but who isn't in this weather?"

They reached Adam's destination. He thought it'd be good for her to get off the hot street and hoped she'd agree to step into the air conditioned building and join him at the meeting. He was also looking forward to seeing his friend, Camille, and to hearing stories about her daughters.

CHAPTER TWO

Camille was wrapping up the first half of rehearsal at Academy Theatre, ten blocks west of Gabby and Adam. She planned to leave for a commitment while her assistant director ran the second half, then return near the end. But first, she wanted to find out what was going on with eleven-year-old Becky. Becky normally showed energy and happiness, but today, she appeared sad and unengaged.

Camille loved working at Academy. The company produced sold-out shows, attracted young performers from as far away as Chicago, paid its employees well, and had a prominent standing in Terrace. She even loved the building – a new venue with a large lobby, two hundred cushioned seats, and the latest in sound and lighting equipment. It's location on Granville Street, about a ten-minute stroll west of her apartment downtown, enabled her to walk to work.

She shared a mutual respect with Academy's founder and owner, Cindy Baker. She admired the success that Cindy had achieved despite being only in her mid-thirties – just a couple of years older than Camille. She knew that Cindy appreciated Camille's popularity with the young performers and their parents, as well as her credentials, including a Bachelor of Theatre degree and a Master of Performing Arts degree, both from Université Laval in Montreal.

"Okay, five-minute break, then Mr. Kyle will run the second half," Camille announced. She asked Kyle if anything unusual had occurred prior to her arrival.

"Now that you mention it, some of the kids went into the dressing rooms to check out the new costumes. I thought I heard a couple of the girls saying Becky wouldn't fit into the Annie clothes. I might have misheard though, so I didn't pursue it." Kyle had graduated just last spring. Perhaps his lack of experience had prevented him from probing into the situation.

Becky was indeed heavier than most kids her age. She also had a beautiful voice, an energetic and joyful demeanor, and a hunger to learn. She was perfect for the role of Annie.

Camille approached Lily and Hannah. When she asked them to go to the front lobby with her, they looked at each other like they'd been found out.

"You're not in trouble." Camille said, which produced a look of relief. "One of the things we believe in at Academy is kindness toward each other. I heard that maybe some of us forgot that earlier today." Concern returned to the girls' faces.

"We didn't say anything mean," said Lily.

"Okay, did you say *anything* to Becky today?"

After a pause, Hannah spoke. "Maybe it was a little mean."

"What did you say?" Camille's voice remained soft, but she looked at the girls, letting them know that the conversation was serious.

Hannah continued. "We said some stuff about her weight."

"How do you think that made her feel?"

"Not good," she said as she began to tear up.

Lily spoke again. "My mother told me they might as well call this show *Fat Annie*."

Camille took a breath. "We all have differences from each other. That's what makes the world exciting. It's nice to have those differences in our musicals, but it's not nice when someone makes fun of someone. I'm going to call Becky over, and I need you to say you're sorry."

Becky came over, and both girls apologized to her, Hannah more sincerely than Lily. Camille asked Becky to stay while the others returned to the stage.

"Becky, I'm sorry that some unkind things were said to you. Sometimes people criticize others. People make fun of me for my accent." She exaggerated her French accent as she said it. Becky returned a small smile while Camille continued. "As a performer, you don't have to worry about what people think. You just need to tell the story to the audience."

Frank Morhan entered the lobby and began listening.

"Okay, I guess," said Becky, giving a puzzled look to Camille. "Tell the story?"

"Yes. Musicals are fun to watch, but they also tell stories. And stories teach people. Can you think of a lesson from *Annie*?"

"Um, I guess that life can be hard, but things can get better?"

"Sure, that's a good one." Camille shifted to singing. "The sun will come up … tomorrow."

Becky smiled naturally.

"I'm proud of you. Let's make the rest of rehearsal great, yes?"

"Yes. Thank you, Miss Camille."

She knew that Becky didn't feel much better. She felt guilty for casting her in the starring role, since she suspected something like this could happen. However, she also knew that playing the role would be a positive experience overall.

Camille looked at Frank.

In recent years, Cindy Baker had stepped back from management of Academy as she became busy with her growing family, so she hired Frank Morhan as general manager. Frank was in his early fifties and thought highly of his own credentials. He once worked as an assistant director for a short-run Broadway production. He was so fond of telling everyone about his Broadway experience that years ago, people started calling him "Broadway Frank." He didn't reject the nickname. In fact, he seemed to like it.

Camille never felt the same level of connection with Broadway Frank as she did with Cindy. He had a good resume, but he didn't have Cindy's artistic, teaching, or business sense. Also, Cindy and Camille usually agreed on topics like casting, blocking, lighting, and script interpretation. Frank and Camille spent much time debating. Camille knew that at his previous employer, a small theater in Chicago, Frank had a director of whom he was fond. She often thought that he'd prefer to work with him.

"What was that all about?" he asked.

"A couple of the kids were making fun of her weight."

Frank gasped and covered his mouth, never missing an opportunity to be melodramatic, especially if he thought it made Camille look bad. He lowered his hand and lifted his chin. "I'm not surprised. You may recall that I disagreed with that casting decision."

"She's doing a great job and learning a lot."

"Yes, but look at the problems it created. Can't say I didn't warn you." He pranced away mumbling, "What a mess."

As Camille left to walk to her appointment, she saw an older model Chevrolet pull into the parking lot. She recognized neither the car nor the driver in it. She was already late, though, so she kept walking.

Shoppers, commuters, and diners shuffled toward their destinations on Granville Street. Camille fit in with these people, but she also related to the less fortunate folks scattered along the street.

A group of three stylish girls, perhaps ten years younger than her, were standing on the sidewalk, looking around. One of them spotted her and said, "Excuse me, can you recommend a good restaurant around here?" She was polite and pretty.

Despite being in a hurry, Camille took a moment. "My favorite place is Mio Posto, just west of Prospect. Great Italian food. You should call to make a reservation though because it takes a while to get in."

"Great, thanks," the girl replied.

"Good job, Brooke," said one of the friends.

CHAPTER THREE

Gabby was surprised to find herself at a Narcotics Anonymous meeting. She thought NA would do her about as much good as cigarette package warnings do for an addicted smoker. But Adam had been persistent, and she owed him. Their walk had brought them close to the meeting location – a conference room above the chic Lapis Lazuli clothing store, and his suggestion about sitting in an air-conditioned room and having a cookie sounded appealing. So here she was.

She and Adam were occupying consecutive chairs within a large circle. Gabby counted twelve other people – eight men and four women. A few were in their twenties and thirties, but most were older. They looked healthy and clean, at least healthier and cleaner than her. Perhaps most were in recovery. Adam greeted several by name, and it appeared he hadn't seen them for a while. He glanced at the door a few times, like he was expecting someone who hadn't yet arrived.

The leader, a solid man with a calm voice called the meeting to order at precisely five o'clock. He remained seated and said, "Hello, I'm an addict, and my name is James."

"Hello, James," the group answered.

"Can we open this meeting with a moment of silence for the addict who still suffers and for our brothers and sisters who have perished?" After a few silent seconds, James lifted his head. "Please join me in the Serenity Prayer."

The attendees recited the words in unison, though Gabby remained silent and glanced at each of her neighbors. "God, grant me the serenity to accept the things I cannot change, courage to change the things I can, and wisdom to know the difference."

After a few more announcements and readings, James asked, "Is there anyone here attending their first meeting?"

Gabby looked around for others, but hers was the lone hand raised.

"Welcome. You're the most important person here. Please introduce yourself if you'd like."

"Uh … I'm Gabby, and I'm an addict."

"Hello, Gabby," said the group.

"I'm afraid I don't feel important but thank you." She appreciated the camaraderie.

James continued. "I asked Adam to share his recent experiences. I know that some of us have had similar experiences, but some have not, so I thought the topic would be useful."

Adam remained seated. He wore black shoes on his large feet, black pants and a white button-down, long-sleeve shirt. He looked like he was dressed for work and that he'd probably be more comfortable in sneakers, jeans, and a T-shirt. Gabby was eager to learn why James had asked him to speak.

"Hello, my name's Adam and I'm an addict." His voice was deep, strong, and gentle. He maintained a small smile as he spoke. He was tall, and he was handsome, in a masculine way. His dark hair was thick and unfussed. His eyes were kind, and he had an inviting, contented look, like he was always about to laugh.

"Hello, Adam," responded the group.

"Uh, I wrote down a couple of notes." He looked at his paper. So did Gabby. The handwriting was a forced neat, like someone not used to wearing a suit and tie but had donned one because it was important for the occasion. "I got out of jail yesterday. James asked me to talk about how I ended up there, my time there, and getting out."

Gabby's eyes opened wider. This pleasant young man who had rescued her had just been released from jail? He must be on probation, which meant that he had taken a risk by calling 911 for her and interacting with police.

"Okay. Going to jail." Adam said it like a chapter heading. "Well, about five months ago, I met some kid here on Granville Street."

Gabby tried to place his age and thought he appeared to be about twenty-four.

"We bought some stuff, and the kid said there was an abandoned building nearby where we could use. After we were in the building, he stepped out to take a leak. All the stuff was inside with me. As soon as he was out, some cops came in and arrested me for possession. I never saw the kid again. I guess he was an informant. I was already on probation for another possession charge, so that violated my probation, and I went to jail. My parents could have bailed me out for three thousand, but I guess they thought I was safer in jail. That's it, man. That's how I ended up there."

Gabby always knew there was a risk of being arrested and incarcerated. Seeing an in-the-flesh example made it salient.

Adam looked at his notes. "Jail. Well, I guess it's kinda like you imagine. It sucks. Not seeing the sun sucks. Not having your freedom sucks. I missed my family and my friends. My parents visited me every Sunday. My brother and sister came as much as they could."

Gabby felt like asking him if friends visited him but surmised the answer was no. He would have mentioned them.

"It was county jail, not state pen, so there wasn't a lot of fights and rapes 'n stuff. I mean, there were *some* fights and some stuff goin' on, but if you mind your business, you can avoid it. The jail had drug meetings, and I went to those. Main thing is, you gotta kill time. I played basketball and cards with the guys. Sometimes I made stuff to eat from things you buy at the commissary. My dad bought me books from Amazon and had them shipped to the jail. I read four of *The Cartel* series. I'd sell them for commissary stuff after I read them. It took five months for my lawyer to work out a settlement. I pled guilty, and the penalty was time served, two years of probation with random drug testing, and a monthly shot of Vivitrol."

Adam smiled less as he talked about his experience. The time served was probably more difficult than he was portraying. One of the meeting attendees asked how the Vivitrol made him feel.

"I haven't had the shot yet," answered Adam.

Another attendee asked if he had urges to use in jail.

"No. And I don't now, man. I'm done with that. I swear to God, I'm gonna do whatever it takes to stay sober." The group applauded.

Gabby had read enough about addiction to know that urges can recede when the drug is not available. The heroin brain can go dormant from lack of access. Although she had just met Adam, she already felt connected to him, and she wondered about his ability to fight his cravings, when they returned. She was happy, though, to see his fierce determination.

"Third topic. Getting out. My dad picked me up yesterday. He drove me to the building where you see your probation officer. I saw my PO for just a minute. He told me to come back in two weeks and that's when everything will start, including the Vivitrol and random drug testing, and he said he'll probably recommend that I take an outpatient rehab program. My dad was mad that I wasn't getting the Vivitrol shot right away. I wasn't too worried about it because I was planning to go to rehab the next day."

"Are you still going?" asked one of the attendees.

"We found out that our insurance won't cover rehab 'cause I'm clean. Also, I thought about it more after I got home. My lawyer told me to make sure I did whatever the PO said to do. If I break my probation, then next step for me is state pen. No way I'm goin' there. The PO told me to look for an outpatient program, so that's what I'm gonna do. My dad and I have appointments to check out a couple tomorrow."

As a former English teacher, Gabby had experience listening to people talk and understanding the feelings behind the words. The way Adam spoke about his father gave her the impression that he was close to him.

"Have you ever done an *in*patient program?" asked one of the attendees.

"Yeah, I did rehab seven times."

James complimented Adam on the effort that he had put into his sobriety over the years. A woman in her early thirties walked into the meeting room wearing fashionable blue jeans, a tan blouse, and a sharp black blazer. Gabby couldn't see her face, only her long dark hair. Adam's smile returned as he interrupted his talk and said, "Hey, Camille."

With a French accent and a soft voice that sounded familiar to Gabby, Camille apologized to the group for being late and tried to be discreet as she found an open chair, across the circle from where Gabby and Adam were sitting.

Gabby saw her face and added to her list of today's surprises. Camille spotted Gabby, and they gave each other a look of disbelief, both showing their palms as if to say, "What, in God's name, are *you* doing here?"

Adam resumed. "The PO also told me to get back to work as soon as possible. I called my old boss when I got home, and she said one cook was out and asked me to work for a couple of hours tonight. So I'm goin' there after the meeting." He paused for a moment. "That's about it."

Someone asked what it was like seeing his family after being locked up.

"It was great. When my parents visited me in jail, they always said we'd go for a steak dinner the night I got out. We went to Morton's down the street." Several in the group smiled and nodded. "It was great. My brother and my sister and her husband joined us. It was nice to see family not through a glass window."

Gabby patted Adam on the back of the shoulder, and James thanked him. "Today's second discussion topic is having a higher power," James said. "Each person is welcome to tell the group the entity that is bigger and more enduring than yourself that gives you strength and direction."

Several people said their higher power was God.

"My daughters and the love we share are my higher power," said Camille.

"Mine is nature and the outdoors. It gives me peace," said Adam.

A couple more people spoke. Gabby thought if she believed in a higher power, hers might be community. Community saved her today.

The meeting wrapped up at six. Finally, Gabby would have a chance to see what was going on with her old friend.

CHAPTER FOUR

Gabby jumped up and walked toward Camille, while James came to speak to Adam.

"Camille, my God, it's been a long time!" she said. They hugged and pulled away with the same dumfounded expression. "I had no idea that you suffered from this," Gabby said.

"Likewise. I'm sorry to hear."

Adam joined them, looking confused that they knew each other. Adam and Camille hugged. "And I haven't seen *you* for a while," she said to Adam.

"I know. Good to see you."

Camille went to introduce Adam to Gabby.

"We've met," said Gabby before she told her about the incident on the street.

"My Lord!" said Camille. "Let me get you some water."

Gabby raised her glass to indicate she already had some.

"So, how do *you* two know each other?" Adam asked.

Camille answered, "We met when I first came here from Quebec. I took English lessons at night, and Gabby was my teacher. We became good friends, but we haven't seen each other for a couple of years."

"Lousy place to have a reunion," said Gabby. She looked at Adam and back to Camille. "Your turn. How do you two know each other?"

"We met a couple of years ago at his restaurant. I eat there often because it's just around the corner from my apartment. When I go there with my daughters, Adam gives them a gift – a small piece of grilled filet."

"My boss approves, of course," added Adam. He continued. "Camille also comes to my home to teach my mother piano. Sometimes she stays for dinner. She's become a friend of the family." He reached his right arm around her back and gently squeezed her right shoulder then let go. "How are your girls? Any birthdays since I last saw them?"

"Mia turned five a month ago. She got two parties – one from my ex-husband and one from me. Rosalie is still seven."

Adam looked at the clock on the wall. "Well, I need to head to work."

"Actually, so do I," said Camille. She turned to Gabby. "Adam and I are heading in the same direction. Do you want to walk with us … if you're feeling okay?"

Before they left, James said he overhead them talking about the overdose and asked Gabby and Adam if they'd come back tomorrow and discuss how to handle that situation. Adam agreed, and Gabby said she'd try.

The three walked west on Granville Street, which was busier and louder than before the meeting. There were more homeless people getting ready for the night, more young people playing guitar, and more well-off shoppers and diners.

When they reached the corner of Granville and Prospect, Camille pointed to the second building north, a five-story apartment complex on Prospect. "Gabby, that's where I live. Feel free to drop by anytime."

"Thank you. I'll do that." However, she had no plans to do that. Although she and Camille had the same addiction, it seemed that Camille was in recovery, had her life together, and surely had to keep an orderly home for when her daughters visited. Gabby even wondered if Camille was embarrassed walking with her, although she showed no sign of that.

Adam pointed west. "Mio Posto is just ahead."

"And Academy is five more blocks," added Camille. She looked at Gabby. "Where are you staying?"

"I have a place."

Camille put a hand on her shoulder. "Are you going to be okay?"

"Yes. It was wonderful to see you."

"Remember, the meeting tomorrow is at six. I have rehearsal, but I think I'll be able to get away to attend the meeting. Will you both be there?" Camille asked.

"I will," Adam replied.

Gabby doubted the usefulness of NA. On the other hand, she always enjoyed the company of Camille, and she liked her new friend Adam. "I suppose I can go, since I get to tell a story. But isn't NA for people who are no longer using?" She wondered if she belonged there.

"It's for people who *want to stop* using," answered Camille.

"They seemed like a good group. Maybe," she answered.

Adam looked like he was nervous about getting to work on time. "Hey, it's my first day back at work, so I better go."

Gabby thanked him again for calling 911 and for convincing her to attend the NA meeting. She was starting to feel nauseated and wondered what repercussions were in store for her from the overdose and the Narcan.

CHAPTER FIVE

Adam arrived at Mio Posto fifteen minutes early for his six-thirty start time. He wanted time to get an updated sense of his workstation and review the cooking instructions.

Walking in sparked a number of memories: how his mother had discovered the job opportunity and coached him for the interviews, how proud his parents were that he worked there, how the management treated him with respect, and how he liked sneaking looks at diners' faces to see how they enjoyed what he cooked.

A less pleasant memory popped into his mind. Once, after work, he'd gone to a public bathroom nearby and used. He'd passed out on a dirty floor until his father finally found him. He shook that memory off and turned his grill on. The manager welcomed him back with a friendly handshake and a light hug, and she thanked him for coming in on short notice.

The kitchen hadn't changed: a large frying area, several ovens, and the grill, Adam's spot. The kitchen was one step up from the dining area and was separated from it by a marble tiled wall that rose about three feet from the floor, then a glass panel extending another three feet, and open space above the glass. The layout enabled diners to see inside the kitchen and enabled Adam to look out at his customers.

Adam felt nerves in his stomach, but the familiarity of the surroundings and of the work eased his anxiety somewhat. He set up his grill station, and another cook came by to remind him of the most important menu items and how to cook them.

After the lesson, Adam looked around at the customers. His eyes were pulled to a young woman as she and two friends were being seated. He found it hopeless to pry his stare away. She wore a loose grey top and tight black jeans, and her blonde hair hung just below her shoulders. The girl noticed him as well, which made his heart thump.

He finally succeeded at withdrawing his gaze to focus on grilling his first orders: two whitefish, and one chicken limone. A few minutes later, he saw drinks being delivered to the three young women. The two friends of the girl each received a fancy cocktail served in a large martini glass, and the girl received a beer. The three clinked glasses and took their first sips. Their server eventually brought Adam one order of truffle-crusted filets and one order of herb-roasted salmon and gave the pasta chef an order for angel hair pomodoro.

Adam desperately wanted to meet her, but more than shyness made him hesitant. He wondered if he should just focus on his sobriety and stay away from dating. He also knew that any normal girl wouldn't be interested in him if she knew his situation. He turned his thoughts and his eyes back to his grill.

While he cooked, he tried to guess which of his orders were going to which girl, predicting that the steak was going to the girl he liked, and the salmon was going to the friend in the blue summer dress. The server delivered the dishes, and he saw that he was right, and that the small pasta dish went to the friend in the tight, revealing top.

The occasional back and forth glances continued while Adam grilled, and while the girl spoke with her friends. When the meals were finished, she got up and walked toward the restroom. As she passed him, they checked each other out more closely. Seeing her full body in motion made him even more attracted to her. She walked back, this time not making eye contact with him, as if to say, "Your move, shy boy."

Finally, Adam was so drawn to her that nothing else mattered. He had to meet her. He had a pause in the orders, so he went to their table with his heart pounding hard enough to bruise his ribs. Up close, he saw how soft her blonde hair was and how she seemed to have the perfect amount of makeup. In fact, everything about her was perfect.

"Excuse me. I'm one of the cooks. How were the meals?" he asked, struggling to keep his voice steady and confident.

The blue summer dress friend complimented him on the salmon. The tight revealing top friend frowned. The girl he liked smiled and rolled her shoulder toward him. "My steak was a bit overdone."

His smile shrank. "Really?"

"Yeah, had you cooked it less, you could have come by sooner. How much direct eye contact does it take for you to walk up to a girl?"

Adam liked her playful flirtation. He shot back, "I think you know."

"Well, it was almost too much," she replied.

"I'm glad you said almost."

"So, the restaurant lets you stop cooking to come and talk to a table of girls?"

"No, they don't," he fired back, proud of the irony of his answer.

"And you always do things you shouldn't?"

Now, he felt a bit jarred by the irony of *her* question about doing things he shouldn't. He also felt he was getting out of his league with the verbal sparring, and he knew that he had to get back to his station. "Well, I hope you come back," he said, immediately realizing what a dumb line that was. Hoping to gain back some respect, he added, "Where are you guys goin' after this?"

The blue dress friend said, "Havana's."

"Why don't you stop by after work?" suggested the girl he liked.

Adam didn't like the idea of going to a bar. Even if he could drink, he didn't like it. In the half-second he had to respond, he wondered how he'd be able to go and not seem weird for not drinking. He'd figure it out later. He made a mental note of the club's name because he'd never heard of it but didn't want them to know that.

"Cool, I'll be there. My name's Adam."

"Nice to meet you, Adam. I'm Brooke. This is my friend, Beth," as she motioned toward the friendly brunette in the blue dress. "And this is Kate," as she looked at the blonde girl remaining quiet in the revealing top.

"Alright, see you guys around ten?"

"Yeah, see you there," said Brooke.

Adam had a bounce in his step as he headed back to his station. On the way there, he noticed a man and a woman entering the restaurant. The man was African American, and she was white. He was wearing a dark blue expensive-looking suit. She wore a short-sleeve, beige dress with some wrinkles.

The man spoke to the hostess with a smart-sounding voice. "I'm John Tylor. I have a reservation, and we need a table in a private area please."

CHAPTER SIX

John Tylor was with Jackie Cowden. They were both partners at Harris Clark, a high-profile law firm that represented large companies and public organizations against lawsuits of wrongdoing. Their jobs were straight-forward: keep their clients from incurring settlement payouts.

Harris Clark was founded in 1979 by Jay Harris and Michael Clark. They were brilliant, brazen, young lawyers who had become friends at Yale Law School, and after graduation, spent a couple of years together backpacking the world, reading and discussing law books, and volunteering. They then each worked at preeminent law firms in New York City for eight years, amassing impressive win rates before founding Harris Clark in Stamford, Connecticut.

From the beginning, they fostered a culture that included aggressive growth, a quota of charitable cases in addition to the big lucrative clients, and a low tolerance for losing. Unlike the older firms, they located their offices in suburban areas where rent was about half that of the major cities. They preferred to allocate the money to partner earnings and salaries to attract the smartest lawyers. Inspired by tech startups of a few years earlier like Apple and Microsoft, their firm would be a leader in the use of technology. By 2016, the firm employed over five hundred lawyers in eight offices across the country and still maintained their aggressive culture.

Harris Clark's office in the Chicago area was in Terrace, at the distinguished address of 551 Granville. It was a landmark five-story building, with a commanding front of white cement blocks, large windows and an eminent Harris Clark logo.

John was in his mid-forties and Jackie, late thirties. Jackie had been admitted to the partnership only three years ago but was fast climbing the partner hierarchy. Recently, she'd become Office Managing Partner, which made her John's superior.

It was Jackie's suggestion to meet at Mio Posto. Many of the local Harris Clark partners treated the restaurant as a licensed extension of 551 Granville. With the exception of the quarterly practice review meeting, spending business hours on internal meetings was frowned upon at Harris Clark. But spending evening hours without wine was frowned upon by many of the partners. Most hostesses at Mio Posto knew to give Harris Clark staff good tables in private areas.

At the best of times, John didn't enjoy Jackie's company. He didn't respect her. Although she often got decent results on her cases, it was seldom because of her own proficiency. She was good at pulling teams together and relying on them to get into the details and to come up with the arguments.

There was also history between them. John had joined the firm prior to her and had made partner before her. Three years ago, he was on the partner admissions committee when her candidacy was being considered. He had argued against admitting her because he thought she lacked the intellect and discipline required to be a successful partner. The discussion within the committee should have been private, but Jackie had learned of his view and, he believed, still held it against him.

They took their seats, and Jackie put her phone face-up on the table in front of her, like a parent keeping a baby monitor nearby. John kept his on silent in the inside pocket of his jacket. They engaged in some strained small talk until the server came by and took their orders.

"Alright, John, you know the last two years have not gone well for you," Jackie began, speaking at her normal quick pace.

John's speech pattern was moderate and precise. "Jackie, we didn't get the results our clients wanted. That's true, but …"

"I'd say that's an understatement. The pharma client paid twenty million dollars, and the retailer paid four million in damages. Those were pretty bad outcomes." Harris Clark lawyers never uttered the name of a client in public, even at a private table with minimal risk of being overhead. "Bad for the firm, bad for our clients, and bad for you. Our clients pay us to *avoid* payouts, not *incur* them."

John had decided early in his life that good grades, hard work, and strict discipline would get him to a better life than he had as a child. He eventually made it to Harvard law school and graduated with honors, although he was a few years older than most graduates because he had worked for two years between high school and college and then again between undergrad and law school. With his savings from working and a huge student loan, he was able to pay for university. He was proud of his long journey and considered himself a self-made man. He believed that Jackie, on the other hand, got into university, then into Harris Clark, more from her parents' connections than from her own competence.

At university, John had been active in various social causes. He joined Harris Clark and rose fast, making partner after seven years. His intelligence, work ethic, and discipline enabled him to deliver good results for his clients, even though he sometimes felt they bore some responsibility for the wrongdoing of which they were accused. His last two cases, which he had worked on over two years, had thrown his career off track.

The server brought two glasses of wine. Jackie took a substantial sip immediately, leaving a semi-circle of red lipstick on the glass. John made the motion of having a sip without taking more than a few drops.

“My record prior to these two cases is stellar,” he disputed. “Those cases were unwinnable. The pharma company was in fact lax in providing warnings about the risks of their anti-diabetic medication. People suffered heart attacks from the drug. And the evidence that the retailer discriminated against that pregnant employee was overwhelming.”

While he spoke, Jackie monitored the steady stream of texts and emails entering her phone. She lifted her eyes and looked back at John. “You know, John, when your heart’s in a case, you’re unbeatable. Un freaking beatable. But, it seems you weren’t ‘all in’ for the last two. You still have some supporters on the executive committee, though, and they want you to have one more chance.”

He felt himself grinding his teeth. “Is that the term they used – one more chance?”

“We’re giving you an opportunity to start rebuilding your reputation. We have a case that can help you do that. If you succeed, that’ll be the first step to getting back on track.” Jackie leaned forward a little. “But if you lose… Well, that’ll be strike three, and we’d have to have a serious talk about your future with the firm.”

John couldn't believe what he was hearing. He knew, though, that the firm did have a history of moving out partners quickly if their performances faltered. He knew that Jackie would be delighted to see him leave, given their history.

Departing the firm at this time would be disastrous financially. He was the sole breadwinner. He had cleared away his large student debt only a few years earlier. He and his wife had to pay for at least three more years of tuition for their son, who had just finished his first year of engineering at MIT, and they'd be paying tuition for their two daughters soon. On top of that, they had just purchased a new home, and were paying for an elder care facility for John's father.

He didn't feel like he was in a position to challenge Jackie too strongly. Besides his financial obligations, he happened to be currently without clients. Given the challenges of the last two cases, he had focused entirely on them, and had not spent much time developing new business. Now those cases were over, and he had few prospects for new clients.

However, he needed to say *something*. "I have to tell you, Jackie, I'm surprised at this conversation. We should discuss that at some point, but for now, I would just like to hear about the case."

Jackie took another sip of wine, leaving a second, fainter semi-circle of lipstick on the rim. She picked up her phone, tapped the screen a couple of times, and passed it to him, pointing at a name. He saw an email from the sheriff of Carlane County and nodded.

"He's a friend of my father's. He and the county are being sued by three families claiming wrongful death of loved ones," she said.

"Did people die in his jail? I haven't heard about that."

"No. All three died after *leaving* the jail. The families are claiming that the jail's policies caused the deaths."

John slid his chair closer. "How could that be?" He took the blue pen out of his shirt pocket and removed a tiny notebook from his suit pocket.

"A frivolous suit, if I've ever seen one. These inmates were drug addicts – heroin, I think. The families are saying that they were on addiction medicine when they entered. I can't remember the name of it, but the jail classifies it as a narcotic, so they didn't allow the inmates to continue taking it."

"I can understand that," said John.

"So these people get out, shoot up, and die. That's what addicts do, isn't it?" She grabbed a bread roll, broke it in half, dipped it in olive oil and parmesan cheese, and bit into it.

John made notes: "proximate cause … deliberate indifference … immunity."

After a few chews, Jackie continued. "And the families blame the jail. There's much in favor of our client. There's no way the families could prove that 'but for' the jail policies, their drug-pumping loved ones would still be alive. Plus, as a public official, he has some protection, as you know."

"Indeed. Why are the families even bothering to try?"

"Maybe they don't know any better."

"How far along is it?"

"The suit was filed, and discovery is complete. We should be able to get to a settlement or a dismissal without it going to trial. A trial would be bad for our client, with his election coming up."

"I agree. Why didn't he come to us from the start? Who had the case before?"

She bit another piece of bread off the roll. "They had some small firm to try to keep their costs low, but our client didn't like the lawyer.

Told me he was 'a pony-tail liberal'. The discovery papers have been moved to us."

"Who is representing the families?"

"Apparently a brother-in-law of one of the plaintiffs. On his website, he boasts about personal injury wins of twenty or forty thousand dollars. Small-timer. Another reason this should be easy."

He thought the case indeed sounded easy to win. "What are the families looking for?"

"Three million dollars in compensatory damages for grief, sorrow and mental suffering – one million for each death."

Now he understood why she didn't just keep the case for herself. A three million dollar suit was smaller than the cases that interested Jackie. Normally the same applied to him, but without other current prospects, he couldn't afford to be picky.

She continued. "Plus they want a change in policy. They want the jail to let addicts continue taking medicine that was prescribed before incarceration. The judge has ordered a settlement conference for Thursday."

John swallowed as he realized the limited amount of time he had to prepare.

Another bite of bread, another few chews, and she continued. "Your job is to simply persuade their two-bit lawyer that this suit will be painful for his clients and will not result in anything of value because they would lose at trial. Or just try to get the judge to dismiss the whole thing. Do you know much about drug addicts?"

John thought of his son, who had experimented with marijuana, much to John's dismay. Once or twice, he wondered if Daniel had ever tried anything more, but he knew that he was too smart to try anything hard or addictive.

John had always viewed drug users as losers, from the potheads he had seen in high school to the heroin addicts he now occasionally saw on the streets. In his opinion, either they prioritized getting high over more important things, or they lacked the discipline to quit.

"Not really. I seem to see more and more of them around town, which isn't pleasant for the rest of us. I'll never understand why someone would choose that type of life."

"Well, it would be good to learn about them, so you can get into the heads of your opponents. By the way, the other area where you've fallen behind is in your pro bono work. We all have to do them, so you need to find one."

As John walked toward his 2012 Tesla, he seethed about his partnership being on the line over a pair of cases that the firm should not have even taken. However, he knew that anger would not be useful, that his situation was serious, and that he had to succeed. He was glad, at least, that he didn't have a moral dilemma with this one. He agreed that narcotics should not be allowed in jails and prisons.

He suspected that Jackie's description of the case was superficial. It sounded too easy. He wondered if there was more to it and what challenges he would find as soon as he dug into it.

CHAPTER SEVEN

Camille arrived back at the Academy building. The car she'd seen earlier was still there. As she walked into the lobby, she was followed in by the driver, who was carrying a manila envelope with a photograph clipped onto it.

The man smiled and said, "Are you Camille Simard?"

"Yes I am. Who are you?"

He thrust the envelope into her hands. "You've been served." He kept the photograph, which Camille noticed was of her.

She opened the envelope and could barely read its contents without shaking in shock and fury. The papers were some sort of emergency application filed by her ex-husband, Robert, to eliminate her visitations with her daughters. She was to appear in court the next day!

Camille became addicted to opioids early in their marriage but was able to stop when she became pregnant, and she managed to avoid using for seven years. To her enormous disappointment, she relapsed six months ago – several weeks before her divorce finalization. Robert got physical custody, but they shared legal custody, so Camille was entitled to participate in all important decisions regarding her daughters' lives.

The divorce terms entitled her to two days of visitation per week, but no overnights. However, her ex-husband typically worked three days a week and had been okay to have Camille watch the girls on those days because it was easier for him than arranging and paying for childcare. Camille also watched them on the days he golfed – usually once a week in the summer. She was delighted to have the girls whenever she could, and schedule-wise, it worked out since her weekday rehearsals were in the evenings.

Camille walked to an area in the lobby where she could get some privacy. She placed the papers on a bench, remained standing, and called the same lawyer she used for her divorce. He was a private attorney, and not cheap, but she'd do whatever was necessary. Rosalie and Mia needed her, and she was not about to let Robert keep them away.

Jerry Murphy didn't answer, so she left him a voicemail. Her knees shook while she continued to review the papers until he called her back a few minutes later.

"Hello, Jerry," she answered.

"Camille, girl. It's been a while. I listened to your voicemail. We'll get this worked out."

Jerry was a scrappy lawyer in his fifties. He interacted with her as if he were a protective uncle or something. "Do you still have the court papers in front of you?" he asked.

"Yes." She scraped them off the bench. "How can he do this? And it's tomorrow that I have to be in court. Is that normal?"

"Unfortunately, it can happen, yes. Tell me, does it say, 'Order to Show Cause' somewhere in the document?"

She partly spoke and partly read. “Yes, it says I have to show cause why an order should not be issued immediately suspending my visits with the girls.” She lowered the papers out of sight.

“Okay, that’s what we call an emergency application, and it can be used when there are allegations that require the immediate attention of the courts.”

“But his allegations are complete lies. He says I’m using drugs again and that the girls are in danger when they’re with me. I haven’t used in six months. They love spending time with me. How can he lie like this?”

“Okay, if you haven’t used, then the drug test tomorrow will come back negative and that’ll help our case. Yeah, it’s a bunch of crap, but the judge may decide to suspend visitation until an investigation is complete. Unfortunately, with your drug history, your word against his is not a battle you’ll win.”

“He has some history too, you know? He has a record for assault from when he hit a woman over a disagreement about a parking spot.” Camille remembered feeling shocked about that incident two years ago. She told him then that if he ever threatened their daughters or her, they would all leave immediately. She wondered, though, if she would have been able to follow through if it had happened.

“I know. I’m afraid that doesn’t matter,” Jerry answered.

“You said there may be an investigation. What does that mean?”

“They’re likely to investigate the safety and security of your home, order frequent drug tests, you name it. They’ll also assign an attorney to represent your daughters. The attorney will meet with them in private, ask them questions about you and how they spend their time with you, and report back to the judge. Just be prepared for the visits to be temporarily suspended tomorrow. I’ll try to prevent it, but it’s a possibility. With allegations of drug use, visitations often get reduced to one or two hours a week, supervised."

"That would be devastating! How long could the suspension last?"

"Could be a few weeks. Could be months. The courts tend to err on the side of caution whenever there are such allegations, particularly if there is an actual history of drug use."

"But I haven't used for six months – and for seven years prior to that."

"Camille, they look at this and see that you used heroin, stopped, then used again. Even though it was seven years later, you relapsed. Any allegation against you needs to be thoroughly investigated. I know it sounds awful, but you need to keep a level head, girl. Once we finish talking, take a picture of every piece of paper you received and send them to me."

"Okay."

"I assume you want me there tomorrow?"

"Yes, absolutely."

"Do you have any idea about your ex-husband's motivation? Has anything happened lately?"

One possibility came to mind. "I think his girlfriend is moving in with him, and she can watch the girls when he works. He only tolerated my time with them because it was convenient."

"I suppose that could be the case," said Jerry.

"Maybe he wants the girls to get close to his girlfriend by spending time only with her. Or maybe he's doing it just to spite me. Do you think I should talk to him before court tomorrow? Maybe there's some other way to resolve this."

"I'd advise against it. He's decided to take you to court with a petition full of lies. I think talking to him will only get you more upset."

"I guess."

"Is he using the same lawyer he did for the divorce?"

Camille scanned the first page with her finger. "Yes, I see his name on these papers. Tim Lund."

"I remember him. He acts all proper, but he plays dirty. That's okay. I've dealt with bigger and badder. We'll work under the same rates we had for the divorce, but don't worry about that right now. Let's focus on tomorrow's court appearance. Since you're being summoned at eleven, meet me there twenty minutes early, so I can prepare you a little more. Okay?"

"Yes. Thank you again."

"No problem. Try to get some rest tonight, and I'll see you tomorrow. I'm gonna look after you. Don't worry."

"Thanks, Jerry."

She finally sat down. She needed a minute before getting back to the rehearsal. She couldn't imagine her life without the girls, or their lives without her. She also thought about her own childhood and how growing up, she had always wanted more time with her own mother, who had travelled for work for extended periods of time. Even now, Camille seldom saw her parents. She had always sworn that she'd be a better mother to her own children. These papers, and the risk they represented, were now the most important thing in her life.

CHAPTER EIGHT

Gabby had started to feel dope sick after the NA meeting because her daily routine had been interrupted. Since becoming homeless a few months ago, her life had fallen into a pattern. In the morning, she'd find a way to get some money, although she avoided things like shoplifting or stealing people's possessions. Other than her addiction, she tried to stay on the clean side of the law.

Sometimes, she'd go to a department store, find a discarded receipt in the parking lot, go in, find the item that was on the receipt, and ask for a refund. She found the most effective tactic, though, was going to downtown Chicago to panhandle. In a couple of hours, she could collect ten to twenty dollars. She always feared being seen by a former student or a teacher colleague, but that was the risk she had to take.

With cash, she'd buy a cheap sandwich and a hit. About a month ago, she'd found a dealer in Terrace who went by the name Base. Unlike buying in the city, where dealers posted up in regular spots, it took some effort to find Base or one of his runners whenever she wanted to buy. He did most of his selling via texts, and his runners delivered the merchandise and collected payment. She frequently saw them moving around town, and it seemed they were not bad off. Base paid them, supplied the drugs they needed, and provided protection when necessary.

Since she didn't own a phone, her transactions had to be face-to-face. Base seemed like a dangerous person, but his merchandise was safe. It seemed in the last few months, Base had become the predominant point of contact for users in or around Terrace. Earlier today, she had not been able to find him, so she'd purchased from a stranger closer to Chicago.

New dealers were not hard to find near Chicago. Just get off the train at one of the spots along Heroin Highway, look for someone with the "seller's look" – decent clothes, hands in pockets, eyes shifting, looking for someone with the "buyer's look" – run-down, desperate, eyes shifting, looking for a seller. With new dealers, though, you always had the risk of getting a bad dose – crap mixed in with the heroin, so you don't get what you need, or, worse, you get fentanyl mixed in, which was lethal more often than heroin.

She normally injected once a day, late afternoon in a private place, like a restroom. She avoided using the same restroom twice in one or two weeks to avoid suspicion. After injecting, she'd find a place to lay low for a couple of hours – a park bench, a coffee shop, a book store, or the library. There were plenty of places where she could sit and be inconspicuous.

She normally administered just enough to feel closer to normal for the rest of the day and night. By mid-morning the following day, she'd have cravings. The knowledge that she'd be using later got her through.

She used her relatively sober time to do a couple of normal things. During her visits to the library, she read fiction. Crime stories were her favorite, but she'd read anything that hooked her or helped her understand the world. The library environment reminded her of her teaching days. She also volunteered at the Parkdale hospital one morning a week.

For sleeping, she made use of a charitable organization called Night Off The Streets, or NOTS for short. On a rotating basis, each night, a different church permitted the organization to use their building as a homeless shelter. Volunteers from NOTS would prepare food and set up foam mattresses and blankets to welcome and feed homeless people who arrived before nine in the evening.

There were no shower facilities, but Gabby had learned to wash using the soap and paper towels in church restrooms. She could do it in just a few minutes because there were often people waiting. She also carried a toothbrush and toothpaste in her bag along with a change of clothes, which she would sometimes try to wash in the restroom, then hang somewhere near her to partially dry overnight.

This evening was different. She was no longer sure what was in the baggie that she had cooked and injected. Perhaps there had been *some* heroin in it, but far less than her normal dose. She reasoned it must have been fentanyl which caused the overdose. Whatever the situation, her body had not received what it had become used to – what it had to have. Withdrawal was upon her. Her muscles and bones ached. She fluctuated between hot and cold flashes with matching bouts of sweat, and she felt like vomiting every time she moved. She knew that all of these symptoms would get about a hundred times worse over the coming hours.

Plus, it wasn't just physical. Her brain no longer produced enough dopamine to fill the additional opioid receptors that had developed. She was beginning to feel nervous, detached, and depressed. Memories of the worst events of her life started filling her mind. She thought of her husband and the night of his accident and how much she missed him.

Her close call with death earlier and the NA meeting made her think that this may be a good time to try to get clean again, but this withdrawal seemed like it would be worse than any she had previously experienced. She doubted she'd get through it without help.

She walked two of blocks south to Terrace General Hospital and entered through Emergency. The attendant at the check-in desk was dealing with another patient, so Gabby leaned on the back of a nearby chair to keep upright while she waited.

She scanned the six people sitting in the waiting room. Two of them were coughing and sneezing, one had her leg up and rubbed her ankle, and the other three seemed to be healthy people there with their loved ones. The attendant finally became free. Gabby lurched forward and put her palms on the counter. The cold blue surface didn't sooth her clammy skin as much as she'd hoped.

"I'm very sick," said Gabby.

"Step into Room B. A nurse will triage you, then you can come back into the waiting room to wait to be seen by a doctor," said the attendant.

Gabby careened to the room, just a few steps from the front counter. She sat and hoped that she wouldn't have to wait long. The nausea, pains, and aches were becoming more severe. After about a minute, a nurse walked in.

"What seems to be the problem?" he asked.

"I'm aching all over. I'm hot and cold. I feel nauseous. I can barely stand."

The nurse looked concerned. "That sounds serious." He measured her temperature in her ear. "How long have you felt like this?"

"It started getting bad about a half an hour ago."

"Extend your arm."

Gabby extended her left arm, but had trouble keeping it steady. The nurse wrapped a pad around her bicep to measure her blood pressure. As he did that, he noticed the track marks on her arm, and his countenance changed. He now looked like someone who had just discovered dog feces on the bottom of his shoe.

"Are you a heroin addict?" he asked.

"Yes."

"Well, you're probably just experiencing withdrawal symptoms."

"That *is* what I'm experiencing."

"I'm afraid we don't treat for heroin withdrawal."

"Why? I have insurance."

"Heroin withdrawal is not life-threatening. Therefore, the policy of this hospital is to not treat it." He stood up to leave.

She grabbed his shoulder, looked him in the eyes, and begged. "Please help me!"

His voice became indignant. "Ma'am, just go home and wait it out. Now excuse me, I have patients to attend to. Please leave the hospital."

"I was revived by paramedics earlier, and they advised me to go to the hospital."

The nurse paused. "When was that?"

"About two hours ago."

The nurse frowned and sighed. "We take a patient's vitals an hour after any Narcan treatment. We dismiss the patient if their situation is not life-threatening. I just took your vitals and deemed you okay to leave. So please leave."

She'd have to find care elsewhere. She left the hospital and started walking back toward Granville Street. Clouds were moving in, and the air was cooling. She didn't get far before she felt a sudden and irrepressible onset of diarrhea. She scanned for a hiding spot but there was none. She saw a sewer grate on the side of the road about five steps away. She rushed to it, pulled down her pants and emitted into the sewer. A passing motorist laid on his horn for an eternity. She grabbed some tissues from her bag and quickly cleaned herself as well as she could, while another motorist coming from the other direction also used his horn to express displeasure as he drove perilously close to her.

She reached Granville Street and was desperate to find a restroom where she could relieve herself more and clean herself better. She spotted the awning for the Cosmos Hotel. She'd be watched and asked to leave, but she hoped she'd make it into the restroom. That was all that mattered. One of the doormen said hello as she walked in, and she saw him immediately report her to security. She scanned the lobby and spotted the sign for the lady's room. As she approached the restroom door, she heard a male voice call, "Excuse me ma'am." She ignored it and walked in. After a few minutes, she left the restroom, feeling better and cleaner but knowing her relief would be short-lived.

The security guard was waiting for her outside the restroom door. "Excuse me ma'am, can I help you with something?" he asked.

"No, I'm good." She continued walking toward the front door. He walked with her.

"Are you a guest at the hotel?"

"I was for a few minutes. Thank you for your hospitality."

"Do you have a room in the hotel?" he persisted.

"I used your restroom. Does that count?"

"Please don't come back into this hotel," he scowled.

"I won't. Your restrooms are not clean enough," she retorted as she walked out the front door.

The stomach pain was fast returning. She was certain that she wouldn't be able to detox. She needed heroin. She needed Base.

CHAPTER NINE

Gabby walked to Rosi's Char House, where she sometimes found Base, but he wasn't there. She checked out the coffee shops and bars. No success. While Terrace's downtown area was big for a suburb, it was centered in ten blocks on Granville Street, so she was confident she'd find him if she kept looking, and if he was out. He was usually somewhere where his runners could get to him.

She eventually spotted him near the Mobil gas station. He was off to the side, twisting the arm of some guy, who walked away, clutching at his shoulder. Base was tall and fit. He was not huge but looked like he would always dominate a fight. He wore a light jacket with nothing underneath it. He lit a cigarette, started texting, and nodded approval for Gabby to approach.

"Two?" he asked. Gabby frequently bought enough for two days.

"I don't have money tonight," she replied.

"Then leave."

"I swear I'll get you the money tomorrow."

"Don't ever ask me for something if you got no money." Base paused and looked at her like he was sizing her up for something.

"Actually, I might be able to help you out. If you run an errand for me, you can have a baggie. And I'll give you ten bucks."

Gabby inhaled and fought to remain standing. She had never imagined working for Base. She realized now why Base continued to take some customers directly rather than through one of his runners. It gave him an opportunity to find new runners. Her symptoms were getting worse, and she didn't have enough energy to go downtown and panhandle before getting a fix.

"I can't run an errand. I've bought from you for months. Just give me credit for one day. I'll pay you ten times as much tomorrow."

"No. Leave." He turned back to his phone.

Her knees buckled, but she fought to regain her standing position. "What's the errand?" she asked.

"You walk to the Terrace East station, take the train to Terrace West, and walk three blocks south." He scrolled through his texts and stopped. "Address is 561 Rosewood Avenue. Put the baggie under the mat at the front door, grab the forty bucks under the mat, and come back." He continued to read texts as he spoke.

Even though she badly needed a hit, she did not want to take Base up on his offer. Becoming part of the drug trade was a line she did not want to cross.

Base's phone dinged in his hand. "Actually, he's in a hurry, so he'll just meet you at the train station. I gotta let him know. You in or out?"

"Can I have the hit now?" She barely got the question out before she ran to another sewer four steps away and vomited violently.

"Damn, bitch! What the hell? I don't want that shit near me. Here," he said as he tossed a baggie at her feet. "Go shoot up outta my sight and come back in three minutes. I'm telling my customer you're gonna deliver."

Gabby picked up the baggie. "Thank you," she said in a weak and grateful voice. "I need a rig too."

"Do I look like fuckin' Walgreens?" Despite his verbal protest, he reached into one of his thigh pockets and pulled out a small paper bag, pushed it onto her chest, and pulled back his arm. She grabbed the bag as soon as he released it, preventing the teamwork of gravity and concrete from breaking the syringe inside. She opened the bag and also saw a spoon and a lighter. Base took a cigarette out of its package, broke off the filter, and gave it to her along with his half-empty bottle of water.

"Bring back the lighter and spoon," he ordered.

She ran to the back of the gas station and vomited again. She opened the baggie like a suffocating diver opening a container of oxygen. She cooked her remedy, drew it into the syringe, tied her arm with a shoelace, poked the syringe into a vein on her right arm, then injected the relief into her body.

Done. Base had rescued her.

He wasted no time upon her return. "Your train is at eight o'clock. Remember, get off at Terrace West." He glanced at his Joe Rodeo watch. "You can still make it. When you get off, the customer will be there. He's wearing a hoodie and black jeans."

Her body was transmuting back to normal, but her voice was still strained and groggy. "What color hoodie?"

"How the fuck should I know? Get the forty bucks from him, then give him this." He handed her two baggies. "Here's the train pass. Take the eight twenty-five back. Then I'll give you your ten bucks. I'm trusting you and helping you. If you break that trust, my guys will find you."

Gabby felt she owed Base the delivery. It certainly was true that he had helped her, and she appreciated it. She wanted to get out of her predicament and concluded the risk of getting caught was less than the risk of Base hurting her, so she walked the two blocks to Terrace East and boarded just before the doors closed. After the errand, she'd still have time to make it to tonight's NOTS church just before nine.

During the short ride, she looked at the train route map to take her mind off what she was doing. "This stop, Terrace West," stated the prerecorded voice. She exited on the far west side of the long platform. She didn't see anyone in a hoodie, so she walked toward the two buildings near the center of the station. The first building held the ticket office and the indoor waiting area, while the other contained a coffee shop.

In the walkway between the two buildings, she saw a man and a woman talking to each other and checking paper copies of the train schedule. They were both wearing jeans and short-sleeved shirts. She also saw a tall man in an orange hoodie and black jeans. He leaned against the outside wall of the coffee shop, holding a backpack with one hand. She couldn't see his face since the hood blocked much of it.

"Hey, are you Base's friend?" she asked.

"Yeah," he said. He handed her two twenties. She took the money and gave him the baggies. She stepped toward the direction of the platform, preparing to wait for the train back, while he headed in the opposite direction.

"Ma'am, sir, could you both wait a minute, please?"

Gabby froze. She turned in the direction of the authoritative woman's voice and saw the woman and man who'd been checking the train schedule. They both flashed police badges. From the other side of the building, another pair of police officers emerged – these two in uniform.

The plainclothes officers guided Gabby a few steps away, and the two uniformed officers guided her customer in the other direction.

"Just wait with us for a couple of seconds, ma'am," said the female officer.

"What's going on?" asked Gabby.

"We'll explain in just a second."

The officers with Gabby watched the two officers with the customer. The customer lowered his hood, revealing his face, and Gabby could now see that he looked to be about twenty. She rubbed her neck, feeling guilty for providing drugs to someone so young.

The young man handed the baggie to one of the officers with him. The officer examined it and gave a nod to the police with Gabby.

"You're under arrest for the sale of a controlled substance," said the woman officer to Gabby. She read Gabby her Miranda rights as they handcuffed her. "We're going to need you to come with us." They guided her to a nearby police car as she watched the customer enter the back of a separate car.

Gabby lowered her head and slumped in the seat. The heroin in her brain kept her from feeling the pain of the handcuffs. It did not, however, assuage the shame, shock, and fear of what she had just done, what had just happened, and what might come next.

CHAPTER TEN

Gabby was alone in an interrogation room that contained a grey table, six chairs, and no windows. No longer handcuffed, she rubbed her temples, thinking about how to get out of the situation but coming up with no answers.

The two police officers came back into the room after a couple of minutes and placed a sheet of paper face down on the table. The man sat across from Gabby and introduced himself as Officer Gray. He was in his early thirties with a serious demeanor, and he sat with a straight posture. He introduced his partner as Officer Jenkins. She looked to be in her late thirties and exuded calm confidence as she took a seat. They seemed to know who was going to ask what.

Gray pulled out a notepad and pen, looked at Gabby, and said, "The package you delivered appears to be heroin. We're getting it tested, but we all know it's heroin, don't we?" He seemed to enjoy his job.

Gabby remained silent.

"Sale of a Schedule One controlled substance is a felony punishable by up to twenty years in prison and 375 thousand dollars in fines. Do you understand?"

"Yes. You probably won't believe me, but this is my first time." She mentally tried to piece together how she had sunk so low so quickly. Two years ago, she was a middle school English teacher at a Blue Ribbon-winning school. Now, she was in a police station, arrested for selling drugs and facing felony charges.

Gray's face remained stern. "Today's your lucky day, though."

"I'd hate to have an unlucky day."

"We witnessed the transaction, so there's no doubt that you're guilty." He paused, presumably to let that sink in. "However, we may be able help get your sentence reduced if you help us."

"What do you mean by help you?"

"Have you heard of the confidential informant program?"

"No, but it sounds like I'm about to."

"We'd like to arrest the dealer who gave you the heroin, and hopefully, get a couple of additional arrests from that. If you agree to be an informant, we'll talk to the district attorney about a lighter sentence."

Gabby scratched at her arms. "I'd be backstabbing my dealer."

"If you're uncomfortable with that, we can end this conversation now, and you'll be behind bars for many years."

Jenkins stepped in. "I don't know who this dealer is, but since you're now working for him, he'll hurt you at some point. It's their way of keeping their people in line."

Gabby harbored no ill will toward Base. However, she also thought about him twisting that guy's arm at the gas station. Furthermore, she didn't like the idea of many years in prison. "What would I need to do?"

"We need you to identify this dealer to us and testify in court," said Jenkins.

"What if he gets released on bail? He'll know I ratted him out."

"There's risk involved. But none of our informants have ever been killed," answered Gray.

"How reassuring. How would I identify him to you?"

Jenkins stepped back in. "Tonight, tell him you'd like to run for him again. Tomorrow, do everything you were planning to do during the day. We'll meet up with you at eleven p.m., just outside Einstein Bagels on Granville Street. We'll be in plain clothes. We'll keep our distance, and you'll identify him to us by talking to him and giving us a signal."

Gabby shook her head. "He doesn't have a set place. He moves around. Sometimes I try to find one of his runners."

"Let's hope, for your sake, you can find him tomorrow," said Gray.

"We'll maintain visual contact," said Jenkins. "When you give us a signal, we'll step in and arrest him. We're betting that he'll have a lot in his possession. Do you have any idea how much he carries?"

"I know he has runners making deliveries for him." She pursed her lips. "I never thought that I'd be one of them." Awareness of the danger was permeating her body. "Won't it be obvious to him that I'm the snitch?"

"We'll wait a few minutes after your interaction. He shouldn't know it was you," said Jenkins.

"Why don't you just come back with me tonight? I have to meet up with him."

"We need more time. And we need to arrange for backup. So … if you're willing to work with us, we'll set things up so you I-bond yourself out of jail tonight, and we'll move forward with our plan tomorrow."

"So, my options are rat out my dealer and risk retaliation or go to jail for years?"

"This is the world you built for yourself when you decided to do heroin and got involved in selling drugs, said Gray. What's the name of this dealer?"

"Base. I'm guessing that's not his real name."

The two officers glanced at each other.

"What does he look like?" Jenkins asked, as she flipped a page in her notebook and lifted her pen.

"White guy, tall, late thirties, dark hair, no beard. Usually wearing jeans with pockets on the thighs. Always angry. His stuff is clean, though."

"What a professional," quipped Gray. He looked at Gabby and made a circular motion with his index finger as if to say, "let's get this show moving." He added, "We don't have all night. Are you going to jail or back to the streets?"

"Maybe I should get a lawyer," said Gabby.

Gray responded, "You're welcome to do that. You'll need to wait in jail to get a court-appointed one. We'll likely move on to the next case while you wait though, which means you can forget about any help from us."

"It sounds like I don't really have a choice."

"There's always a choice. Now, if you want to do this, we have some paperwork for you to sign," said Gray as he motioned his head at the paper on the table.

"Can I see it?"

Jenkins turned the paper face up, wrote something on it and handed it to Gabby. Gray continued. "It's an I-bond. Doesn't require any bail money. You sign it and you leave tonight."

Gabby read the paper thoroughly. It appeared to be a standard form saying that she promised to show up for court.

"It doesn't say anything about our arrangement," said Gabby.

"Of course not. We don't document those," responded Gray.

Jenkins added, "Also, if you do this, for your safety, don't tell anyone, even close friends, about it."

Gabby was scared. She was also worried about taking so long to get back to Base and about what he might be thinking. But more than anything, she was afraid of going through withdrawal in jail.

"I'll do it. I still would like to have a lawyer."

"Of course. When it's time for the court case, you'll have one appointed," said Jenkins.

Gabby signed the I-bond. Jenkins passed her a small aerosol container slightly larger than a lipstick tube, told her it was pepper spray, and told her to use it if anyone gave her trouble.

CHAPTER ELEVEN

Gabby made the nine twenty-five back to Terrace East, but only after convincing the officers to drive her to the station to minimize how late she'd be. To not blow her cover, they let her keep the forty dollars to give to Base. She'd be an hour late getting back to him and didn't know what she'd say.

She reached Terrace East and started walking west to find him. The storm clouds that had been menacing for the last few hours finally started to drop hard rain, and the temperature dropped. She was soaked.

She reached the Mobil gas station where she had left him. He wasn't there, so she walked further, looking inside all the restaurants and finally spotted him sitting alone, texting, inside Culver's. The smell of hamburgers and milkshakes reminded her of when she'd taken her students there for frozen custard ice cream during a school outing. She approached him and handed him the cash, concentrating on keeping her hand steady. "Sorry I'm late," she said.

There were three or four customers in the restaurant. In a low but threatening voice, Base began. "What did the cops say?"

"What are you talking about?"

"You're late. And I didn't get a text from my customer. Customers always text me when they receive delivery."

"There were no police."

Base's phone dinged. He looked down to read the text, and Gabby read it upside down.

got the shit. sorry dint txt earlier. I used near station. Left phone home.

Gabby kept her breath steady, trying to avoid displaying the relief she was feeling. Perhaps the police had suggested the customer text Base.

"Why you late?"

"I'm really sorry. I got on the wrong train coming back."

"What wrong train did you take?"

"It was heading west. I got off at the first stop – Hampwood. I had to wait an hour for the next eastbound one."

"No police?"

"No."

Base grabbed her arm and held it tight enough to hurt her. "Well that's good because police try to recruit snitches. And snitches don't do good around me."

"If I was a snitch, wouldn't you be arrested by now?"

"I'm connected. I got friends. I tried to help you, but you cross me, and you'll be praying to be in jail rather than on the street."

"Base, I'm part of your team now."

"Prove it. You wanna deliver again?"

"If I still get money and a hit, then yes."

Base leaned forward. "Some of my runners have become dealers in other towns. I supply them. Tomorrow, you'll deliver to one of them. If you get arrested with that size shipment, you'll be in jail for decades. You up for that?"

She was about to say yes. The cops would be working with her, so there was no risk. But she realized that he might be testing her. Saying yes would reveal a lack of concern for legal ramifications.

"I don't think I'm ready for that. Can we just keep it small for now, like delivering a hit or two?"

He grumbled, then said, "Find me tomorrow. Maybe I'll have a delivery for you. Maybe not."

"Can I have my ten dollars?"

"When you're late, you don't get paid. Leave."

Gabby got up and left. By now, she wouldn't be able to get into the church hosting NOTS. She had nowhere to sleep. The weather had evolved into one of those Chicago area storms where the rain fell so hard in such a short time that the suburban sewers overflowed, basements flooded, and the winds snapped branches off trees. She was exhausted and afraid from the day's activities. She needed somewhere she could feel safe.

She had previously, on occasion, spent the night at a vacant retail spot several blocks south of Granville Street. However, sometimes a guard dog was present, preventing intruders. She walked there, and as she approached it, she heard a dog bark at her viciously.

She knew that Camille's apartment was about a half a mile away – head back up to Granville, go west to Prospect. As much as she hated to impose on her, she had to survive the night. She walked there and pressed the buzzer for her friend's unit.

"Hello?" said Camille, her voice coming out of the speaker next to the front door.

"Camille, it's Gabby."

"My friend. Are you okay?"

"I've had much better days. I can tell you that. I feel horrible for coming here, but do you mind if I come in for a while."

Camille paused then said, "Uh, sure. I'll buzz you in."

Gabby opened the front door then heard the buzzer that unlocked it. Apparently, it was unlocked before Camille buzzed it.

Once in Camille's apartment, Gabby told her the situation, and Camille listened. Gabby concluded by saying, "Normally I'm okay to find a place to sleep when I can't get into a church, but I think the dealer suspects I'm helping the police and—" Gabby started to feel dizzy. The room was spinning then she felt the floor hit her head and everything went black.

—

"Hey, you scared me," said Camille as Gabby woke up.

"Sorry. How long was I out? I guess the day's events caught up with me."

"A few minutes. Gabby, I don't think you could survive tonight on the streets. Just stay here."

"I appreciate it. It'll be only one night."

Gabby had a shower, then went to the guest room. The clean pajamas that Camille lent her felt soft and smelled like flowers. The single bed looked majestic. It had been some time since she'd slept on something horizontal more than two inches off the ground. The plain sheets were inviting and magnificent. She knelt near the bed, made the sign of the cross, and thanked God that he was watching over her.

She crawled under the sheets and realized that she had forgotten the splendor of a clean bed. She enjoyed the breeze and the sound of the rain coming in from the window. She was still terrified about what tomorrow would bring, but fatigue, comfort, and the proximity of a true friend drew her to sleep.

CHAPTER TWELVE

Adam ordered an Uber from the restaurant. He'd googled the location of Havana's, and one of his waiter friends told him that the club opened five months ago and became popular thanks to its extravagant cocktails and energetic dance music. It was on the outskirts of Terrace, about a five-minute ride from the restaurant.

Adam had worked an hour longer than he expected, so he wasn't able to run home and change before heading to the club. He was thankful that his cooking smock had protected his shirt from the grill's spatter, so he at least looked clean, if not fashionable.

While waiting for the car, he called his father. Adam's arrangement with his parents was that they would pay for his Ubers as long as he remained drug-free.

"Hey, Adam."

"Dad. I'm finished work, and—"

"Okay, I'll come and get you. How did it go?" His father sounded happy and eager to pick him up.

"No. I met a girl. I'm gonna go see her and her friends at this club." He swallowed and hoped the conversation wouldn't turn into a confrontation.

"Adam, I know what you do when you don't come home. Your second day out, and you're already going downtown to get stuff?"

"I'm serious. I'm meeting a girl at this place called Havana's."

"I don't believe you. Stay at the restaurant. I'm coming to get you."

The Uber arrived, and Adam got in. Despite the tense conversation, even the act of jumping into the back seat of an Uber was a thrill after his time in jail.

"Dad, you can check the email that Uber will send. It'll just show me going from the restaurant to this club. Then I'll take one home later." He hoped his father would believe him.

"Adam, your tolerance is low because you haven't used in months, and you're no longer on Suboxone. You can't relapse."

"Dad, I'm in the car. You can talk to the driver to see where we're goin'."

"I guess I can just look at the app. Maybe Mom or I will go to the club and make sure you're there."

His parents had indeed followed him in the past when they thought he was lying and might be in danger. His father showing up at the club would be a nightmare. He squeezed the phone tightly and raised his voice a little. "That's so freakin' creepy!"

"After everything we've been through, we have the right."

"Dad, you're freakin' me out. Promise me you won't do that."

"Okay, but if it turns out you're lying, that'll be a problem."

"I'm not lying. I'll be home around midnight."

Walking into Havana's, Adam was concerned that he only had a bit of money, and he was still worried that he'd look odd for not drinking. He spotted the table with Brooke and Kate. There were also two guys sitting at their table. He presumed Brooke's nicer friend, Beth, was on the dance floor.

He walked toward the table, looking around to get a sense of the club. The place was crowded, music was blaring, and servers rushed around with trays of colorful cocktails.

"Adam!" shouted Brooke. "You made it!"

Adam felt different from the two other guys at the table. One of them had huge biceps that were accentuated by a tight T-shirt. The other appeared to have spent an enormous amount of time and gel preparing his hair. Adam had a normal build from playing a good amount of sports, but he seldom pumped iron, and although he washed his hair daily, he seldom used a comb, much less hair products.

"Of course I made it," said Adam. Brooke looked even prettier than he recalled.

"You remember Kate, of course." Kate nodded in his direction, and Adam greeted her. "And these guys are ... sorry, what are your names again?" asked Brooke.

The muscle dude had an air like he thought he was in charge. He extended a hand to Adam, introduced himself, and said, "Pleased to meet you." His handshake was viselike and clammy. The hair guy also introduced himself. Adam forgot their names as soon as they said them and silently dubbed them Muscles and Hair.

"Sup," he said to both.

He saw a glass of some sort of whiskey that seemed to belong to Muscles, a cocktail in a tall glass close to Hair, a fancy martini drink in front of Kate, and a clear, carbonated something in front of Brooke.

"What can we get you to drink, buddy?" said Muscles.

"I'm thirsty as hell. Been cooking all night. I'll just get some water."

"Oh yeah, I thought I noticed the cook pants and shoes!" said Hair, displaying an unusual level of interest in clothes.

Adam now wished he'd taken the time to go home and change.

"Here, sit down," Brooke said as she slid to the left of the bench to make room.

As he sat, he felt his hip touching hers and relished it. Muscles and Kate went to dance, leaving Adam, Brooke, and Hair at the table. Adam wanted to get to know Brooke, not Hair. He noticed that a girl, who also seemed to have taken hours to get ready for the club, was checking out Hair, who didn't have a clear line of sight to her.

Adam excused himself, approached the girl, and told her that Hair thought she was great but was too shy to come over himself."

"Ahhh, that's sooo sweet. I'll come over in a sec," she said.

Adam returned to his seat by Brooke. After a minute, the girl came over, and she and Hair started talking, then left. He grinned.

"So, tell me about yourself," suggested Brooke.

Adam took a drink of his ice water and wondered how he'd get through this conversation without revealing that he'd just gotten out of jail and was a felon. He decided that if he and Brooke saw each other again, he'd reveal more. "Well, to start with, I enjoy goin' to nightclubs dressed as a cook to meet up with pretty girls." They both chuckled.

He continued. "I'm studying culinary arts at Carlane College part-time, but I'm taking a term off right now. I plan to start up again in the winter term." He had completed about half of the courses for his Associate Degree. He'd been taking two courses during the spring term when he was arrested and jailed, so he hadn't been able to complete them.

"And, as you know, I work at Mio Posto."

"Right. What do you do for fun?"

"I love doin' anything outside – snowboarding, snowmobiling, swimming, tennis, pickleball, fishing, wakeboarding, dirt biking."

"Wow. You must have a lot of friends to do all that with."

Adam shrugged. "I suppose. We do a lot of that stuff at my parent's lake house. It's my favorite place in the world. I wish I could live there."

"It sounds nice. Where is it?"

"Just a couple of hours south of here. Alright, your turn. Tell me about yourself."

"Well, I like flirting with cooks in restaurants."

"I guess today was your lucky day."

"Yes, it was." She smiled. Adam had never seen such a pleasant smile. "I'm studying to be a radiography technician. I go to CC too. I don't live in Carlane County anymore, but I did when I started. Now I live in Belmare with Beth."

"I know that place – about halfway between here and Chicago?" Adam had frequently been in that area to buy heroin. "Maybe we'll run into each other at CC when I'm back," he said.

"I'm sure we will. It's a three-year program, and I have one year left."

"Cool. So you'll take X-rays and stuff?"

"And ultrasounds and mammograms and CAT scans. I also work part-time at a hospital. It's nice because I can actually use the things that I'm learning at school."

Adam was impressed. She seemed like she had everything – brains, ambition, looks, poise. He felt privileged that she was interested in him.

"Beth is in my program too" she added.

"That's not the one dancing with Muscles, right?"

Brooke laughed, "You're terrible. No, the one with 'Muscles' is Kate." She started laughing again.

"You got any brothers and sisters?" Adam wanted to keep watching her talk. It gave him an opportunity to get lost in her eyes. He just wanted to stare into her large brown eyes and never stop.

"Yes, two brothers."

Adam also noticed her sexy lips. Everything about her seemed soft and confident – like she could calmly solve any problem and be pretty while she did it.

"Protective brothers?"

"Yes. Big and protective."

"Noted. What are you drinking?"

"Just soda water." Adam was relieved that she was also not drinking. She continued. "I had a beer at the restaurant and my friends insisted I have a mojito here. That's more than enough for me." She looked over her shoulder at the gyrating couples behind them. "Do you dance?"

"Not well," he replied.

She smirked and pulled his hand to the dance floor. They danced three songs. He was uncomfortable dancing but thrilled to be close to her.

Adam could see that there were several people back at the table, and he wanted to get more time alone with her, so he suggested they step into the patio area in the back under the canopy. They talked for about fifteen minutes, which felt like fifteen seconds. He could have talked to her all night.

Brooke said she had class in the morning and had to get going. Even the way she moved to the table and said goodbye to her friends was graceful. It seemed the world was her home and she was comfortable in it.

Waiting for the Ubers inside the entrance to avoid the rain, Adam said, "I'd love to see you again. You wanna do something tomorrow night?"

"Sure. I can be home around eight-thirty. Would that work?" she asked.

"Yeah, how 'bout dinner?"

"Sounds good."

They exchanged numbers. When the cars arrived, Adam awkwardly extended his hand for a handshake. She held it with both hands, which comforted him. Her hands were soft. She held him for a few more seconds, let go, tapped his arm and said, "See you tomorrow."

Adam smiled naturally and helped her get into her Uber. His smile wouldn't leave. He anticipated his father would still be up when he got home, and he could hardly wait to tell him about her.

CHAPTER THIRTEEN

Adam jumped out of the car and rushed under the rain to his front door. He stepped in and saw his father, David, sitting at the kitchen table, working on his computer – a typical situation. Either David or Adam's mother, Sharon, usually stayed up until Adam got home. Adam always thought that was odd because when he used, it was typically at home, so he was at more risk there than out.

"Dad, I met the most amazing girl," he said before even closing the front door.

"That's nice. What's her name?" David lowered the screen on his computer. It seemed his father had calmed down from the earlier argument, probably from having seen the maps of the Uber routes.

Adam smiled, and as he arrived in the kitchen, he said, "Brooke."

"I'd like to hear about her, but first tell me about work. How was it to be back?"

Business first. Okay. "It was decent. It took a few minutes to remember everything, but it all came back. They asked me to stay an extra hour."

"That's good. When do you work next?"

Adam sat at the table. "Tomorrow – short, early shift, two to five-thirty, then I have the NA meeting. After that, I'm seeing Brooke again."

"Don't forget, we're checking out some outpatient programs tomorrow morning."

"I know."

"Okay, so who's this girl?"

Adam's face lit up. "She goes to CC, studying to be a radiography technician. She's gonna do mammograms and x-rays and stuff. She's beautiful and smart and nice."

"Are you sure that seeing a girl right now is the best thing for your sobriety?"

"I think the more normal I can be, the less likely I am to relapse."

"Perhaps, but a relationship can cause stress. And stress can cause a relapse, can't it?"

"Dad, not seeing her would be stressful. If I have something good in my life, that'll help with my sobriety. I really, really like her." He thought for a few seconds. "But maybe you're right. Maybe I shouldn't be getting involved so soon."

"Well, you can think about it. I'm going to bed. You should too – it's a big day tomorrow."

"Yeah. I might grab a bite to eat first."

"Don't leave the kitchen a mess."

"I won't. Remember when you and I had that apartment in Edmonton, and we'd make stuff together?" When there wasn't a confrontation, Adam enjoyed spending time with his father and held many pleasant memories.

"Yeah, I think we made about a million crepes," said David.

"Let's make something now."

David laughed. "You're crazy, man. It's almost one."

"So? C'mon. I'll show you how to make a brick."

"The thing you made in jail?"

"Yeah."

David groaned but agreed.

Adam rifled through the pantry, finding Doritos, potato chips, and Ramen. "With the money you put in my jail account every week, I bought stuff like this at the commissary."

"Yeah, I remember you telling me. It sounded like you amassed quite a collection."

"Yeah, the guys took dibs on my stuff when I told them I was being released." Adam kept rummaging through the pantry. "Got any Slim Jims?"

"I don't think so."

Adam found some sliced salami in the fridge. "I'll use this instead. So, you crunch up the Ramen and Doritos and chips inside their bags. You break the salami and some pickles into pieces. Put it all in a large Ziploc bag. Put in whatever spices and sauces that you can buy, or in this case, that you can find in the pantry. You put a tiny bit of hot water in the bag – we had hot water in our cells. You close the bag, soak a towel in hot water, wrap it around the bag a few times, then wait till it gets kinda hard, so you can break pieces off and share it."

"That's cool. How long do we wait?" asked David.

"About ten minutes. Smoke while we wait?" Adam particularly enjoyed smoking with his father. They could hang and talk or not talk. It was just time together. He believed his father felt the same way. He only smoked when he was with Adam.

"Dude, I haven't smoked since you went to jail."

"Yeah," Adam said with a smile. "But I'm home now. C'mon. It's good for you," quoting a line from a movie he'd watched several times with David – *Alpha Dog*.

Paradoxically, Adam's addiction had brought him and his father closer. David was an independent technology consultant who helped large companies implement new computer systems. His assignments usually lasted more than a year and were in cities that required weekly flights. On several occasions, to get Adam away from home and its associated triggers and dangers, David and Adam got an apartment in the city where David was working. Adam would find a job cooking in a nearby restaurant. In the evenings, they'd have dinner together, go work out together or watch TV shows together. On weekends, they'd ski, snowboard, fish, or go catch a football game.

David would fly home every few weeks. He'd missed his wife and other children but knew it was best for Adam. During his weekend trips home, David worried about leaving Adam alone but felt he was safer away.

Adam and David walked into the double garage. Adam pushed the buttons to open the two large doors. The open garage allowed them to watch the hard rain and provided a place for the smoke to exit.

Adam lit one of his Marlboro Reds, and they continued talking. They moved toward the driveway, almost reaching the rain, but staying in the garage to avoid it. The speed and size of the raindrops were impressive, as was the pounding noise of thousands of them hitting the cement every second.

"So, this girl. When are you going to tell her about your sickness?" asked David.

"I'll find the right time, but Dad, I'm not doin' that shit no more."

"I know, but to be fair to her, shouldn't she know your situation?"

"Yeah, but I just want a few days of normal – just a few freakin' days of normal."

"I know you do. If you can stay sober, your life will be normal. I love you, Adam, and your mom and I want you to have a normal life as much as you do."

"I know. I love you too."

When Adam's cigarette was almost done, David extended his hand "Okay, give me the last puff."

"Take a full one, man!" Adam started to remove a fresh cigarette from the package.

"No. Just give me that," said David, as he looked at the remainder of the lit cigarette.

Adam passed it to him. David took a drag, inhaled and exhaled. "Oh yeah. I miss it … But I'm not going to start again." He extinguished it, and they both went back into the house.

Adam touched the food he'd created. "It's going to need another few minutes."

"Alright, I'm going to bed. I promise I'll try the brick tomorrow," said David.

"Okay. Thanks for hangin' with me, Dad."

"It was fun." He and Adam hugged, and David said, "It's good to have you home."

"Thanks."

David looked at Adam's phone. "Remember our deal?"

"What?"

David extended an open hand. "You give me your phone at night."

"I just want to text Brooke goodnight."

David nodded once. "Do it fast."

Adam typed a few things, looked at his phone for a couple of seconds, and handed it to his father.

WEDNESDAY

CHAPTER FOURTEEN

John Tylor got to his office around seven Wednesday morning. He understood the importance of the case and the gravity of his situation. He had done some research at home last night and planned to get into more detail this morning. He sat at his computer to review the case files. Harris Clark lawyers used a digital tool named "Harry", which was a derivation of the acronym HAIRE, or Harris Artificial Intelligence Research Engine.

He touched the icon for Harry. A pleasant male computer voice said, "Awaiting instructions."

"Harry, show me the discovery papers for the case against Sheriff Mason."

"Here are the discovery papers," responded the Harry system as several documents appeared on John's forty-two-inch computer screen. John reviewed the situations of the deceased and their families. One set of parents was suing for the death of their twenty-three-year-old son who died six days after being released. A second set of parents was suing for their twenty-five-year-old daughter, who perished four days after she got out. One man was suing for the death of his fiancé, a twenty-nine-year-old man who died six days after being released.

The depositions from the families showed a consistent pattern leading up to the deaths. First, the people got charged two or three times for possession. John wondered why these drug abusers didn't learn their lesson after one possession charge. The second step was spending several months in Carlane County Jail awaiting a final outcome. The last step was getting out and passing away within a week.

The deceased had all been on medicine prior to incarceration – two of them on Suboxone and one on Methadone. John knew of Methadone as a prescribed drug that heroin addicts took in order to stop taking heroin. He had not heard of Suboxone, however.

"Harry, what is Suboxone?"

"Suboxone is the brand name of a medicine whose primary ingredient is Buprenorphine. It is used to treat people with opioid use disorder."

John had heard the terms "opioid" and "opiate" and was not sure what the difference was. "What is an opiate, and what is an opioid?"

"An opiate is a natural medicine derived from opium poppies. Examples include heroin, morphine, and codeine. The term opioid includes those natural opiates and the synthetic versions, like Hydrocodone and Oxycodone."

The names sounded only vaguely familiar to him. "What are the brand names for the last two?

"Vicodin and OxyContin."

Now he remembered. He had been prescribed OxyContin after his back surgery last winter. He despised the feeling it generated, so he had taken only two pills. After several months, he had flushed the rest down the toilet.

"What does Suboxone do?" asked John.

"Suboxone reduces the urge to use opioids."

"Give me more detail."

"Use of opioids changes the structure of the patient's brain by increasing the number of opioid receptors and reducing the patient's ability to produce dopamine. The patient cannot fill the increased number of receptors on their own and therefore feels pain and dysphoria. The patient requires more opioids to feel better. Taking more opioids compounds the problem. Buprenorphine fills the receptors, reducing the requirement for the patient to fill them with heroin or other opioids."

"Does it work? Does it stop addicts from using?"

"People with opioid use disorder might still relapse, even when on the medicine. However, the frequency of relapse and mortality rates are significantly lower."

"What research did you review to draw that conclusion."

"I reviewed 1,384 documents since January 1, 2015, including articles from the American Medical Association, the National Institute on Drug Abuse, and the Canadian Medical Association." The Harry system scrolled the list of document titles on John's computer. John glanced at it, then swiped it away.

John thought about the word "disease" that he had noticed in the depositions and Harry's use of the term "opioid use disorder." Fancy terms for bad character, poor choices, and lack of discipline, he thought.

"Harry, why do some people call drug abuse a disease?"

"The American Medical Association defined substance abuse as a disease in 1956. The American Society of Addiction Medicine defines addiction as a primary, chronic disease of the brain."

John shook his head and returned to reading the discovery papers.

Part of the suit was a claim for damages posthumously for the pain and suffering the addicts faced as they were forced to withdraw from their medicine in jail. The families presented quotes they had received when visiting their loved ones.

The first one read, "I threw up blood and convulsed. They put me in the sick room. The entire room was not much more than the width of a narrow bed. They just gave me Tums."

The second one: "I couldn't help but scream at the aching in my bones. My stomach felt like it was full of razor blades, and my skin was piercing."

The third: "I've been through heroin withdrawals, and now I've been through a Methadone withdrawal. Cold-turkey Methadone withdrawal was worse."

John thought about these people and about all addicts. Since it's so horrendous to withdraw, why do they do it? Why would they destroy their lives like that? They knew it was illegal. They knew they could get caught.

He read the deposition by the sheriff: "It's a shame that people died once they were free to do what they wanted. My heart goes out to these families. However, that's obviously not something we can control. These families think we should give the inmates Suboxone. Imagine how that would work. These are little strips of a narcotic. They would be hidden, sold, and abused. These people abuse drugs. That's why they're in jail. If we make narcotics available, we'd have overdoses and deaths inside my jail. Not on my watch."

He pondered the sheriff's statement. While it was a little crass, it made sense.

"Show me studies on opioid death rates after incarceration," he ordered.

Harry answered, "A study by *The New England Journal of Medicine* concluded that former inmates' risk of fatal overdose is 129 times higher than for the general population."

"Print it … More," John commanded.

"A study by the Canadian Medical Association found life expectancy for people who were incarcerated was significantly lower than for the general population. For incarcerated addicts, the life expectancy is even lower."

"Print it … More."

"The Journal of the American Medical Association—"

"Stop. Are any states trying to reduce these death rates?"

"Searching … Rhode Island provides inmates with medical assisted treatment, giving them Methadone, Buprenorphine, or Naltrexone, then continuing the treatment after release through treatment centers."

"Any results reported?"

"There was a sixty percent decrease in mortality rate."

"More examples," commanded John.

"California allowed drug offenders to go to treatment rather than jail. They saw reduced crime which resulted in savings of one hundred million dollars to the state."

"Have there been any wrongful death suits against jails or prisons where the death occurred post-release?"

"Searching … None found."

So, the studies showed that providing medicine to inmates had positive effects. Not good for his case. He was glad to have this information though, so he could prepare a defense if the opposing party quoted such studies.

He asked Harry to research the downside and risks of jails

providing such medicine. He wanted information to support his case. Unfortunately, the system did not come up with much.

"Harry, send a note to my legal assistants letting them know what research and documents you reviewed with me and tell them to read the rest of the discovery papers and summarize them for me."

"Emails have been sent to your team," Harry responded.

In his most successful cases, John had spent time getting into the minds of his adversaries. Jackie's suggestion was nothing new. The more he could understand their point of view and way of thinking, the more he could anticipate their moves and what might be acceptable to them.

He knew of the Alcoholics Anonymous organization from seeing AA meeting scenes on TV and in movies and wondered if there was something similar for drug addicts.

"Harry, is there an Alcoholics Anonymous for opioid addicts?"

"There is an organization called Narcotics Anonymous."

"Do they have meetings?"

"Yes, NA has closed and open meetings."

"What does that mean?" Even though John had used the Harry system for several months, he was still amazed at its ability to understand questions, sift through thousands of web pages and documents and provide answers.

"Closed meetings are only for people with substance use disorder. Open meetings can be attended by other people, typically family members or close friends."

"Are there any open NA meetings nearby tonight?"

"There is an open NA meeting at six p.m. at 341 Granville Street in Terrace."

John's wife was out of town, and his son was always busy in the evenings, so he decided that he'd go and listen in after work. "Mark it on my calendar."

"Done."

He called the sheriff's private office number. He didn't expect to reach him, but thought he'd leave a message introducing himself, to let him know that he was on the case and that he'd like to meet in person.

"Sheriff Mason here."

John was surprised that he answered. "Sheriff Mason, this is John Tylor from Harris Clark."

"Hello, John. Yes, Jackie told me about you. I've known Jackie's family for many years. I trust she assigned someone who will make this bullshit go away."

"We'll make sure to get you the best result possible."

"Christ. That's not same as 'go away'. I guess that's how you lawyers talk."

"It may take a bit of work, though." John liked to manage expectations.

"What are you talking about? This is a bullshit case. The last firm was giving me the same crap. That's why I fired that goddamn ponytail. You don't have a ponytail, do you?"

John considered telling him that that was none of his business but thought better of it. "I do not."

"Good."

"Sheriff Mason, I'd like to meet you in person as soon as possible to understand what a successful outcome would look like to you and to prepare for tomorrow's settlement conference."

"Sure, let's meet, but I can tell you right now that a successful outcome, as you call it, is that this suit gets dropped. Like I said, it's bullshit, and it needs to go away. I will not change policy, and I will not have the county pay damages. For what? These people were safe in my jail. They died after they were released because they went back to shooting up. Pretty cut and dry."

"Okay, we'll talk more about that when we meet."

"I can meet at nine. That's forty-five minutes from now. Can you come over here?"

"Oh. Yes, I'll be there."

John was surprised, but glad, that the sheriff wanted to meet so quickly. Before leaving, he called the lawyer representing the families to introduce himself and to get a sense for how flexible the families might be.

"Hello?" said the male voice on the phone.

"Hello, my name is John Tylor. I'm a lawyer with Harris Clark. I'm representing Sheriff Mason on the wrongful death suit."

"Hello, Mr. Tylor. I'm no longer representing the families."

"Oh?"

"They concluded they wanted someone more experienced, and I guess, more expensive."

"Who is the new firm?"

"Parker and Associates. The lawyer's name is Angela Parker."

John tightened his lips. "Okay, thanks for the information."

He knew of Angela Parker. She was young, but she had already developed a reputation for winning high-profile cases against governments and large corporations. She had a face that news cameras loved, and she played that to her advantage. Parker and Associates had been featured in the magazines, *Life in Terrace* and *Chicago Life*. The "Associates" consisted of one other lawyer – an employee of Angela's, not a partner. Apparently, the other lawyer was as sharp as Angela, but had no desire to be in the spotlight. The firm also employed a well-regarded researcher and an experienced paralegal. A small but powerful dream team.

John surmised that Angela Parker knew the chances of winning this case at trial were low, but that public attention could force a satisfactory outcome for the families without a trial.

A call came in on John's mobile, and he answered it.

"Hello, Mr. Tylor. This is Angela Parker. I just received a text with your name and phone number from the previous counsel for the families."

"Hello, Ms. Parker. You move fast. Pleased to meet you, at least by phone."

"I guess we'll be seeing each other at the settlement conference tomorrow," she said.

"Yes. It seems that the legal case for your clients is not strong."

"Weaker cases have been won. By me." Her confidence was as large as her reputation.

"How eager are your clients to reach a settlement?" asked John.

"They may be flexible on the compensatory damages, but not on the policy change. They want inmates to have their prescribed medicine. They want to save lives. How much flexibility does the sheriff have?"

"I'm just getting up to speed on the case and on his position, but at this point, he's not willing to concede anything."

"Sounds like we won't have a conclusion tomorrow. Which is good because then I'll have a story to provide to the news."

"See you tomorrow, Ms. Parker."

"Indeed."

With the sheriff holding firm and the plaintiffs not yielding on the policy change, maybe this wouldn't be the layup that Jackie thought.

CHAPTER FIFTEEN

Camille's two-bedroom apartment was not lavish, but it was clean and neat. She earned a decent income from Academy and supplemented it with private piano and voice lessons. Hanging on her bedroom walls were several framed pictures of her with her daughters, a picture of her as a child with her own parents, and one of her with her grandparents.

In the living room, an upright Yamaha piano stood against one wall under a window that looked out onto Prospect Street and also provided a partial view of Granville Street. On the surface of the piano top were sheets of music and lyrics handwritten in pencil. Two of the living room walls featured a continuous row of fourteen framed posters of the musicals she'd directed over the years, starting with *Beauty and the Beast* and ending with *Rent*. She turned the television on to CNN to see the morning headlines but muted the volume.

She entered the kitchen, made coffee, unwrapped a strip of Suboxone, and put it under her tongue. She heard Gabby in the guest room getting her things in order. Camille touched the FaceTime icon on her phone.

"Hi, Mommy!" said Rosalie, sitting in her kitchen. She pushed her long brown hair behind her ears and called out to her younger sister, "Mia, it's Mommy!" Camille had purchased an iPhone for Rosalie a few months back and installed parental controls so she could use it only for calls and for FaceTime.

Mia's little face entered the phone screen. Rosalie tenderly moved Mia's dark hair away from her eyes. "Hi Mommy! Freda's coming over today," she said in her little, five-year-old voice.

"Oh, that's nice," Camille said.

"Freda might take us to the pool," said Rosalie.

"That sounds like fun since the weather is nicer now. Make sure you put sunscreen on."

"Freda said she has a new bathing suit she wants to wear," added Mia.

Gabby hurried into the kitchen when she heard the girls' voices. Camille pointed the phone camera at her. "Girls, this is an old friend. Her name is Mrs. Jones."

"Hi, Mrs. Jones," they both said.

"Mrs. Jones taught me how to speak English better when daddy and I first moved here."

Rosalie looked confused. "A teacher teaching a grown-up?"

Camille laughed. "Yes, she taught English as a Second Language. At night."

"During the day, I taught at a school, with children a little older than you," interjected Gabby.

Mia asked in her tentative voice, "Will you be my teacher one day?"

"That would be nice, but I don't think so, honey."

"Mrs. Jones reads and writes a lot. She and I wrote a few songs together years ago," said Camille.

"Well, I just wrote the lyrics. Your mom is the brilliant musician. Anyway, nice talking with you, girls. I better go get my things together."

"Gabby, put some apples and bananas in your bag," Camille said, briefly turning away from her daughters. Gabby nodded.

"Girls, I have something I want to sing for you." Camille walked to the living room and positioned her phone in a large cup sitting on top of the piano, which allowed her to look at the camera without tilting her head.

"What song is it?" asked Rosalie.

"A new one that I've been working on just for you two."

Camille played chords then began to sing.

"You're my reason for living
Every day and every hour
You guide all my actions
You're my higher power

Your love lifts me up
When things can seem so dour
You're much bigger than me
You're my higher power

A love so deep
An everlasting flower
I stay strong for you
cause you're my higher power"

"What do you think?" asked Camille.

"I love it!" shouted Rosalie.

"Me too!" agreed Mia.

"What's a higher power?" asked Rosalie.

"It is something bigger than ourselves. It's something that guides our actions and keeps us healthy."

"We're not bigger than you," said Mia.

"And we don't keep you healthy," suggested Rosalie.

"It's just a way to say how much I love you."

"I can't believe Mommy's writing us another song!" said Rosalie.

Mia jumped up and down. "Me too!"

Meanwhile, Gabby had entered the living room, removed a few items from her bag, and put them into her pockets to make room for the fruit.

Through the phone, Camille noticed that her ex-husband had been watching the video conversation. Robert's doorbell rang, and he walked away from the phone. Camille heard him say, "Hello, my love. Girls, come say hi to Mommy-Freda." Mia said bye to Camille and walked away.

Rosalie lowered her voice, "Mommy, sometimes Daddy isn't very nice to us."

"What do you mean?"

"Sometimes, he yells at us for no reason."

"Why?"

"I don't know. I guess mostly when he thinks we're not nice enough to Freda. He wants us to call her Mommy-Freda. I don't do that. Or when he wants to be alone with her."

"Does he do anything besides yell?"

"What do you mean?"

"Like a spanking or anything?"

Rosalie paused, then said, "No."

Camille said the opposite of what she was thinking. "Well, he has a lot of stress. He's raising you and your sister mainly on his own, and that's a big job. I'll speak to him."

"Okay."

"Rosalie, come and help Mommy-Freda with her things," Robert said in the background.

"I'm talking to Mom."

"I know. I don't care." Through the phone video, Camille caught a glimpse of Freda. She was an attractive woman, and she was carrying several suitcases.

Robert added, "Actually, I want to talk to Mom," then took the phone.

Robert was also from Quebec, but his first language was English. "I assume you got my papers?"

"Yes. I'll see you there. I need to hang up now."

"Hey, was that your old friend Gabby I saw in your apartment? Is she a junkie too now?"

"You don't need to use that word, especially if the girls might hear."

"They're walking upstairs with Freda."

Camille was still eager to end the conversation but thought she'd speak to him about what Rosalie said. "Robert, you know how Rosalie hates yelling. You can be mean to me all you want, but could you watch it with them?"

"They need to learn to be nicer to Freda. By the way, did you see how hot she is? And she doesn't do drugs. Anyway, it's none of your goddamn business how I raise my kids in my home."

Camille could see his anger starting to rise, like she had seen many times. His tirades often paralleled a classical music composition.

"I have custody, not you. You're the one who decided to start using heroin," he said like a slow adagio. Then he increased tempo and volume, "Pain pills weren't enough for you. You chose heroin over your girls, you goddamn junkie!" Finally, the thunderous cadenza, "You're pissing me off. I'm calling ICE to let them know that an immigrant is in possession of a controlled substance. Good luck trying to keep your green card and staying in the country. Bitch." He always managed to land the last word right on the button for a solid finality. He disconnected the call.

"Quite a piece," said Gabby.

"He served me with papers yesterday to stop seeing the girls. I'm going to a visitation hearing today."

"Oh, God. I'm so sorry to hear that."

"And it's not like he takes great care of them. I don't know how they would ever get cleaned or dressed properly if I didn't see them."

"Was he ever violent to you or the girls?" asked Gabby.

"He came close a few times. He thought spanking was acceptable. I was always able to convince him otherwise. I know that he was spanked as a child."

"Well, hopefully this Freda lady will also convince him not to hit."

"I pray so. That's another reason they need to visit me. It gives me a chance to check on them." Camille shook her head, appalled at her situation. "Let's go to the kitchen and grab some coffee."

As Camille poured the coffees, Gabby pointed to the empty Suboxone wrapper, "You find that medicine helps?"

"Yes. I do everything I can to avoid relapsing. It was almost impossible to find a doctor to prescribe it, but I'm glad I was able to."

Gabby sipped her coffee and said, "It's astounding that it's already been five years since we first met, and over two years since we've seen each other."

"Yes, I tried to contact you a few times, but the number I had didn't work, and I couldn't find you on Facebook or anything," said Camille.

"Yes, I suppose I've been incommunicado. You never mentioned anything about addiction back when we were friends. How did it start for you?"

Camille continued to hold her coffee in one hand as she spoke. "Well, when Robert and I were first married, we were at a party, and a girl was handing out Vicodin. I had never done any drugs, but it just seemed harmless. A painkiller. A pill that doctors prescribe. Once I took it, I couldn't believe the feeling. Like the anxiety I had all my life was gone. The feeling reminded me of how I felt when my mother would hold me when I was five or six years old. The girl gave us four pills to take home."

"Did Robert use any of the pills you took home?"

"He tried one again. They didn't do much for him."

"Fortunate man."

"But for me, I was a new person. No more nerves or anxiety. A classmate at Laval told me that he took OxyContin, which was stronger. He showed me where to get some – a guy who sold from his apartment nearby."

"Expensive pills, aren't they?"

"Yes, like forty bucks! Besides school, I was waitressing at an expensive restaurant and making good tip money, which was going to the habit, tuition for Robert and me, a cheap apartment for us, and food."

"And then your kind dealer suggested something more affordable, right?" said Gabby.

"Yes, I never thought I would snort heroin, but I did. Then I never thought I'd inject heroin, but I did, every few days. Robert knew what

I was doing. He was taking a program to become an electrician, and he didn't care that I quit school since it gave me more time to work and make money."

"He sounds like a winner from day one. Someday, you'll have to tell me why you married him."

"He *is* handsome and very good at certain things." She smirked. "In the early days, he was a good cuddler too. But the marriage was difficult from the start. Anyway, then I got pregnant. We were not trying to have children, but I guess we weren't trying not to either."

"Babies bechance."

"I stopped using immediately. Detoxing was tough, but it's amazing what people can do for their kids. I eventually finished my Master's degree and stayed clean for seven years. About ten months ago, Robert and I started discussing divorce. He'd been having girlfriends, and he had a temper. I was focused on Rosalie and Mia and my music and theater work. A couple of months later, I relapsed. Because of that, I thought that I should be the one to move out. After the divorce, I went back to my former surname."

"I'm so sorry to hear all that, Camille."

"I don't know why I relapsed. I think I just let my guard down. When you've been clean for a long time, you forget that you still have to work at it. That heroin brain is always there trying to take control, I think."

"Well, I haven't been clean for that long a time, so I wouldn't know from experience," said Gabby.

"I continued using about every ten days or so. One day, I was in the restaurant where Adam works, and he told me you could get medicine for addiction."

"Is it still difficult to stay clean?"

"Every day, I remind myself to not let my guard down. I wear this wristband that Rosalie gave me, as a constant reminder to stay healthy for them. They need me. I can't become one of those numbers." Camille pointed at a copy of a newspaper article on her coffee table. "Someone handed that out at a meeting." The headline read "60,000 people died of overdose last year – 160 every day."

"Let's refill our coffees and go sit in the living room," suggested Camille.

The CNN headline read, "New outbreak in the Ebola epidemic. 7 people treated in Congo." It was swept away and replaced by, "Shocking car pile-up. 6 people killed."

Camille sat in her leather chair and Gabby sat in the matching sofa.

"So, what's going on with you? I had no idea you had this problem," said Camille.

"Yes … Well, I use regularly. Every so often, I get enough fortitude to withdraw. On the street, that's tough. I don't know why I force myself through it. After a few days, I recidivate."

Camille was reminded of Gabby's large vocabulary, which she sometimes forgot to suppress. "How did it begin for you?" asked Camille.

"Two and a half years ago, near the end of the school year, I was teaching a self-defense course as an extracurricular at the private middle school where I taught English."

"I didn't know you did self-defense."

"I used to practice a bit of karate. Nothing intense. Anyway, I was showing the girls how to throw a punch, and I dislocated my shoulder. The doctor fixed my shoulder and prescribed me a thirty-day supply of Oxy. I'm not even sure why. The pain was bad, but bearable. Like you,

I couldn't believe how much better life seemed with the painkillers."

"Exactly."

"I got another prescription. Then another. I became dependent. When I couldn't get any more from doctors, I started buying them on the street. Over the summer, I progressed to heroin. I returned to work the following September but kept missing days, and the school terminated me in October. One nice thing they did was agree to keep my health insurance going for two years."

Gabby sipped her coffee and continued. "With no income, I had to sell my home, get what little equity there was and rent a place. I went through rehab twice, on my dime, since my insurance didn't cover it. I fell behind in my rent and got evicted about four months ago."

"I remember that your parents and your sister live in Chicago. Can't they help?"

"They're disgusted with me. They've asked me to not contact them until I've decided to change my lifestyle." She paused. "Mark would have understood."

"How long has it been?"

"Almost six years. He was the love of my life."

"It was a car accident, right?"

"Yes."

"I'm so sorry," said Camille.

"Thank you. After he died, I was blessed to have my work. I savored being part of the school." Gabby went on to tell Camille about the legal troubles she was in, how the cops wanted her to be an informant, and how unsafe that seemed to be.

"I'm so very sorry to hear about your situation. You know that I'd let you keep staying here if I could, but I'm fighting for visitation–"

Gabby waved her hand. "No, I wouldn't dream of it."

"Gabby, I need to get going to my hearing."

"Sure. Could you drop me off at Parkdale Hospital? I do some volunteer work there every Wednesday. Even amidst this quandary, I'd like to do it."

As they walked to the car and during the drive, Camille continued to think about Rosalie's comment that Robert was sometimes mean to her and Mia. She wondered what exactly was behind it.

CHAPTER SIXTEEN

Gabby walked through the front doors of the hospital. She was worried about her task with the police later in the day and the prospect of many years in jail. However, she was glad to be free for now. Physically, she wasn't feeling bad. She'd had a good sleep, and she was still a few hours away from serious withdrawal symptoms.

She stopped at the front desk to get her volunteer badge and walked down several hallways until she reached children's hospice. She entered a room that contained eight girls around middle school age, some of them thin and weak.

Large windows looked out onto the full green foliage of the healthy maple tree outside. A combination of teen beauty, science, and health magazines blanketed a coffee table.

The girls had been waiting for her. Some who were strong enough called out.

"Hey, Gabby!"

"Miss Gabrielle!"

"Sup, Teach?"

"Hello, girls. I missed you." She proceeded to ask each girl how they were doing. She reached into her bag and pulled out a well-worn book. It was a teen thriller with enough bad words that it wouldn't be on a middle school reading list and that only Gabby could bring to life in her humorous, street-wise way.

"Where did we leave off last week?" asked Gabby, knowing the answer.

"You finished Chapter Thirteen," yelled one of the girls.

As Gabby started reading Chapter Fourteen, her voice was the only sound in the room. She was in her element, providing some joy and education to these kids. She continued to read expressively, occasionally pausing for questions about what a certain word meant or to wait for the smirks and snickers to finish at the racy parts. After thirty minutes, she closed the book, and said, "Discussion time!" For another fifteen minutes, she led a conversation, letting the girls know why the author wrote things the way she did and answering questions on any topic. Despite their circumstances, the girls enjoyed the conversation.

"Okay, I have to go now." She proceeded to say goodbye to each girl and wished them the best. As she was walking out of the lounge, several girls said, "See you next week."

"Absolutely," she responded, knowing she probably wouldn't be back.

Outside the lounge, a young man sitting at the nursing station popped up and approached her. She remembered him as the person she had interviewed with about six months ago, when she applied for the volunteer role of hospice reader.

"Gabby, you may remember me. My name is Terry O'Neil." His voice was high-pitched.

Gabby nodded.

"I'm an assistant business manager here at the hospital," he boasted. "I direct the volunteer force. We met when you applied for this role."

"I recall." She wondered where the conversation was going.

"One of my other responsibilities is to review potentially uncollectible accounts. That includes ambulance and paramedic services."

"Okay."

"Well this morning, I saw a paramedic bill for reviving a drug addict with no address. The paramedics suggested it go into the uncollectible pile. The document had your name on it. And the signature on the waiver matched the signature on your volunteer application form."

She was now concerned. "I thought that ambulance was from Terrace General."

"TG was overbooked last night, so we were helping them out."

"I'm not in a position to pay for that ambulance service."

"That's an issue, but that's not what I want to talk to you about right now."

"Okay."

He attempted to smile at her as if they were friends. "Gabby … You're a drug addict. Heroin." He said the word as if it trumped every other word in the English language.

"I'm afraid I know that."

"Well, we can't have a heroin addict spending time with our child patients."

"Why?"

"It's just not something that's allowed, of course. No hospital would allow it."

"Why?"

"Isn't it obvious – a hospital allowing a heroin addict to come in and read to children? Good God. What would the parents think?"

"I've met several of the parents. They like me and are grateful that I come in and take their children's minds off their unspeakable situations for a short time. They thanked me many times."

"Well, they don't know that you're an addict."

"They know that I bring joy and intelligent discussion into the little time these kids have left."

"You could steal drugs from the hospital to support your habit."

"If that's true, the hospital needs to lock down its drugs more securely."

"You could steal other things."

"There's not a lot of street value in Styrofoam cups and bendable straws."

"Well, it's hospital policy – people abusing drugs cannot be part of our volunteer force. You can no longer volunteer at this hospital. Here's a letter saying you're not allowed on the hospital's property – unless it's for your own medical treatment."

Gabby took the letter and left. More arguing wouldn't change the situation. She also knew that he had a point. Most importantly, she knew that the day would bring bigger and more menacing problems.

CHAPTER SEVENTEEN

John arrived at the Carlane County buildings about twenty minutes before his meeting with Sheriff Mason. The campus was located on Granville Street, in a less populated area, about ten miles west of downtown Terrace. He was somewhat familiar with the property, but as a civil lawyer, he didn't come here as often as criminal lawyers did.

The campus was a sprawling set of five large, modern buildings. Four of them housed county administration offices and courtrooms. The fifth building contained the jail and the sheriff's office. It wasn't connected to the other buildings, and there was only one public entrance. John parked in one of the three lots and decided to stroll inside one of the court buildings for a few minutes as he gathered his thoughts.

The large hallways were filled with criminal lawyers in cheap suits dashing from courtroom to courtroom as they juggled appearances for multiple clients and talked on their camera-less phones. The majority of the defendants were nervous men and women in their twenties and thirties fighting drug possession charges. Some had also been charged with crimes related to getting money for drugs, like shoplifting, theft, and prostitution.

John could hear discussions between lawyers and clients because they occurred in the hallways without privacy. Most of the conversations were one-sided, with the lawyer using legal terms and descriptions of procedure that their clients didn't understand. The conversations usually ended along the lines of, "We're going to file a motion for continuance."

He stepped outside and walked across the street to the building featuring the words "Carlane County Sheriff's Office and Jail" above the front door.

"I have an appointment with Sheriff Mason," he announced to the officer at the security desk, a solid-looking woman in uniform.

"There's only one."

"Excuse me?"

"There's only one sheriff. You can just say 'I'm here to see the sheriff' and we'll know who you're taking about."

John wasn't sure if this was a feeble attempt at humor or an effort to be condescending. Either way, she sported a small grin conveying she was proud of herself.

"Okay," John said.

"Are you John Tylor?"

"Yes."

With her quip out of the way, she became more helpful. "The sheriff is expecting you. Please follow me."

The sheriff's office was large, housing a desk, credenza, bookcase, and a small table with accompanying chairs. There were several certificates framed on the wall, although John couldn't make out what they were for. On the floor, leaning against the wall, was a framed document with a large title at the top, "Favorite Quotes from Sheriff Joe." John had time to read one of the quotes as he stepped toward the chair facing the sheriff's desk. "I needed a place to put the dogs. I put the prisoners in the tents, and I had a nice place to put the dogs. We treat the cats nice too, and horses. I have the inmates take care of the animals."

The sheriff stood up, stayed behind his clean desk and extended his hand. "Pleased to meet you, young man," he said without smiling. He wore a putty colored short-sleeve police shirt with his badge fastened on the left side of his chest. He was stocky, with some fat that probably used to be muscle and hair that had partially turned grey. His chest was out, and his chin was high.

"Likewise, Sheriff Mason. Thank you for trusting our firm with this important matter."

"Cut the crap and the lawyer talk. I trust no one. Make this goddamn thing go away, and fast. I got a jail to run and an election to win."

His speed and bluntness surprised John. "I need to tell you that the families have moved their legal counsel to Parker and Associates."

"Is that that pretty girl who likes to go on TV?"

"Yes."

"Has she gone on TV about this?"

"Not yet. She wants to see if we can come to a settlement at the conference. I suspect that if we don't, she will indeed leverage the press."

"Your boss told me the families have a weak case – that there's no way they can prove wrongful death for a fatality that occurred when the person was not in our custody."

"It would indeed be difficult for the families to win at trial.

However, *going* to trial during your election campaign is what could cause damage."

"I know that, for Christ's sake. That's why you need to make it go away."

"Do you have any flexibility in your position?"

"Like what?"

"Well, is changing the policy so addicts can have their prescribed medicine an option?"

"I guess you didn't hear me earlier, and you didn't read my deposition. I will not do that. I run a tight ship. My safety record is better than ninety-one percent of the jails in this country. I know what I'm doing."

Reaching a settlement without trial would be unlikely if the sheriff had no flexibility. "I needed to know if there was any room for a compromise."

"No, there isn't. I get elected because people know I'm tough on crime. Do you know what 'tough on crime' means?"

"I believe so." John felt he was not making a good impression.

"It means tough on criminals. Punish them for what they did to society. This place is not supposed to be a luxury stay at the Ritz. These are criminals. I saw you noticing the quotes from Sheriff Joe. One of the deputies gave me that as a gag. But Sheriff Joe kept getting re-elected because he was tough. He made the inmates wear pink underwear, gave them two twenty-cent meals a day, moved them out of the air-conditioned jails and into the sweltering Arizona heat in tents, put the addicts on chain gangs. Don't you think someone's gonna stop being an addict when they discover it involves almost suffocating in tents and working on chain gangs?"

"I suppose ..." John was starting to dislike the crassness of the sheriff, but he mostly agreed with him. "Well, Sheriff Mason, we likely will be going to trial if we don't settle tomorrow."

"Do your job. Let them know where I stand and that they have no hope in hell of winning. That should keep this stupid thing from going to trial."

John wrapped up the conversation and left. He needed to think about the next moves, given the Sheriff's unmovable position. He planned to spend the rest of the day and evening figuring out a path to a settlement.

CHAPTER EIGHTEEN

Adam woke up smiling, thinking about Brooke. He also marveled at being home and being sober. He stood in his closet looking at his clothes and appreciating the opportunity to wear something other than an orange jumpsuit. He pushed aside the many white work shirts and found a short-sleeve, blue shirt that his mother had purchased for him and that he liked. There was no need for him to hide his arms this morning, since he'd just be visiting a number of outpatient programs. He put on jeans and his blue, size eleven Nike Airs, which he'd purchased for ten bags of Doritos and twelve honey buns from an incoming inmate.

The sound of Carter's folksy guitar playing made him smirk, and he decided to go razz his younger brother. They hadn't spent much time together in recent years but had been close when they were young boys. Since Adam's addiction, they'd had their share of altercations, but Carter had been the first in the family to show empathy for Adam's condition. He was kind to Adam, despite the disruption that he caused. For his part, although Adam felt a bit envious of Carter's talents, he respected him and was proud to be his brother. Carter had graduated

Electrical Engineering and was working on a Master's degree. He was an avid musician and had written several good songs with his band. He was also one of those understated popular types. In high school, he had many friends but seldom brought them home, probably because he'd been afraid of them seeing Adam high or witnessing one of the many arguments Adam had with his parents.

Adam opened the door to Carter's room. Posters of The Beatles, Leonardo Da Vinci, and Patrick Kane hung on the walls, left over from Carter's teenage days. His prom king hat and his hockey and basketball trophies sat on bookshelves. Carter was sitting in his desk chair facing the bed and was still holding his guitar. Adam sat on the bed.

"Dude, is that a song you wrote?" Adam asked.

"It's one I'm working on. It's good to have you home."

Carter had a steady girlfriend. Adam thought he'd tell him about Brooke.

"I met a cool girl."

"That's great, man. Where? What's she like?"

"At my restaurant. Then I met up with her at Havana's. She's freakin' awesome. We're goin' out tonight."

"I'm happy, bro. And it's so good to see you like this."

"Like this" meant sober. Adam was okay with the compliment. He got up to leave. "Thanks. Good luck with the song. Sounds like it needs some work, though. I think your band jumped the shark."

With the razzing complete, Adam strolled downstairs. He appreciated the pictures on the wall, ranging from early pictures of his older sister, Meghan, pulling him in a wagon when he was a toddler, to Adam pulling Carter in the same wagon, to high school graduations of each of the kids, to the most current – the entire family and Meghan's husband at Meghan's wedding.

David was sitting at the kitchen table tapping on his phone, arranging the routes to the two inpatient programs they were going to visit. Sharon was emptying the dishwasher. Adam inhaled through his nose, enjoying the smell of the fresh-brewed coffee.

"Good morning, Adam," said Sharon.

"Morning."

"It's nice to have you home."

Adam's three years of heroin addiction had made his family's life hell – lying, stealing, using in their home. However, he knew that when he wasn't being disruptive, his parents liked having him there. He'd also seen his parents become less angry with him and more understanding over the years. "Thanks. I'm sorry about all the shit I caused you guys. That's over."

"Let's hope so," both parents seemed to say.

David and Adam got into the BMW that showed a few dents and scratches.

"Have you had any urges since being out?" asked David, as they pulled out of the driveway.

"No. I'm done." Adam had no interest in returning to his former life.

"Well, you may start to have urges at some point, I suppose. How do you think you'll do without Suboxone?"

"I'm gonna be okay. It's actually nice to not be on anything."

"I'm still angry that the jail wouldn't let you have it. You didn't say much when we visited you, but I know the withdrawal must have been bad."

Adam clenched his fist. "Yeah it sucked, but you get through it." He looked out the window as they drove through Parkdale. "It's good to be on the outside and see normal houses and stuff."

Most of the older houses in Parkdale had been replaced over the last twenty years with larger, more modern versions. While the town avoided the cookie cutter house look through variations in exteriors, there was still the impression of sameness across the homes. The cookies had been made with different molds, but from the same batch of enriched white flour, sugar, and baking powder.

The receptionist at the first outpatient center gave Adam some forms to complete and said someone would be out to speak with them. They sat in the waiting area, and Adam began to fill out the forms.

"Dad, there's a question here about who referred me." Adam smiled as he thought of the inmate who suggested he check out this place. Adam knew him only by his nickname. "Should I just write in 'Big Al'?" He laughed, picturing how it would look on the form, and David smiled with him.

A father and daughter walked in and approached the receptionist. The young woman was pretty and looked to be about Adam's age. She was wearing shorts and a sleeveless shirt. She sat across from Adam, crossed her legs, and she and Adam said hi to each other.

In the manager's office, David and Adam asked several questions, and the manager asked Adam a few questions. After about fifteen minutes, Adam told the manager that he was going to check out a couple more programs, then call and let him know.

Driving to the second appointment, David said, "That was a pretty girl who said hi to you."

"Yes, she was."

"She seemed interested in you."

"Well, she wasn't Brooke." Adam looked outside and had fun imagining his date later this evening. What should they do? What will she be wearing? What should he wear? Should he tell her about his situation?

CHAPTER NINETEEN

Camille rocked back and forth in her seat in the courtroom as she waited for the hearing to begin. The butterflies in her stomach reminded her of the feelings she used to have waiting for her turn at piano competitions. She was seated to the right of her lawyer at a small table facing the judge's quarters. About twelve feet to the left of her table was another table with two seats. The seat on the right was occupied by her ex-husband's attorney, who was applying Chapstick, and to the left of him was Robert.

"This is case number DR01821, the Honorable Judge Castle presiding. Attorneys, please state your appearances," said a court officer.

Both attorneys stood up. "Tim Lund for the Petitioner, Robert Cauchon. Good afternoon, Your Honor." Lund somehow looked both thin and flabby. He also looked confident, which made Camille nervous. He had round eyeglasses, trimmed hair, and a tailored suit. He sat and removed his glasses to clean them. Robert was wearing a fashionable dark suit, white shirt, and a yellow tie. He looked like he had gotten a haircut for the occasion. He was handsome, and he knew it.

"Jerry Murphy for the respondent, Camille Simard. Hello, your Honor," said Jerry.

Judge Castle was looking grim and reviewing papers.

The court officer looked at Camille's ex-husband and said, "Sir, please state your full name and address for the record."

"Robert Cauchon. My address is 122 Spruce Lane, Terrace."

"What is your relationship to the children in this matter: Rosalie Cauchon, age seven and Mia Cauchon, age five?" asked the court officer.

"I'm their father."

The court officer directed her attention to Camille. "Ma'am, please state your full name and address for the record."

In a shaky voice, Camille said, "I am Camille Simard. I live at 378 Prospect Lane, Terrace. I'm the mother of the girls." Jerry touched her back and nodded as if to say, "good job."

The judge finally looked up. "Officer Park, please summon Ms. Flores. I'm assigning her as attorney for the children in this case."

"Yes, your Honor." The officer walked out of the courtroom through the back door.

"If I may, your Honor," said Jerry. The judge didn't stop him. "There may not be a need to assign an attorney to represent the children. This is a frivolous application on the petitioner's part. It is not supported by any facts and is an attempt by the petitioner to deny my client access to her children. Their divorce was finalized only six months ago when the parties entered into a custody agreement that has been beneficial to the children. There is no change in circumstances warranting a modification of that agreement. I would respectfully ask that the court dismiss this petition."

Camille thought his words sounded convincing and crossed

her fingers, hoping the judge might agree.

"Mr. Murphy, as far as I understand it, the reason your client does not have physical custody of the children is because she abuses drugs. Heroin, no less. So it is for me to decide whether to assign an attorney for the children, and I have already decided I will."

Jerry added, "May I also point out that although Ms. Simard was personally served with the petition, the service happened less than twenty-four hours ago, thereby making it defective."

The judge gave him a stern look, but Jerry appeared confident. With sarcasm, the judge said, "Are you contesting the court's jurisdiction, Mr. Murphy? We are all here, and I would like to be able to make some progress, if you will allow it."

"I apologize, your Honor, and yes, we will consent to the court's jurisdiction."

Camille's hopes for a quick dismissal were dashed. Robert leaned back so Camille could see him, even though there were two attorneys between them. He smirked at her, and she turned her head away.

The court officer returned and whispered to the judge. He nodded, and the officer stood by the railing separating the judge's bench from the two tables.

"Mr. Lund, the allegations your client is making in this petition are serious. He claims Ms. Simard is using drugs again, possibly in the presence of the children, and he is concerned they may be in danger of neglect or abuse while under her custody. What happened to make him bring this petition now?"

Lund stood. "Several things, your Honor. First, this has happened before. Ms. Simard admitted to using heroin six months ago. In the past couple of weeks, she has been acting erratic, having bouts of anger toward my client for no apparent reason, and has even refused to spend additional time with the girls when my client offered on Saturday last week. The girls also mentioned to my client that some of the songs she sings to them are odd."

Camille started whispering to Jerry. She wanted to tell him that her songs were about her love for her daughters and that the reason she didn't have the girls last Saturday was because she had rehearsal all day. Jerry whispered back, "Write it down. I need to listen." He pushed a notepad and pen toward her, and she started to write quickly.

Lund continued. "So until recently, all my client had was circumstantial evidence, your Honor. It all appeared to add up to continued drug abuse on Ms. Simard's part, and he felt responsible to do something about it – to protect his children. Then just this morning, your Honor, he was witness to an additional piece of evidence which confirmed his suspicions."

"What was that?" asked the judge.

"When the girls were using FaceTime to speak with the respondent, my client saw someone in the background inside Ms. Simard's home. She was clearly a current drug user, based on her wasted, drawn out look. Ms. Simard introduced the woman to the girls as her friend. That woman said hello to the children, then, in the background, withdrew a syringe and other items from her purse and put them into her pocket. My client was shocked and appalled. For these reasons, your Honor, we request that …"

The rest of the attorney's words were lost on Camille. Did that actually happen or had Robert made it up?

Camille regretted letting Gabby stay the night. Jerry appeared surprised at what Lund was saying and tapped the notepad. Camille scrawled, "Gabby is an old friend who was in trouble last night. I let her sleep over. That's all!"

Jerry skimmed her comments. He gave her an assured look then stood up and said, "May I respond, your Honor?"

"I thought you might, Mr. Murphy."

"It's no secret that my client had a problem with drugs in the past. In fact, she recognized it to the point where she agreed to give up physical custody of her daughters. Since then, she has had a stellar recovery. She has held stable employment, and she gives private piano and voice lessons to students of all ages. She is well-paid and is appreciated by her clients, and she attends Narcotics Anonymous meetings regularly. She takes medication for her addiction. She has not suffered a relapse in the last six months and is willing to take a drug test today. These ridiculous allegations of bouts of anger and erratic behavior are nothing but misrepresentations by the petitioner."

He hesitated, then continued. "And this statement about strange songs, well, she could sing for your Honor the same songs she sings for her daughters."

Judge Castle seemed to hold back a smile. Camille swallowed and wondered if she could really be asked to sing in a courtroom.

"That won't be necessary," responded the judge.

Jerry continued. "Last Saturday, my client could not spend the afternoon with the girls because the petitioner notified her of their availability at the last minute, while my client was already at rehearsal at her employer. My client is not using drugs and is actually slowly but surely becoming a candidate for shared physical custody. Suspending her visitation based upon these misrepresentations would be devastating to the children. They rely on her love and affection and the regularity of their visits with her."

The judge responded, "Having stable employment is important, and—" He was about to continue, but the courtroom door at the back opened, and a woman, around Camille's age, walked in. She was well-dressed and carried a briefcase. She stopped and stood at a third table that was between the other two tables but a little further behind.

Camille could see Robert staring at the woman, probably assuring himself that he could win her over in a minute with a few flattering comments.

"Ms. Flores. Please have a seat. I have made copies of the Order to Show Cause and the petition in this case for you. They are on your table. I have appointed you as attorney for the children," said the judge.

"Yes, your Honor," responded Ms. Flores.

The judge spoke to Jerry. "I agree that most of the arguments are circumstantial, but you haven't addressed the allegations of what happened this morning regarding your client having active drug users as guests in her home. What does your client have to say about that, Mr. Murphy?"

"Simply that the petitioner saw what he wanted to see, your Honor. He may think he can tell by a person's appearance, if that person is an active drug user or not, but most people would not swear to that with such certainty. And the syringe? Well, was it really a syringe he saw – again through a phone screen from a distance? And a syringe is not a drug. Or is the petitioner alleging he saw drugs too?"

Camille started to feel more confident.

Jerry continued. "This is a manipulation of the truth. The real truth here is that Mr. Cauchon just had his girlfriend move in with him and is looking for a way to get my client out of the picture. He probably wants the girls to bond with this woman and slowly but surely remove my client from their lives. It is in the children's best interest to have a relationship with their mother. So we respectfully ask the court to deny the request for a suspension of the visits."

"Ms. Flores, I know you just walked into this case, but do you have anything to add?" asked the judge.

"Not at this time, your Honor."

"I understand. I will give you an opportunity to meet with your clients, and we will reconvene very soon. Mr. Lund, your client shall make the children available to Ms. Flores at her convenience."

"Yes, your Honor."

"I am ordering that both parents submit to a drug and alcohol test today before leaving the courthouse. Any objections to that?"

The attorneys did not object.

"I am also ordering that Ms. Simard take a parenting class this weekend. It takes place here in the courthouse on Saturdays from eight a.m. to four p.m. She can sign up today."

"Yes, your Honor," said Jerry.

Camille scrawled another note. "I have rehearsal all day Saturday!" Jerry read the note and whispered, "Since he ordered it, you must get it done before we reconvene."

The judge continued. "I am also ordering a home study of Ms. Simard's residence. I will put in an expedited order to see if they can do the visit this week. Ms. Simard will be notified no more than one hour before the inspection, so make sure she is available."

"Yes, your Honor."

Camille worried about missing the all-day rehearsal on Saturday. Assistant Director Kyle wouldn't be able to handle it. Nor could Broadway Frank, since he had not been involved in the show. She'd have to cancel it, and Frank would be furious. She'd been concerned that her job was on thin ice already because Broadway Frank seemed to want to replace her, and she knew that losing her employment would be bad for her case.

Judge Castle looked at her and said, "Ms. Simard, at this point, it is your word against Mr. Cauchon's. Let us consider the facts. You are a heroin addict. Mr. Cauchon believes you are not staying clean, and he is concerned about the safety of the girls. I need to take his allegations seriously. My job is to protect your daughters, so I am temporarily suspending your visits, with one exception. If your drug test today comes back negative, then you can see them tomorrow for ninety minutes with an approved supervisor. Your attorney will explain how to go about scheduling that visit, and Mr. Cauchon will bring the children to and from the scheduled visit.

Camille's lips trembled. She whispered into Jerry's ear, "How will I explain this to them? I'd rather not see them this week than subject them to a supervised visit. Please do something!"

Jerry said, "Your Honor, when will we be returning to court? My client is concerned about the negative impact that a supervised visit may have on her relationship with her daughters, so if there is any way to avoid this—"

"We are about to pick an adjourn date, Mr. Murphy. I would advise your client to take advantage of the time I have given her with her daughters. The court-approved supervisor will make the experience as positive as possible for the children. Moreover, I want a report from the supervisor about your client's interaction with the children, so this is not an optional request."

"Understood, your Honor."

Camille sensed a real risk of losing her daughters. Her addiction medicine could create a positive drug test result. The home inspector might not like her home. The visitation supervisor might not like her. It seemed her life was at the mercy of strangers who were to make recommendations based on arbitrary criteria.

"Is everyone available next Tuesday at four o'clock?" asked the judge.

All agreed.

Camille got into her Ford Fusion, covered her face with her hands and began crying – moderately at first, then uncontrollably. She said to herself, out loud, "Why did you have to be such a screw-up? Why? Why? The girls need me. They're living with that jackass and his floozy!"

She cried a bit longer but eventually straightened herself out as best she could. She had no choice. She had another critical task to complete.

CHAPTER TWENTY

Camille started the car and began driving to her doctor's office. Every two weeks, she had to take a drug test there to get a fourteen-day refill of Suboxone.

During the twenty-five minute drive, she called Broadway Frank, thinking the sooner she told him about the Saturday rehearsal issue, the better. He answered after two rings, and they exchanged unpleasant pleasantries. She then said, "Frank, I have a problem."

"What is it this time?" he groaned.

"I have a personal situation that I'll need to attend to on Saturday."

"Are you and your family okay?" he asked.

"Yes. But I'm going to have to cancel the rehearsal."

She heard Frank perform one of his fake gasps before he began speaking. "The show is in poor shape and the kids need every rehearsal they can get. Kyle can't run a full-day rehearsal by himself. Unless you have some major medical problem to deal with, we can't cancel."

"Frank, this can't be helped."

"This is a problem," he said before hanging up.

She arrived at the medical building and went to the doctor's office on the third floor. These visits infrequently involved seeing the actual doctor. Usually, she would provide her urine sample, speak with a counselor for a couple of minutes then get her medicine. This time, the receptionist said the doctor wanted to see her. She provided the sample, then waited half an hour before being called in. The doctor was a pudgy middle-aged man who spoke in a soft, condescending voice and rarely made eye contact. He didn't wear a doctor's smock or anything else that would make him look like a doctor. There were, however, framed degrees and licenses hanging on his wall. He was eating brownies out of a Tupperware container.

He glanced at her file. "So how are things going … Camille?"

Camille needed to stay on his good side because it was almost impossible to find a doctor to prescribe Suboxone. She answered politely. "Things are going well, Dr. Morgan. You probably saw that my drug tests have been clean for six months." She knew that he didn't look at the results himself, but maybe he'd appreciate her thinking he did.

"Yes. You need to keep everything else in your life as low stress as possible – an easy job that you like, lots of time with family and friends, that kind of thing. Are you doing that?"

"My time with my daughters is nice. And I have a job that I love."

"Okay, good." Camille thought she could have said anything, and he would have responded in the same way. He cleared his throat, paused, then said, "Camille, you may know that I'm restricted in how many patients I can prescribe Suboxone to."

From discussions at the NA meetings, she understood that most doctors were limited to one hundred Suboxone patients, although they could prescribe other medicines without restrictions.

"Yes, and I'm grateful to be one of your patients."

"Well, I've found that the best success comes from a holistic program of medication assisted treatment, private counseling, and group counseling."

"Yes, I have a counsellor that I see here, and I go to NA meetings regularly."

"Good, but you should have group counseling as well."

"I'm not sure I have time for another thing."

"Staying sober requires you to make time. We have a program here that I'm recommending you attend. Without embracing the full program, you run a higher risk of relapsing."

"Can you tell me the cost and the time requirement of the program?" Given her fear of losing her prescription, perhaps she could fit in the extra counseling, even though driving here and back more often would be challenging.

"Here's a brochure." Dr. Morgan handed her a pamphlet that had a picture of a beautiful beach and a blue sky on the front and the words, "New Beginnings." "You'll see a description of the program. A discussion leader is at each session. You can do Tuesday, Thursday, or both nights; the cost is the same – one hundred dollars a month. For new patients, by the way, the cost is a hundred and fifty dollars a month." He finished eating his brownie while he waited for her response.

"Dr. Morgan, evenings are when I work. I'd have to quit my job to do this."

"You work every evening of the week?"

"Well, no, but—"

"Like I said, you only need to come one night per week. What's your sobriety worth to you?"

She was certain that she couldn't do the program without

impacting her job. She tried to buy time, given her legal situation with her daughters. "How about I think about this and give you an answer when I come back in two weeks?"

"Camille, I have a long line of people who want to be my patients and get the prescription, a waiting list of several hundred. Most of them would jump at the opportunity. They need care and they're desperate for it. It's not fair to them to wait two weeks."

"Dr. Morgan, I am so very grateful to be your patient. But doing this program would be extremely difficult for me. Maybe—"

He interrupted. "That's no problem, Camille. Here is your fourteen-day supply. Please know that I will not be able to give you a positive reference if another doctor calls asking if you're serious about your recovery."

"I'm not sure I understand."

"I told you that I only keep patients who are committed. You'll need to find another doctor."

She hadn't anticipated such a final reaction. Now she wished she'd agreed to pay the ransom, even if she planned to not attend. She tried to recover.

"Well, perhaps I could—"

He interrupted again. She tried once more, and he interrupted once more. "Ms. Simard, I gave you the opportunity. A new patient will be delighted to take your spot. You can go now."

She stood up, dumfounded. She wasn't sure how this happened, and so quickly. One thing was certain: she needed to find another doctor, fast.

CHAPTER TWENTY-ONE

Camille thought about the situation while she drove home and wondered if Adam had ever faced similar situations with his medicine. She commanded her phone to call him.

"Hey, Camille."

"Adam. How are you?

"Good, I'm in the car with my dad."

She asked him to put her on speakerphone, and she said hello to David. She told them about her predicament and asked if Adam had faced anything similar.

"That hasn't happened to me, but I've heard of it from another dude who sees Dr. Morgan. I did have a situation where the first doctor I had moved his office a couple of times. I think he was exceeding his limit or something. Eventually, we couldn't find him anymore."

"I can't imagine finding a new doctor and getting an appointment within two weeks. Maybe I should just taper off it altogether."

Adam responded immediately. "You can't taper off in two weeks. You gotta find a new doctor, Camille."

David added, "I know that Sharon made a ton of calls to help

Adam find a new doctor. She got a list off the internet and just started calling."

They talked a little more before ending the call. Camille had rehearsal in less than three hours. Until then, she'd call doctors and try to get an emergency appointment. Starting tomorrow, she'd take only half a strip of Suboxone. Cutting her dose by half would be challenging, but she was worried that she might need at least a month to find a new doctor, and she didn't want to run out completely.

She got to her apartment, googled several search terms and eventually found a list of twenty-two doctors who prescribed the medicine in Carlane County. Twenty-two, in a county of a million people. She imagined there were probably several *thousand* doctors in the county who could prescribe most other medication.

She called the doctor whose office appeared to be closest to her home. No luck. He was not taking new patients. She continued down the list, calling eighteen of the twenty-two and was now at the point of calling doctors who were twenty miles away – about a forty-minute drive. She dialed the next one and heard better news.

"Yes, Doctor Singh recently got approval to take additional patients."

"Oh. Uh, how soon can I get an appointment with him or her?"

"It looks like she's available about one month from now – on Friday, September thirtieth at eleven in the morning. Does that work for you?"

Camille explained the situation then asked, "Would it help if I came in sometime and just waited for an appointment?"

"That works sometimes if there's a cancellation, but—"

"What if I went there and waited *today*?" Camille had only about two and a half hours before rehearsal, but getting a new doctor was critical.

“If she gets a cancellation, it’s possible, but unlikely. She only sees patients until four today.”

“I’ll be there.”

By two forty-five, Camille walked into the doctor’s office. It was on the ground floor of a four-story building. “I’m Camille Simard,” she announced to the receptionist.

“Yes, hello, Ms. Simard. I’m afraid you probably wasted your time. Dr. Singh is with a patient now, has several in the waiting room as you can see, and more will be arriving.”

“I’ll just sit down, in case she can see me.”

Camille waited as each patient went through the door to the office, then re-emerged and left some time later. It was a little before three-thirty when she heard a woman’s voice behind the door talking to the receptionist. She couldn’t see the other person or make out what the two were saying.

“Ms. Simard, could you step up to the window?” said the receptionist.

As Camille approached the receptionist’s window, the other woman came into view. She was wearing a doctor’s smock and had a warm, motherly disposition.

“Ms. Simard, I am Dr. Singh,” she said with an Indian accent.

“Hello, Dr. Singh.”

“I heard about your situation. I’d like to help you, but I’m afraid I have to leave for an engagement. I cannot prescribe anything without assessing you first, and that takes some time.”

The doctor turned to the receptionist, “Get her prioritized on the waiting list.” She turned back to Camille, “We’ll do our best to accommodate your requirements, Ms. Simard."

Camille was grateful that they were going to at least try. However, she wanted to avoid a repeat of the situation with Dr. Morgan. "Do you require your addiction patients to take a program of some sort from you?"

"I require them to be serious about their recovery. That would include successful drug tests, counseling, and perhaps a group program, but the program doesn't need to be from me."

Camille left, happy that she may have indeed found a new doctor, but still concerned about her short supply, and praying that she'd get an appointment soon. The clock in the car read three-thirty – more than enough time to make it to rehearsal. Her phone rang and displayed a number that she didn't recognize.

CHAPTER TWENTY-TWO

Camille answered, and the woman's voice said, "Is this Ms. Camille Simard?"

"Yes, who is this?"

"This is Laticia Rivers. I work for Illinois Child Services. I'm a home inspector, and I have an order from Judge Castle to inspect your home at my earliest opportunity."

"Of course, Ms. Rivers. Yes. Thank you for doing this so quickly."

"Ms. Simard, I will arrive at your home at four-thirty to perform the inspection. I need you to be in your home before I arrive. Is that possible for you?"

"I have to be at work then." Camille didn't even know why she said that, since she knew this was not optional.

"The inspection cannot be rescheduled. If you refuse to have it, the judge will make his decision knowing that."

"I understand. I'll be there." She ended the call and shouted, "Merde!" She called her assistant director. "Kyle, it's Camille."

"Hey, Camille."

"A situation came up, and I can't make it to rehearsal on time."

"Oh. When will you be there?"

"Probably around five-thirty. I need you to take care of things until then."

"Yeah, Sure. Everything will be fine."

"Keep all of them in your sight. Do some warm-ups then run through Act Two."

"Sure, don't worry."

Worried is exactly what she was. She liked Kyle and had given him the opportunity to be assistant director as a learning experience, but he'd need to perform this role a few more times before being proficient. At least Broadway Frank had no reason to be at the theater, so he might not even find out about her being late.

When she arrived home, she started to clean up from Gabby's visit and stayed on alert for the front door buzzer. She wished her place were tidier and worried that the inspector might notice that a guest had been over. She wondered what kind of questions she might get about the guest and started preparing answers in her mind.

It was after four-thirty, and the buzzer hadn't sounded. She looked at her door and saw the knob turning. Frightened, she jumped at the door, stopped the knob from moving and turned the deadbolt to lock it. She then heard a knock on the door.

"Yes?" she yelled.

"This is Laticia Rivers from Child Services."

Camille let her in. The inspector held up a wallet with her badge behind some clear plastic. Camille noticed on the other side of the wallet fold, a picture of two teenage girls who resembled Laticia, and she presumed they were her daughters.

"Apologies for the scare. I would not have opened your apartment door, but I was checking to see if it was locked. It wasn't. Also, I was able to open the front door of the building without you buzzing me in."

"I've been after the superintendent to fix that. Usually it locks, but sometimes it doesn't. My apartment door wasn't locked because I knew you'd be arriving soon."

The inspector had a serious demeanor and didn't engage in small talk, but Camille sensed there was compassion behind the stern face.

"Who lives here besides you?"

"No one. Just me."

Camille's phone rang, and she saw the caller was Cindy. She couldn't imagine what the Academy founder would be calling about, but she knew to not interrupt the interview, so she let it go to voicemail.

"Sorry," Camille said as she silenced her phone.

"No problem. I'll continue. Do you ever have guests stay over?"

"Very rarely."

"Do you have any pets?"

"No."

"Where are the fire alarms?"

The questions and answers continued for a few minutes. The inspector examined all the physical aspects of the apartment – the windows, the electrical plugs, corners, and doors. She turned the stove on and off and looked inside the fridge. She touched her tablet computer several times, apparently answering yes/no questions. After she finished the walkthrough, she sat in the living room and asked Camille about her daily schedule, work hours, and other habits. She asked if Camille drank alcohol, smoked cigarettes, or used drugs. She also asked whether she allowed her guests to do so. Camille answered all the questions honestly and Laticia Rivers took notes on her tablet.

When the inspector was finished, Camille looked at her with imploring eyes. "Will I pass?"

"I can't answer that. I send my report to the judge. I will tell you, though, that it is difficult to pass a home where strangers can walk through the front door of the building."

Camille understood the message. She also knew that failing the inspection could be a deal breaker for the judge. "What can I do?"

"Well, it's unfortunate that the front door was not repaired prior to my arrival. I'm afraid I need to go. Goodbye, Ms. Simard."

"What if the superintendent fixes it tomorrow?"

"I'll be filing my report tomorrow. When you reconvene in court, you can appeal and say there were extenuating circumstances."

"That will be too late!"

Camille thought about what, if anything, could be done at this point, but she also needed to get to rehearsal as soon as she could, and she wanted to return Cindy's call. After Laticia Rivers left, Camille listened to Cindy's voicemail.

"Hey, Camille, I was hoping to reach you before losing cell phone service for a couple of days. We're just leaving Banff on a bus to Yoho National Park to do some hiking in the mountains. Please call me as soon as you can."

She called Cindy, but it went to voicemail. She tried a few more times with the same result.

She arrived at the theater about forty-five minutes late. As she parked her car, she saw Broadway Frank's car in the lot. *Merdre!*

She could see that the young cast was already disorganized under Kyle's leadership. She walked onto the stage as several kids from the cast yelled her name, excited to see her. Broadway Frank's voice came through the speakers, "Ms. Simard, could I see you in my office for a minute?" She was alarmed that a request like that would be made in such a public manner. She looked up at the sound booth at the back of the theater and saw Frank putting down the microphone then walking out of the booth.

Broadway Frank's office walls were adorned with pictures of himself with semi-famous people, and with small circulation newspaper articles that praised his shows.

"That was an unusual way to call me to your office," Camille said.

"Well, we're having some unusual times, aren't we – you being late to rehearsals and having to cancel this Saturday's altogether."

"I told you that I have a personal situation this Saturday."

"Yes … A personal situation. So, I spoke with Cindy earlier." Camille was happy to hear that, given her good relationship with Cindy. "We'd like to help you out."

"What do you mean? Help me with what?"

"We think you need a break. We'd like you to take a leave for six months. So you can focus—"

"What are you talking about? You're firing me for being late a couple of times and for missing a rehearsal?"

"We're not firing you. We're telling you to take some time away. We'll take you off the payroll, then in six months, you can re-apply, and we'll see if it makes sense to bring you back at that time."

"In my language, that's firing."

"Camille, we know that you struggled with drugs. You've never hidden that from us, and we respect that. But we thought it was behind you."

Camille resented his saying "we." She couldn't imagine that Cindy agreed with this.

"I don't know what you're talking about. I've been clean for six months."

"Your former husband came by earlier today."

Camille felt like she'd been punched in the stomach. "What was the purpose of his visit?"

"Since we work with children, he wanted to warn me that you were using again. In fact, he said he had some legal papers substantiating it. And I saw that guy yesterday serving you papers."

"Those legal papers are just a bunch of stupidity. His evidence of drug use is that I sing to my daughters!" She wondered how Robert misrepresented the papers to Frank, how Frank may have misunderstood them even further, and how Frank may have misrepresented them to Cindy. A vicious version of telephone game.

"Well, I suppose things like that happen when one abuses drugs," he said.

"Frank, I can't imagine that Cindy agrees with this."

"Cindy supported the idea of giving you a break."

"Did she agree to take me off the payroll? That's a termination."

"She agreed to leave the administrative details with me."

"Why now? Can't you wait one more week? I have a visitation hearing on Tuesday."

"The new director is available now. He was about to accept a position with another theater, but I was able to snag him. I've worked with him before. Academy is lucky to have him. He'll start immediately, and we won't have to cancel the Saturday rehearsal."

"Did Cindy interview him?"

"She's met him before. He'll be on a contract until Cindy gets back and can see his work. I'm sure she'll love him as much as I do."

Camille asked about the rest of today's rehearsal, and Frank said he would tell the cast that she was no longer directing, and he would handle the remainder of the rehearsal himself. He handed her some papers that outlined the terms of the termination. She refused to take them.

Before starting her car, she called Cindy. Voicemail again. She sat, not sure what to do or where to go. This was bad for her court case. Very bad. A failed home inspection and a job termination based on alleged drug use would severely hurt her case. Her arms and legs were trembling. She desperately needed something to calm herself down. She looked at the band from Rosalie on her wrist and decided to go to the NA meeting.

She was about fifteen minutes early when she walked into the meeting room and saw that Adam and Gabby had already arrived. They were standing at the back and Adam was showing Gabby something on his phone.

He looked up. "Hey, Camille. I was just showing Gabby this app that I heard about. It calls police and sends them to your location if you're in trouble. I'm tryin' to convince Gabby to get a cheap phone and install it."

"That's a good idea, Gabby," Camille said. She then told them about her firing, and they expressed their regret.

"I bet the parents will be angry, 'cause I know they loved you," said Adam.

"I suppose," she responded. Adam's comment gave her an idea.

CHAPTER TWENTY-THREE

John arrived at the NA meeting a few minutes early, not sure what to expect. Most people were already sitting and engaged in conversations. There seemed to be addicts and a small number of family members present. He found a friendly-looking young man standing and speaking with two women.

"Excuse me," he said.

"Hey."

"Is there a leader for the meeting?"

"Yeah." The man pointed. "That's James. He's the secretary. I'm Adam. These are my friends, Gabby and Camille."

John introduced himself to them. He could tell that Gabby was an addict. Her eyes had bags under them, and her face looked worn out. Camille appeared stylish and healthy, but she looked sad. Perhaps she was an addict too. Adam looked clean and healthy. John wondered if he was there as a friend of one of them, and not an addict himself.

John walked toward James and said, "Excuse me, is it okay if I sit in on this meeting?"

"Yes, sir," James said kindly. "Are you an addict or have a loved one who is suffering?"

"Uh, no. My work involves people who are addicted, so I am trying to learn about it."

"I see. What do you do?"

"I am a lawyer."

"Well, we need lawyers, since our addiction is illegal. Good to have you."

John was embarrassed that James presumed he was working on behalf of addicts when the opposite was true. He looked for a place to sit and saw that Adam, Gabby, and Camille were now sitting, and there was an empty chair next to Adam. He asked him if it was taken.

"No, it's not. Have a seat."

"Thank you."

"So, John. What brings you to this meeting?"

Apparently, Adam had already pegged him as a non-addict. John explained he was here to learn for a legal case he was working on.

"You got clients you're tryin' to keep out of jail?"

"Something like that."

"I hope you do well for them, man. A lot of us end up in jail."

"Spend an hour with me, and I can teach you everything you need to know about addiction. I'm a leading expert," Gabby said.

Adam smirked, looked at John and said, "By the way, how was your fish last night?"

Caught off guard by the question, John wasn't sure how to answer.

Adam smiled and said, "I grill at Mio Posto. I saw you having the whitefish."

"Oh. You have a good memory."

"So? How was it?"

"Well, I plan on coming back with my wife at some point, so I'd say exquisite."

They continued talking as John glanced around the room. He had imagined that a group of addicts would look forlorn, unkept, and threatening. With the exception of Gabby, this group looked clean, personable, and healthy, although most also looked downtrodden.

He was impressed with Adam – a pleasant young man, welcoming and easy to talk to. Adam whispered to John, telling him about several of the people around the room. He knew many of them and told John their stories with enthusiasm and affection. John now thought that Adam too, must be an addict, appearing to have attended this NA meeting regularly.

James started the meeting. "Hello, I'm James, and I'm an addict."

"Hello, James," responded the group.

"May we start this meeting with a moment of silence for the addict who still suffers ..."

John never imagined he'd be observing a moment of silence for drug addicts.

James invited Gabby and Adam to tell the group about Gabby's overdose and the successful reversal. John again pondered why, with all the downside, don't more addicts make a more concerted effort to stop. Gabby basically died and was resurrected, and, despite that, she probably used today. How could anyone be so careless? What an enormous cost to society to revive people who voluntarily inject themselves. What a burden to our first responders who are in place to deal with other emergencies.

As the meeting was wrapping up, John decided he needed more time with Gabby, Adam, and Camille. "I noticed there was a Corner

Bakery next door. Any chance I could buy you each a coffee and talk some more?"

"My next appointment is at eleven, so I have time for a coffee," said Gabby.

John chuckled, assuming Gabby was joking about an appointment.

"I'm afraid I need to go home," said Camille. "But it was nice to meet you, John."

Adam looked at his watch. "I have a little time, and I shouldn't leave my friend Gabby alone with a stranger – especially a lawyer."

John smiled, and said, "Great." As they headed out, he patted his coat pocket to make sure he had his notebook.

CHAPTER TWENTY-FOUR

John paid the cashier at Corner Bakery for their coffees and for Gabby's ham and cheese panini. Gabby appeared to know the cashier, since they talked about his boyfriend. The cashier handed them their coffees and a stand with the number nine at the top to identify their order.

"Thanks for joining me," John began, at their table. He removed the red and blue pens from his shirt pocket and opened a small notebook.

"I don't know if we want you writing down stuff we say," said Adam.

Apparently, Adam really was there to look out for his friend. John put his tools away. "Sorry, force of habit."

"No problem," said Adam. "Do you have a business card or something from your law firm?"

"Of course." John handed each of them his card with the Harris Clark logo. "Well, I'm trying to understand the struggles that people in your situation might have with the police, courts, and jails. Gabby, you mentioned you had some stories?"

His question released a torrent of thoughts from her. "Always. You want to know about our interaction with the law? It's atrocious.

Because of the war on drugs, an active user avoids police at all costs. You don't get arrested for other sicknesses. You get treated. It seems to me it's prejudice. People say we caused our own addiction by trying drugs in the first place. I suppose they have a point. But, sixty percent of the population tries drugs, so lock up sixty percent of the country. They made the same choice we did."

John was surprised at how articulate Gabby was, in addition to being feisty and clearly bitter. He was also surprised at her choice of the word "prejudice."

"I mean, John, you must know a thing or two about prejudice," she added.

John thought about his first experience with racism. He was a child, vacationing with his family – too young to know where, but it was a long drive from their home and a warmer place. They were out for a walk. He was between his father and his older sister, holding their hands. His mother was pushing his younger sister in a stroller. A car drove by, and someone yelled racial slurs out of the passenger window. He had never heard it actually used before that, though he was familiar with the word. He remembered that his parents were appalled and tried to explain the concept of prejudice to him.

He flashed forward to conversations with Jackie, which occasionally contained undertones of bias. He also knew that everything Gabby was describing or was about to describe would be worse for him and his family and any person of color. "I suppose I do," he said.

"That cashier I said hi to ... he's had his share of prejudice. We've come a long way in reducing prejudice against you and against him, at least that's my impression as a straight, white person. But I know we have much further to go. I also know that what I'm describing would be worse for you. I've seen it."

“I’m glad to hear you acknowledge that,” said John.

“Maybe one day, addicts will get treated instead of incarcerated. Maybe doctors will figure out how to repair the broken brains. Maybe over-prescriptions will stop. By then, though, we’ll find yet another group to discriminate against. That seems to be human nature.”

The conversation had become deeper and more philosophical than John had expected or intended. It was, however, interesting, hearing a white person talk about prejudice. He thought he’d let it continue for a bit. “I’ve heard addiction called a disease. With respect, isn’t that unfair to people who have other diseases that were not caused by their own behavior? Someone who contracted cancer or tuberculosis had no choice in the matter,” said John.

“That’s true,” said Gabby. “But I can tell you this: many addicts had no choice in getting the conditions that made them prone to addiction. Things like childhood trauma, social anxiety, depression.”

“I suppose,” said John.

Adam jumped in. “We don’t just accept our situation. Many of us fight like fuck against it. We’re responsible for our recovery, just like a person with any other disease works on *their* recovery.”

“Why don’t you just stop? I mean, the destruction of your lives – it can’t be worth it?”

Adam continued. “Of course it’s not worth it, man. No one says ‘Hey, I think I’ll ruin my life, and the lives of my family, and perhaps die, which would make my family sad for the rest of their lives, … but it’s worth it.’ Willpower can work for a while, and for some people, a long time. But it can’t work forever for many addicts. I don’t know. I guess there’s different levels of this thing. Some addicts have really bad cases and some not so bad.”

John thought about that. Based on what he’d seen at the NA

meeting and Gabby's general behavior and comments, her addiction was clearly one of the more severe cases.

John thought he'd come back to the prejudice topic. "When you say people are prejudiced against addicts, I guess I can understand that because addicts are often involved in crime to support their addiction. Stealing, selling drugs, prostitution."

"That's true. Many addicts do that shit to get money for their drugs. I stole shit and sold it. Sometimes, you do what you gotta do to get what you gotta get," said Adam.

"Well, that's why people have negative views," said John.

Gabby responded. "Isn't that profiling?"

Another loaded word, thought John. He didn't want to get into a discussion on that topic, so he didn't answer.

"There are many addicts who don't commit crimes other than possession of the drug that they're addicted to." She took a drink of her coffee, then raised her index finger. It reminded him of his old high school history teacher. "Portugal made all drugs legal. The addict goes to the doctor to get the drug. That removes the crime and the cost of the crime, the cost of enforcement, and the cost of incarceration. It also removes the deaths."

John asked Gabby to tell him about her personal experiences with the law. She described the events of the previous night. Since he was interested in police interactions, she slowed down at that part. "In a moment of reckless ineptitude, I agreed to deliver a baggie to a kid in an orange hoodie at the Terrace West station and got arrested," she said.

"I'm surprised the police let you out," responded John.

Gabby didn't answer. John asked her if she could share how her addiction started. She told him and Adam the same story she told

Camille that morning: pain pills led to addiction, which led to heroin. Her food arrived. She smiled and thanked the waiter.

John wondered if he could get Adam to also describe his journey to addiction. He decided to appeal to his protective nature.

"Adam, I have a son a few years younger than you. I know he's done some drugs. Nothing close to heroin, but I suppose there is always a risk. Do you mind if I ask how things started with you? Maybe it would help me recognize signs with him, if ever he starts doing harder things."

"I guess I could share a few things." He paused and twisted in his seat. "In my sophomore year of high school, half the school celebrated four-twenty by smoking weed. You know, April twentieth, national pot day? I never tried anything until that day."

"Yes, I've heard of four-twenty."

"It was amazing. Suddenly, I was less shy, I could talk to people, life seemed like it was nice, rather than a struggle. A bunch of my friends and I smoked a lot of weed for a long time after. It got in the way of school work." He looked at his coffee. "Eventually, my friends and I tried harder things. For them, they somehow knew it could be just a phase. For me, it was more. I remember one time, my mother gave my friends hell. She said, 'You guys may be able to get over this, but Adam can't.' After she left, they laughed."

"How did she know?" asked John.

"Moms know, I guess. Anyway, my senior high school year, we were experimenting with pain pills. Oxies were *everywhere*. Everybody had a parent or a grandparent or aunt or uncle who had Oxies or something like them in their medicine cabinet. Kids brought them to parties and stuff. Anyway, my parents put me in a private high school in New York State to get me in a new environment. Teachers found me with some pills and kicked me out. I was happy to be coming home."

"Did you get back into your old school?"

"Yeah, I got through the year and graduated. Back in middle school and in my freshman year of high school, I had gotten really good grades – student of the month, principal's list, all that stuff. But the last couple of years of high school, my grades were shit. Barely good enough to pass."

"Sorry to hear," said John.

"After that, it was a spiral for a couple of years – painkillers, heroin that you snort, then heroin that you inject. Rehabs, counseling, getting clean, and relapsing. I was usually not an everyday user. I used when I could – when I had a few days off."

John reached for his pen, then remembered Adam's request. "Did rehab help?"

"I don't know. A couple of them were good. Some were not. My parents sent me to my first rehab when I was just doin' weed. It was like a four-week advertisement for heroin. When the counselors aren't around, you hear the other guys talkin' about how great it is, where to get it, how cheap it is, how to inject it, all that stuff. One of the guys I met in my rehab took me to Belmare when we got out and showed me where to get it."

While John was captivated with the discussion, he needed to ask about things more related to his case. "Have you ever been prescribed medicine for your addiction?"

"I was on Suboxone for a couple of years. I'm off it now," said Adam.

"Why did you stop?"

Adam seemed to blush. "That's another story. I need to get going. I'm meeting a real special girl."

Gabby added, "I have to go as well. Thanks for the sandwich."

"Yeah, thanks for the coffee, man," said Adam.

"You're welcome. Thanks for talking to me."

John stayed back and considered what he had learned. What if Angela Parker made the case that an addict is powerless over his addiction and is bound to relapse at some point? That seemed to be what Gabby and Adam were describing. John didn't believe that himself. Everyone is capable of deciding what to do for themselves or to themselves. However, if a judge believed it, then taking away the medicine that kept the addict alive might meet the proximate cause test. For the first time, John thought there was a chance that the sheriff could actually *lose* at trial. Yet another reason he had to get the case settled before trial.

CHAPTER TWENTY-FIVE

John arrived home, planning to spend several hours preparing for the hearing the next day. He had to figure out a path to settlement. He spotted his son's orange hoodie hanging on the hook in the entrance closet and stopped. *No way!* The Terrace West train station was near his home.

John found Daniel's backpack in the living room and looked through it. He saw several papers from the summer course that Daniel had taken online to get a jump on his sophomore year. Then he discovered what he was looking for but hoped not to find: a court summons to show up at Carlane County Courtroom on September fourteenth. Shock was John's first visitor. It wrapped his body like a cold snake. John felt so ill, he thought he might throw up.

This can't *be possible. This can*'t *be. Daniel – my son. It's got to be a mistake.* He took a second look at the name on the paper. He read "Daniel Tylor" at the top. *Damn!* He saw his son's future disintegrating.

Shock gave way to anger. *How could he do this? Throw away his life. Waste his brain. Why?*

He went to the basement where Daniel was reading. He held up the court summons. "Were you planning to tell us about this?"

"What the hell? You can't go through my private stuff!"

"What the hell? Yes, I can. And what the hell? What is this?" John's voice was getting louder.

"It's nothing. Some homeless lady tried to hand me drugs. It's bullshit. I'll go to court, and it'll get thrown out." Daniel's voice matched the volume of John's.

"If she gave you drugs and you gave her money, it is not going to be thrown out."

"I'll deal with it. It's a first-time offence. They're not going to put me in jail for it."

"How do you know that? How the hell could you do this? All the work you did to get into MIT, the bright future you have, the support we've given you, and you're willing to throw it away to shoot heroin?"

"I told you, they're not going to send me to jail for a first offense."

John thought that was probably true. Still, Daniel was going to need a lawyer and have to show up at court, probably several times, during the school year in the middle of the week. As John processed the information, it dawned on him that the legal issues were not the biggest problem. The problem was that his son had purchased and had planned to use heroin.

"Were you doing this in college?"

"No … well, once or twice. Do we have to have this conversation right now?"

"Believe me, I have much better things to do as well. When did you start this?" John hoped this was relatively new for Daniel, which might mean his chances of recovery were higher.

Daniel looked at his father. "I guess just after you had back surgery, last winter."

John's mind raced, and his stomach roiled from the conclusion he drew. He now remembered that when he finally threw out his pain pills after his surgery, the container had seemed to contain fewer than he thought it should have. "Are you saying you took some of the pills I was prescribed?"

"It wasn't a big deal. Everybody was taking extra pills out of medicine cabinets. Everybody was trying things. I grabbed a few when I was home for spring break."

There was a lot that John wanted to know, including how pills progressed to heroin. However, emotions were running so high that those questions would have to wait. He did have one critical question that couldn't wait. "Are you addicted?"

"I don't know. I only do it once in a while."

"What's once in a while?"

"Like, maybe once a week or so." Daniel paused then continued. "I don't want to talk about it anymore tonight." He walked up to his bedroom and closed the door.

John went to the study, shell-shocked. Until two days ago, he seldom had occasion to use the words "addict" or "heroin." Now, the topic had invaded his life.

I'll be damned if let a child of mine become a heroin addict. His priorities shifted for the night. Tomorrow's settlement meeting still loomed, and he still had extensive preparation to do, but now, he also needed to help his son.

CHAPTER TWENTY-SIX

Camille had returned to her apartment after the NA meeting, still stunned that Frank had fired her. She needed to solve this. She had to have a job to show stability to the judge. When Adam had commented that she was popular with the parents, she thought that perhaps she could get the parents to rally behind her. Maybe they could convince Broadway Frank to at least postpone the decision until after the Annie performances, which would be after the visitation hearing.

She thought of a list of parents to call and what to say. She decided to start with Laura, Becky's mother. Laura was always grateful for the extra time and coaching that Camille gave Becky, and she was delighted when Becky got the role of Annie. Plus, Laura was well-connected and influential with the other parents. Camille dialed her number and continued to pace.

"Laura, this is Camille."

Laura gushed, "Camille! Hello. It's so nice to hear from you. What's going on at Academy? I was waiting for Becky in the parking lot, and I saw several kids walking out in tears. When Becky got in the car, she told me that this Broadway Frank guy announced you're taking a break. She said he took over the rehearsal, then some new guy showed up and was introduced as the new director. She said both of them were intense – as if these kids were putting on some big professional show. We wanted this to be a fun, educational experience, not a misery."

Camille felt horrible for the kids in the show.

Laura continued. "We're disappointed that you decided to leave, but I guess you must have your reasons. Is everything okay with you?"

"I didn't decide to leave. Frank fired me."

"What? Why?"

"Invalid reasons."

"Well, I could lobby for you. Within minutes, Broadway Frank will be flooded with calls from parents. He has no idea what it's like to deal with an angry mob of theatre moms! Unless you're a child molester or a drug addict or something, we want you back."

Camille paused, sat down, and said nothing for a moment.

"Camille, are you still there?"

"Laura … I'm a recovering heroin addict."

"That's funny, Camille. Seriously, we need you back. I think some of the kids are going to quit."

"Actually, I'm serious."

There were a few more seconds of silence. "Oh … I'm sorry. I thought you were trying to be funny … I see." More silence. Then Laura continued. "You say you're recovering. You mean you're not yet recovered?"

"Addicts never fully recover. It's a chronic disease that stays in your brain for life. For the rest of my life, I'll be in recovery. I take medicine for it, and I go to meetings and counseling."

"Okay … did you stop? Do you plan to use heroin again?"

"I haven't used for six months. I don't plan to use ever again. But I'm afraid I cannot guarantee it. I could relapse one day. It would not be near children, but it could happen."

"I see." More silence. "Well, I appreciate you sharing that with me, Camille." Laura no longer sounded like a friend with an army of "theater moms" to deploy. She sounded like a stern and judgmental school principal. "My goodness. Well, I guess I can understand Academy's perspective. In fact, I'm surprised they didn't disclose that information. Parents might have wanted to know that. No offense, Camille. You're a lovely person, and I suppose you'd never intentionally put our children in danger, but Academy should have disclosed this. They'll be hearing from me and from other parents, I'm sure."

Camille was now concerned about damage to Academy's reputation. "Please know that Academy has a strict drug policy. Staff members are absolutely forbidden from working if intoxicated. All staff members submit to a drug test before their employment is confirmed."

They ended the conversation. Camille's idea to get the parents to rally around her to get her job back had backfired, at least, with that parent. Others may have the same reaction. They had the right to.

She rubbed her face, thinking about what to do next. Her phone rang, and she saw that it was an unfamiliar number. "Hello."

"Hello, this is Peggy Morton. Am I speaking with Camille Simard?"

"Yes."

"I have been assigned to supervise the visit with your daughters tomorrow." She sounded bothered.

"Pleased to meet you, Peggy."

"Please call me Ms. Morton, especially tomorrow, in front of your daughters."

"Oh. Okay. Thank you for doing this, Ms. Morton."

"Yes. I had to scramble to fit it in on such short notice. I understand this is your first supervised visit?"

"Yes, it is."

"Okay, well, I'd like to cover a few things prior to the visit tomorrow. Is now a good time?"

Camille nervously tapped the fingers of her free hand on her leg. She was still shaken from the conversation with Laura, but she wanted to get off to a good start with the supervisor. She had to. "Yes, certainly."

"Okay. First, my fee."

Camille hadn't even thought about a fee. She just assumed it would be paid for by the county – like judges' salaries or the cost of maintaining the courtrooms.

"Okay."

"I charge fifty-five dollars an hour plus mileage. The writing of the report is paid for by the county. With this phone orientation, drive time, and visitation, that'll be two hours, so 110 dollars for my time plus fifteen dollars for mileage will be due tomorrow. I can take cash, check, or credit card."

Turns out, supervised visits were not only demeaning but also expensive. "Sure, I'll bring a check."

Ms. Morton continued as Camille wrote a reminder to herself about the check.

"Now, we usually get assigned to these cases when there is a serious deficiency in a person's parenting skills, or a threat of absconding, or when a parent is a drug abuser. I understand that your situation is drugs?"

Camille was surprised at her matter-of-fact and judgmental tone. Jerry had told her that supervisors usually showed professionalism and compassion. She surmised that like any job, there are a few unpleasant ones, and that Ms. Morton fell into that category. She knew better than to talk back, so she agreed.

Ms. Morton continued. "It's my responsibility to ensure that the meeting goes smoothly and without incident. I'll say hello to the children, introduce myself, and explain why I'm there. I'll stay in the same room and within hearing range. I'll intervene if I see or hear anything inappropriate or something that puts the children in danger. If you have any questions during the visit, let me know. After the meeting, I'll write a report with my observations." She spoke as if she had made this speech a million times, like a bored flight attendant giving the pre-flight safety speech.

She continued. "Refrain from speaking to the children further about my role or about the court case."

"Okay, that all sounds fine," answered Camille.

"I understand the visitation is to take place at Mio Posto between eleven-thirty and one tomorrow?"

Camille had requested Mio Posto because Adam had shown her a private dining room that contained a piano, and since the room was seldom used, the management was happy to let Camille use it with her girls. "Yes, that is correct."

As they ended the conversation, Camille scratched her head and wondered how Ms. Morton's presence would hamper the visit with Mia and Rosalie. She also thought about the supervisor submitting a report to the judge. After the failed home inspection and getting fired, a bad visitation report would be the fatal finale in her attempt to keep her relationship with her girls.

CHAPTER TWENTY-SEVEN

Adam took an Uber from the Corner Bakery to Belmare. On the way there, he closed his eyes and pictured Brooke's face and her smile. He imagined what a bliss it would be if she were sitting next to him right now. He arrived at her address with time to kill, so he decided to walk around, think of things he could talk about with her, plan out where they might have dinner, then call her just a couple of minutes early. He knew the area because he had sometimes taken his father's car late at night when his parents were asleep to come to this neighborhood to buy heroin. Take any of the highway exits around here, and you'd find what you were looking for.

Adam was delighted that his travels tonight were for a different purpose. He'd been thinking about Brooke all day, sneaking glances at her picture that he downloaded from Facebook.

After his stroll, he arrived back at the four-story, eight-unit building, and called her phone. "Hey, Brooke, I'm downstairs."

"Come on up. I'm not quite ready. I'm in 302." The front door buzzed for him to open it. He went up, knocked on the apartment door, and Brooke's friend, Beth, answered. The place was bright and tidy. Standing next to Beth was a sandy-colored Cocker Spaniel wagging its tail and looking eagerly at Adam.

"Hey, Adam," said Beth

"Sup, Beth?"

"That's Daisy. She's Brooke's dog."

He petted Daisy and scratched her behind the ears. "Hey, girl. What a pretty girl," he said to the dog. Daisy absorbed the affection.

"Have a seat," said Beth. "Brooke's still getting ready. That was a great club last night, wasn't it?"

"Yeah, it was cool." Clubs were not his thing, but he wasn't about to disagree with Brooke's friend. "It was nice meeting you guys. Just you and Brooke live here, right?"

"Yes. Kate lives nearby."

"Cool. Why were you guys in Terrace last night?"

"We were shopping there. Then some cool lady recommended your restaurant."

They talked a little more until Brooke came out of her bedroom. In an instant, Adam admired every inch of her – her open-toe red shoes, her skinny jeans, her white V-neck T-shirt that offered to reveal a bit of her stomach if she lifted her arms, her soft blonde hair, and her stunning brown eyes.

"Hi, Adam," she said as she graced toward him and gave him a light hug.

"Hey, Brooke." He hugged her back, being careful to not touch her too much and have her think he was a creep.

"I'm casual. Hope that's okay," she said.

"I'm nervous. Hope that's okay," he responded.

She and Beth smiled and shared a glance that looked like approval.

Brooke looked at him. "Since it's such a nice night, I thought we'd take the train downtown, go for a walk, and maybe just grab some tamales or something. Sound okay?"

"That would be amazing." Adam loved tamales from street vendors.

During their walk to the train station, he noticed a park on the left.

"I see you live near platform tennis courts," he said.

"Yeah, I'm not sure what that is, though."

"If tennis and ping-pong had a baby, it would be platform tennis. You play it on a smaller court than tennis, with a weird racket and a special ball. You can play it in the summer, but it's really cool in the winter because they heat the platform, and all the snow melts and drains away."

"That sounds like fun."

"Yeah, I play it with my dad sometimes. He tries so hard to beat me. Sometimes he does."

"Because you let him?"

"Nah, he earns it, but not often. Maybe you and I can play someday?" As soon as he said that, he regretted it, realizing that they were just on their first date and she might think him too forward.

"Yeah, you'll have to teach me."

Relieved, he continued. "So how 'bout you? Besides school, work, and going to Havana's, do you play sports or anything?"

"I like to snowboard, like you. I also go to yoga sometimes, and of course, I like watching basketball."

"I love watching the Bulls. I can't wait till the season starts. It sucks that they traded Rose."

"Yeah, but he had so many injuries. Oh, and I love to eat," said Brooke.

"We got that in common!"

The more Adam walked and spoke with her, the more he thought she was perfect. She was so poised, like everything she'd encounter in life would be smooth. And her voice – he couldn't get enough of it. It was as if it entered his ears and massaged his brain. He wanted it to never stop. Her eyes were like a magnet that kept pulling his own. Her shirt and tight jeans complemented her attractive figure.

Close to the train station, a less attractive sight interrupted his admiration. The dealer he'd often used was standing on the sidewalk with his back against a building. The dealer gave him a look that Adam interpreted as "Where've you been and how much you want?" He thought the guy might come right out and ask him. Adam shook his head – a slight movement that he hoped the dealer would notice but Brooke would miss. He passed the man, almost bumping into him, but the dealer remained quiet, and Brooke seemed to not notice the silent communication.

Disaster avoided. However, the moment triggered Adam's opioid brain. Urges were creeping in. Brooke's presence kept his mind off them.

"Sorry, this isn't the nicest area," she said.

"What do you mean?"

"I think that guy back there is a drug dealer."

"Oh. I guess that stuff goes on lots of places."

They rode the train to downtown Chicago, using tickets on Brooke's Ventra app. They did the traditional things that first-daters do in Chicago. They walked to the Bean in Millennium Park and made silly reflections. They strolled the Magnificent Mile, while Adam learned about radiography and described how to make Buffalo chicken wing sauce from scratch. They traded snowboarding stories and compared their favorite Lil Wayne lyrics. They found a tamale street vendor with a long line of waiting customers, a sure indication of quality. Adam bought four tamales and two bottles of water.

David had given Adam thirty dollars for his date, which he expected Adam to pay back once he started receiving his paychecks. After paying for dinner, Adam still had fifteen dollars – enough to buy a hit. He was pissed off that the idea entered his mind. He focused on Brooke's eyes to crush the thought.

Brooke and Adam listened to an open-air concert at Millennium Park while they ate. A few minutes before eleven o'clock, Brooke suggested they head home.

When they reached the Belmare train station, Adam ordered an Uber to take them to Brooke's apartment, then to take himself home. At her place, Adam offered to walk her upstairs while the driver waited. This strategy might create an opportunity for him to give her a good-night kiss but let her know that he didn't expected anything else.

At the door of her apartment, Adam touched her shoulder and reached in to kiss her, and she welcomed his advance. He'd never known how sweet a kiss could be. He knew he'd remember the feeling for the rest of his life, and he hoped that she felt the same.

"I'd like to see you again," he said.

"That would be nice."

"Do you have classes tomorrow afternoon?"

"I have one class in the morning. That's all."

"Well, I don't work tomorrow, and it is supposed to be a hot, sunny day." He hesitated then said, "How 'bout we drive down to my parents' lake house? We could swim in the lake, go for a boat ride, cook dinner, all that."

She smiled and said, "We've just met, and you're going to drive me to some remote place on a lake?"

"I think you watch too much Lifetime," Adam responded, thinking of the movies he'd occasionally watch with his mother. "Besides, I'm sure you've googled me, and saw that I lead a pretty unremarkable life." He had previously googled his own name to see if people could find out that he'd been in jail. He found that only by using the specific search criteria "Adam Lambert arrested Parkdale" would people be able to see the news article announcing his arrest.

"Yes, I googled you. You seem safe enough."

"So, that's a yes?"

"Yes. It sounds like fun."

"Pick you up in the morning around ten?"

"I can take an Uber to your place. It sounds like your place is closer to your lake house."

"Okay. Sure. See you then."

Behind her apartment door. Adam could hear Beth, say, "So, how was it?"

"I really like him," Brooke answered. "He's so easy to talk to, and he seems kind. And he's sooo handsome!"

Adam smiled and walked downstairs. He sighed as his elation was counterbalanced by the guilt he felt for keeping his secret from her.

In the car, driving toward the highway, he saw the same dealer in the same spot he'd seen earlier. Instinctively, he asked the driver to stop, and grabbed the door handle to exit. For a second, his mind was flooded with how peaceful it would be to have that feeling that heroin gave him. He paused and tensed the muscles in his arms. He managed to kill the thought, replacing it with thoughts of Brooke, his family, and his freedom. He released the door handle and told the driver to carry on.

He felt triumphant. Never before had he been able to pass up a hit. He had money, and the dealer was right there, but he didn't buy. He crossed his arms, tilted his head upward, and whispered, "Fuck, yes!"

CHAPTER TWENTY-EIGHT

Gabby met the two officers as planned at eleven. They were once again in plain clothes, so Jenkins looked like a regular civilian woman, and Gray looked like a typical young suburban dad.

"Alright, we're all going to split up," Jenkins began. "Gray will stay on the other side of the street, about thirty steps ahead of you. When you find the dealer and stop to talk to him, he'll walk a bit further, then stop and pretend to talk on his phone. I'll stay on your side of the street, about fifty feet behind you. I'll stop and light a cigarette."

"Okay." The fear was making her unsteady, but she was determined to get this task done to get their help with her case.

"Find him and talk to him. As planned, offer to do a delivery. Then walk away and cough. With that signal, we'll know it's him. We'll wait a bit, keeping an eye on him while we let you get far enough away so he doesn't connect you with the arrest. Stay nearby. We'll want to talk to you afterwards."

"Sometimes, I can't find him," warned Gabby.

"Well, if runners are going back and forth to him, he's gotta be somewhere," said Gray.

Gabby started walking east. Granville Street was quieter this late at night. The buskers had stopped, traffic was light, and there were few pedestrians. Her heart was thumping. She had heard rumors about Base – something about a homicide a year ago where he was a suspect. Finally, she spotted him near Morton's walking slowly west, texting.

Her hands were shaking. It occurred to her that there was a problem with offering to make a delivery for him today. If he got released after the arrest, he'd find out that the person she was supposed to deliver to didn't receive the goods, revealing her as the snitch. However, at this point, she had no choice but to move forward with the plan.

"Hey, Base," she started.

He stopped, frowned, and looked at her as if to say "What? I'm a busy man."

"I could use some money and a baggie. Can I do another run for you tonight?"

Base looked around. Gabby thought he saw the plainclothes officers but took them as just other people walking about. He cracked his neck and turned back to his phone. "I'm still pissed off about you screwing up yesterday, being late 'n shit. Leave."

Gabby saw no need to continue the conversation. She resumed walking east and coughed. Her heart pounded even harder. She was glad that the officers said they'd wait before approaching him, perhaps even wait until after he spoke with someone else. That opportunity presented itself as a man with tattoos crawling up his neck and face came to speak to Base. Gabby wasn't sure if he was a runner or a lower-end dealer purchasing inventory, but she was relieved either way that someone was speaking with Base after her. He looked about six feet tall and was wearing sneakers, jeans and a grey hoodie. She'd seen him before with Base.

The situation didn't unfold as planned. After Gabby took only a few steps, she overheard Base tell the tattoo man to get out of sight but to stay close, and Base resumed walking west. The officers' plan assumed that he'd remain stationary. They started moving toward Base as soon as he started walking. Their walk turned into a sprint, one on either side of him approaching him. Gabby was still only about ten steps away and did her best to pretend she didn't notice anything unusual.

The officers reached him, and Gabby ducked into the space in front of a store entrance, where she could hear and see if she peeked around the corner but couldn't be seen. At least she hoped not.

The police showed Base their badges. "Sir, we're officers with Terrace Police, and we've been surveilling this area. We have reason to believe you're in possession of a controlled substance," began Officer Jenkins. "Do you mind turning out all your pockets?"

"Damn right I mind. What makes you think I have drugs?"

"We have probable cause, so we're going to search you anyway."

While Gray searched Base's pockets, Jenkins let their backup know to move in. Gray found about fifty baggies of powder and several containers of pills.

"Sir, you're under arrest for possession of a controlled substance with the intent to distribute," said Jenkins. She read him his Miranda rights as Gray handcuffed him.

A police car and two additional officers arrived. Jenkins and Gray were walking Base to the car, when he began bellowing, "I tried to help you, Gabby. And you set me up! You'll pay for this! You hear me, Gabby? I see you standing there with your stupid brown bag."

Gabby assumed that the yelling wasn't for her benefit. Base was clearly intending for the tattoo guy to hear. She was marked.

"Who's Gabby? Who are you talking to?" asked Gray. Base didn't answer.

"We'll look around for any accomplices," said one of the new officers.

Gray put Base into the back seat of the squad car. A couple of minutes later, the other two police returned and said they couldn't find anyone or anything.

The police car left with Base inside. "Thank God," she mumbled as she walked toward Jenkins and Gray.

"Okay, that's what you wanted, right?"

"Yes, indeed. That's a good start," said Gray.

"What do you mean 'a good start'? You're still going to help me reduce my sentence, right?"

"Of course. You need to help us make three arrests. This was your first, so you're well on your way."

"I didn't know I'd have to do it three times! I don't even know three dealers!"

"We told you. And it doesn't have to be three dealers. We can arrest for smaller amounts of possession. You must know other users."

"I'd be turning in my friends."

"Would you prefer to go to prison for a long time?"

"For God's sake, Base's associates are out here, and by now, they know that I'm the snitch. They're going to kill me!" Anger was layered on top of fear.

"If you get into a dangerous situation, call 911," said Gray.

"That might be difficult if someone is about to stab me. Plus, I don't have a phone."

"Just lay low till tomorrow night. You said you've bought from other dealers, and you know some of this guy's runners. Identify *them*."

Gabby didn't have a choice in the matter. She stood between extensive prison time on one side and dangerous, angry dealers on the other. She needed to think about how to survive this situation and having this argument in the middle of the street wasn't helping.

"I'll try, but I'm telling you, I may not be able to come up with anyone."

"We're trusting that you won't waste our time. We'll start a bit earlier tomorrow. We'll see you at ten-thirty sharp. Same spot. If you're five minutes late, we'll leave and put out a warrant for your arrest," said Gray.

She didn't know how she could accomplish what the police wanted her to do. More urgently, she couldn't risk running into the tattoo guy. She rushed to the train station, and without a ticket, boarded the next train heading toward downtown Chicago. She figured she'd be safer under a bridge on Michigan Avenue for the night. She'd then do some panhandling the next morning and head back to Terrace mid-day and kill time in one of her many hiding spots until it was time to meet the police. One way or another, she had to avoid Base's associates for twenty-four hours.

CHAPTER TWENTY-NINE

Adam got home around eleven-thirty. As he walked into the house, he was happy to see his father still up, so he could tell him more about Brooke.

"Hi, Adam," David said, looking up from his computer at the kitchen table. "Everything okay?"

Adam was used to the question. It really meant, "Are you sober?"

"Yeah, everything's good. This girl is freakin' amazing, Dad. She's beautiful, smart, and nice."

"And she doesn't do any drugs?" asked David.

"No, man!"

"Have you told her about your situation yet?"

Adam felt his chest constrict. "No. I know I need to. Goddamn it, I just wish I could be normal."

"Just stay sober, Adam. That's all you have to do to be normal."

"I know. I'm planning to. You don't know what it's like, Dad."

David closed his laptop, walked to Adam, and put his hand on his shoulder. "I *don*'t know what it's like. I can imagine that fighting this is horrible. I'm proud of you for working on beating this. If you can conquer this, you can do anything. You should be proud. I've never had to do anything so difficult, nor has mom, nor have Carter or Meghan."

Adam thought about his younger brother Carter and his older sister Meghan. He thought about how much more successful they were than him and how proud he was of them. He also thought about all the trouble he'd caused his family over the years. A few years ago, he needed money for a hit. Meghan was home for the summer and so was her computer. He knew the computer's hard drive contained some math paper that she had worked on for a year and was going to try to get published in some journal. Despite that, he took the computer downtown and hawked it. Turns out, she had backed up the paper onto one of those external thumb drives you stick into the USB port. The thumb drive was still in the port when he sold it. She was furious and worked on recreating the paper since then, but never seemed to have enough time to complete it again.

Another time, he'd found out the passcode for his parents' bank card. In the middle of the night, he took their bank card to the ATM and withdrew three hundred dollars. He justified it by saying that was the value of the pills his parents had found and had thrown out.

There had also been yelling, physical confrontations, and property damage. Even today, the front door had cracks from the time his parents locked him out and he tried to get back in.

Dealers had come to the house to collect payments.

Adam had been arrested several times. Multiple court cases required his parents to take time from work to drive him to court, and each seemed to require about ten appearances before getting resolved.

He knew his parents didn't take vacations because they felt they couldn't leave him alone. He knew what a financial burden he was, with multiple rehabs, lawyers, court fees, and medicines. He knew that Carter seldom came home from college because home was not a happy place. He knew that Meghan wanted him to be better and would often talk to him about it but didn't know what to do.

All this, and yet his father tells him that he should be proud. He was ashamed and felt like he didn't deserve his family's respect. However, he went along with the conversation and said, "Thanks, man." He tried to think positively and added, "I've been sober for five months. I've never been sober that long before."

"Have you had urges?"

He was settling down from the memories of his bad behavior. "No … well, maybe a bit, but nothing major."

"Well, you need to decide which outpatient program you're going to do and start it on Monday."

"I know."

"So, anyway, we got off topic. You were telling me how great Brooke is."

His smile returned, his eyes lit up, and his muscles relaxed. "Yeah, she's amazing. And she seems to like me. I told her about our lake house. We're hoping to go there tomorrow, if that's okay."

"I don't mind you using it, but how will you get there?"

"I was hoping to borrow your car." As he said it, the problem dawned on him.

"You're no longer on the insurance, so you can't drive it. Maybe she could drive. Does she have a car?"

"No. How do I get insurance?"

"You don't want to do that. With your criminal record, the cost would be crazy."

"How much?"

"Probably about half your wages."

"How would I get it?"

"Call them up, and tell them to add you, I guess. But you just started working again. You don't have money to pay for it."

"Could I borrow the money?" He knew what the answer would be, but he also knew he had to find a way to make this happen.

"No."

Adam thought for a moment. "How 'bout to pay for it, I'll have my paychecks go to your account until six months of insurance is paid for? I'll go to my work in the morning to fill out the forms to do that."

"Well, I'd want to see those forms completed before you go. And, I'd want to meet Brooke and confirm that your plans are what you say they are or at least have Mom meet her. I think I have an appointment in the morning."

"Dad, you always freakin' want proof … Okay. Tomorrow, I'll get that paperwork done, if there's someone in the restaurant early enough. Brooke is coming here before we go tomorrow, so Mom can meet her and stuff."

"So, you're going to do all this just to go on a date?"

"Yes, I'd do anything to spend more time with her." He needed to push his luck. "One more thing."

"What?"

"I wanna cook her a special dinner. Can I borrow some money to buy some nice steaks and a few other things tomorrow morning? Plus, we might stop for lunch on the way."

"I guess I'm certain to get paid back since I'll be receiving your paychecks, so I suppose I can lend you some. I'll leave you about thirty bucks in the morning."

"I don't think that'll be enough for two steaks and a lunch."

"Well, pack a lunch or get her to pay."

"She probably will, but just in case."

"Thirty should be enough," David said.

"Okay. Thanks. I appreciate you helping me, Dad."

Adam set the alarm in his room for eight o'clock. He wanted to ensure he'd have enough time to get everything done in the morning.

THURSDAY

CHAPTER THIRTY

Adam normally slept late, but Thursday morning, he woke up well before his alarm. He spotted an envelope on the kitchen table with his name in his father's handwriting. He smiled with appreciation when he found thirty-five dollars in the envelope.

He called the insurance company, but they told him that since he wasn't the policy holder, he couldn't add himself. They needed to speak with one of the parents for approval. His father had already left, having taken the train downtown, and his mother was still sleeping.

He tapped on his parents' bedroom door and opened it with one hand while holding his phone connected to the insurance agent in his other hand. "Mom?"

"Whaaat," she said, more as a complaint than a question, and in a voice that blended sleepiness and anger. She didn't move and kept her eyes closed.

"I got the insurance lady on the phone. You need to talk to her."

"What are you talking about?" her voice now containing more anger than sleepiness.

"Oh. Dad said I should call the insurance to get added, so I can use the car. They need your approval to talk to me."

"Why do you need the car, and why did you have to call so early? Why are you even up this early?"

"Because I—"

"Just give me the phone," she commanded. "Hello," she said, her voice shifting back toward sleepiness. "Yes … Okay ... Bye." She handed the phone back to Adam.

"Sorry, Mom." He left the room.

The insurance person went through several questions, to which he answered "no," but then she asked, "Have you ever been convicted of a crime?"

He started to perspire. He realized that he'd be facing this question for the rest of his life. He mustered up enough breath and said, "Yes."

"Have you ever …" She paused and backtracked. "Please state the nature of the offense."

"Possession of a controlled substance." Adam imagined how the insurance lady must now be viewing him – a drug-addict criminal. Friends had told him that the pain of discrimination from having a record exceeded the pain of the jail time itself. He was beginning to understand that. Jail time was finite. The record lives on.

"Are you an *active* user of drugs?"

"No."

She proceeded to ask more questions about his lifestyle and drug use. Then she said, "Give me a few seconds and your quote will be available."

"Okay."

"Alright, it looks like the cost will be 576 dollars per month."

His father was right about the cost. However, the price of insurance would not block his day with Brooke.

"Go ahead and add me," he said.

The insurance conversation had taken longer than he expected. He sat at the table as he tried to think about how to get everything done. He decided to check the freezer to see if there were steaks there that he could take instead of making a trip to the Jewel. He grabbed two T-bones and put them into a cooler. He'd buy two steaks after his date to replace them. He went to the kitchen and got some potatoes and vegetables.

The next task was to move his pay to his parents' account. He considered deferring that until the next time he went to work, but he knew that his father would complain about him not fulfilling his part of the bargain and maybe not lend him the car.

Mio Posto wouldn't be open for business for several hours, but knowing that his boss went in early, Adam called the restaurant. No-one picked up, so he drove there, determined to get everything done in time.

He knocked on the employee entrance door, then the front door. No luck. He looked inside and saw no activity. He took a selfie standing in front of the restaurant and texted it to his father, who texted back a question mark. Adam dialed him.

He held the phone in one hand and fidgeted with the keys in the other. His tone was pleading. "Dad, I just wanted you to know that I came here to move my pay to your account, but there's no one here. They won't be here until probably ten, and Brooke is supposed to be at our place by then."

"I guess you won't be going. We had an agreement about what you'd do before you went."

Why does he always have to be so damn rigid? "Dad, I really, really like this girl. I swear that I'll move my pay to your account as soon as it's possible. I just can't do it right now."

"Then maybe you should go on your date tomorrow."

"It's all set up for today."

"How much was the insurance?" asked David.

"Five hundred and something a month."

"Damn! If you went, how would you stay safe? There's beer and wine at the lake house."

"I'll tell her there's no alcohol there. I don't think she's a big drinker anyway."

"Okay, I guess. Be careful."

Adam had suspected his father would give in after making his point. "I will, Dad. Thanks. I love you."

"I love you too. Have fun. You deserve it."

As he walked to the car, Adam checked Facebook on his phone to see if there were new pictures of Brooke. Scrolling down, he saw an ad for badcrook.com. Like all ads, he ignored it. He discovered no new pictures so put his phone away.

On his drive home, he started thinking more about the ad. His chin trembled, and he accelerated the car.

CHAPTER THIRTY-ONE

Adam arrived home, went to his room, and logged into Facebook. Sure enough, the ad appeared again. This time, he looked at it and saw the slogan, "Find out if they're a crook." Clicking the ad caused a search field to pop up. He swallowed. He had to know. He typed "Adam Lambert." Within a second, the screen changed to a page that said, "We found one Adam Lambert." Below that was his arrest mugshot, followed by the details of his arrest and finally a link that said, "Is This You? Clear Your Name!"

What if Brooke saw the same ad? He assumed he'd been targeted since his name was in their files, but anyone could find out about the site. He also wondered if this website could target his email contacts or Facebook friends somehow.

The site was one of several that scraped publicly available law enforcement websites or got access to mugshots through Freedom of Information requests. They posted them, then charged a fee to remove them. Pure modern extortion.

He clicked the link. For $499, these blackmailers would remove him. He could save up money to get his mugshot removed, but they might just put it back up later, or it might come up again on a similar site. He resigned to the fact that his profile was there, and that people could find it. He was branded.

He washed the car and put the cooler in the back seat. He had a shower and started thinking about what to wear. Dressing in the summer was difficult because he wanted to cover his track marks, even though they were now barely visible. To Adam though, the scars were like dog tags on a soldier. Rank: Addict. Drug: Heroin. Method: Intravenous.

Maybe he could explain long sleeves by saying that he sunburned easily. But he and Brooke would likely be swimming. In fact, he was looking forward to seeing her in a swimsuit. He put on a light blue golf shirt and continued to think about how to hide his marks.

He heard Meghan's voice downstairs, ran to her, and blurted, "Hey, Meghan Anne. I have a girlfriend!" When he wanted her attention, he called her by her first and middle name.

"You mean you went on one date with a girl?"

He had always enjoyed bantering with his older sister. "Yeah, but she's gonna be my girlfriend. She really likes me." He smirked. "What are you doin' here anyway?" Meghan and her husband lived in Chicago, so dropping in was not common.

"I had to pick up some old math books." Meghan was a math teacher at a prominent high school in Chicago. "Plus I wanted to see you. How are you doing?"

"Pretty good, since I'm sober and got a girl." He smiled wide.

"You know that you'll need to keep sober to keep her, right?"

"I'm not doin' that shit no more. I told you guys."

"That's good, Adam. You have to stick to that commitment, no matter what."

"I know. How's Eric?" Adam knew that Meghan and her husband

were trying to have children. He smirked and said, "Is he gonna be able to get you pregnant?"

Her smile switched from being natural to forced. "We may have children, one day."

"Just goofing with you. He's a cool guy."

Sharon walked into the kitchen. She greeted Meghan then turned to Adam. "So, what was all that about the insurance?"

He brought her up to speed, telling her more about Brooke, the date he had planned for today, and the agreements he'd made with his father. Sharon asked questions about whether or not the girl was an addict, and Adam answered them.

Adam showed his forearms to his sister and mother, embarrassed but determined to address the issue. "Hey, do you guys think these marks are noticeable?"

"No … I mean, if you point and I look, I suppose," said Sharon.

"What if Brooke notices them?"

"Tell her the truth," replied Meghan. "You need to anyway."

His mother touched the faint marks on his right arm. "If you're worried about it, I have something that might help."

Meghan grabbed her books, said she had to get going, and left. Adam and Sharon walked to his parents' room, then to where Sharon kept her makeup.

"Give me your arms," she said. She used her index finger to take a bit of makeup out of a container and rubbed it on the spots, making them disappear.

"Cool. What is it?"

"It's some waterproof base. I seldom use it, but I thought it might work for you."

"Seems to. So when I go swimming, it won't come off?"

"It shouldn't."

"Alright! Thanks Mom." He hugged her and thought about the many times she had helped him. She was the one who found out about Suboxone and worked to get it for him; she was the one who set him up to live with his uncle for a while; and she was the one who found him a lawyer. He also thought about the great time they had when she took him to Florida last December.

The doorbell rang, and Adam beamed. He darted downstairs to let Brooke in.

Brooke's blonde hair fell on a green summer dress. Her left hand rested on a white bag that was strapped over her right shoulder. In the other hand, she held a bouquet of three flowers. Adam couldn't believe he was about to spend the day with this woman.

Sharon came to the entrance. "You must be Brooke."

"Yes, hello, Mrs. Lambert."

"Hello, and please, call me Sharon."

"I brought these for you." Brooke handed her the flowers.

"Well, thank you. They're beautiful. Welcome to our home."

"Thank you."

"So what do you do, Brooke?" asked Sharon.

Adam knew that his mother was probing for information. She asked a few more questions and seemed satisfied with Brooke's answers. The three of them talked for a couple of minutes at the front entrance. Brooke's natural grace and confidence were evident, and Sharon seemed to take a liking to her.

Adam kept looking at the door. "Alright, we should get going," he said. He opened the front door and invited Brooke to walk out first. As he exited, he looked back at his mother, who smiled and gave him a thumbs up.

CHAPTER THIRTY-TWO

John hadn't slept much Wednesday night, having talked well into the night with his wife, Velinda, and their son. He and Velinda had no experience dealing with addiction. Internet research only brought up ads and blogs for rehab centers trying to sell their services. They wondered if Daniel should take a term away from school, attend rehab, then live in a sober house.

John and Velinda resumed the discussion early Thursday morning. They decided that John would come home after the settlement meeting, and they would spend a few hours calling different rehab centers.

John had been at the Harris Clark office since nine. He wanted to be there for at least a few minutes of the partner meeting, and he planned to do some final preparation for the settlement conference.

A little before ten, he went to the office kitchen to get a fourth coffee and ran into Jackie. "Good to see you, John. Care to update me on the case? Come, walk with me." It was one of her "this is not a request" statements that she felt she had the right to make. They walked to her corner office.

"Peter didn't call me after his meeting with you yesterday, which I found surprising, but it must mean he's happy. So how'd it go?"

"It went well. You should know that the families are now being represented by Parker and Associates.

Jackie raised her eyebrows. "Dear Angela Parker, huh? This seems like precisely the type of case she'd like. Well, we know what she'll do, which is try this case through the media. It's even more important now that we look good. Are you prepared for the conference?"

"Yes." He actually did not feel prepared, given the events of the last twelve hours.

"Don't screw this up. You can be sure that Angela Parker will deliver all sorts of inflammatory statements and sympathy pushes, so you need to be prepared with the legal arguments. This is about the law and not emotions. Get that through to the judge."

He resented her statement about not screwing it up. Partners didn't usually talk to each other that way. "I know that. Ms. Parker already threatened to go to the media tomorrow if we don't settle today. "

"That's what she does. What's your plan?"

"I'm going to ask the judge for a gag order. The plaintiffs may indeed have a weak case. However, the reality is that we can't settle before trial if the sheriff shows no flexibility."

"Let's head to the partner meeting." They walked toward the boardroom. "If you need to talk strategy or discuss the case law with me, come by. You know what's at stake here."

"Of course," said John, thinking that he'd rather talk strategy with any colleague other than Jackie. "I can go to the partner meeting for only ten minutes because the settlement conference is at eleven."

"Okay. Come by, listen to the announcements, then head out. Are you coming back to the office afterward?"

John paused, then said, "No, I'm afraid I have a personal matter to take care of."

"Is everything okay?"

"Yes, of course. Just something at home that has to be looked after. I might make it back near the end of the day."

"Well, call me if you can after the settlement meeting. I want to know how it went, and we can discuss next steps."

The quarterly practice review meetings were required attendance for all twenty-eight partners of the Terrace office, unless there were extenuating circumstances. The meeting was an opportunity for all partners to hear about significant new clients and outcomes on key cases, welcome any new partners, and conduct a Q & A with Jackie. The long oval table accommodated twenty people, leaving the remaining in-person attendees to sit in a row of chairs at the wall. There was also a large screen at the front for partners offsite to video conference in.

John chose one of the extra seats near the door, since he'd be leaving early. He thought about his situation at home. He really should request a reschedule of the settlement conference and assign someone else so he could focus on his son for a few weeks. However, he knew better than to tell anyone at work that his son shoots heroin.

Jackie stood at the front. "Before we get started with our regular agenda, I just wanted to mention a personal situation that Greg Myers is facing." Greg was another partner about John's age. "Greg will be taking some personal time off. He unfortunately learned that his daughter, who has been home for the summer from her second year of college, has been diagnosed with a serious illness and needs attention."

Soft gasps and concerned murmurs filled the room.

"There is no need to share the details, but I will say this. While serious, the condition is treatable and carries a high chance of recovery, so we can be thankful for that. Greg will be gone for a few months to help her and the rest of his family deal with this situation. Therefore, some of us will pick up a bit of work to cover for Greg." There was a good amount of head nodding and whispering of words like "absolutely" and "of course". "I know everyone will do it happily because that's the kind of firm we are."

John left the meeting and thought about the settlement conference. He continued to think through what the judge might say and how he would respond. Normally, he would have done more preparation and would have been running on more than a couple of hours of sleep.

CHAPTER THIRTY-THREE

John met the sheriff outside the courtroom about ten minutes before the settlement conference. Sheriff Mason was in uniform.

"Good morning, Sheriff."

"Hello, young man. Are we ready to make this go away?"

"Well, your previous motion to dismiss has already been denied. I'm going to make the argument again, but I don't expect it to be successful. Today, the judge, the opposing lawyer, and I are all feeling each other out to see who has flexibility and if a settlement might be possible. I expect this judge wants to hear our position regarding a possible change in policy before he does anything. Since he has his own election to consider, he may not want to be known as the judge who dismissed a wrongful death action."

"So if he won't dismiss it, what's he going to do? Why are we here?"

"He'll twist both parties' arms a little and see if we can meet somewhere in the middle. He'd like to get to an agreement, but he could decide to send this to trial."

Sheriff Mason raised his voice a notch. "You know that I don't want that. And I don't want people telling me to change any policies. And

I absolutely will not be paying damages for something that happened outside my jail."

John was still concerned about the sheriff's lack of flexibility and the impact it would have in the conference. "Let's see how this plays out. And remember, there won't be a need for you to speak in there unless the judge asks you a question. I'll do my job, and perhaps we can discuss our options again once we leave."

Sheriff Mason looked at John with skepticism. "Okay, but I better not be walking out of that room with a trial scheduled. You said they had a weak case, so I thought you'd be able to get this dismissed."

"Are you sure you won't consider a policy change?"

"If it makes the judge happy, sure, I'll consider it … then I'll reject it."

John hoped to be the first ones inside the courtroom. However, the doors were still locked for the lunch break. Angela Parker strolled toward them. She was dressed in a black pant suit and a white collared shirt.

"You must be John Tylor," she said. "I'm Angela Parker. Nice to meet you." The sheriff walked away.

"Good to meet you, Angela. Where are your clients?"

"They're not coming today. There was no point. I know how far they're willing to go in terms of settlement, so I can take care of this myself."

The courtroom doors opened, and everyone walked inside. All the court players were there except the judge – two court officers, one court reporter, the judge's clerk, and the judge's law secretary, all in their appropriate places. John motioned for the sheriff to approach the counsel table on the right side of the room, and they both sat down. John pulled out his file, his pens, and his notepad. Angela

Parker sat on the counsel table on the left.

Approximately ten minutes passed while they waited for the judge. Sheriff Mason looked around and sighed impatiently.

"All rise. The Honorable Judge Foley presiding," exclaimed one of the court officers as the judge appeared from a door on the far side of the courtroom and walked toward his place at the bench.

"This is case number 17-CV-9821, the matter of Rodrigues et al. v. Carlane County, number eighteen in the court's calendar. Counsel, please state your appearances for the record."

"Angela Parker from Parker and Associates for the plaintiffs, your Honor."

"John Tylor from Harris Clark for the defendants. To my right is Sheriff Peter Mason of Carlane County. Good afternoon, your Honor."

"Good afternoon, everyone. Are any of your clients coming in today, Ms. Parker?" asked the judge.

"No, your Honor. I can accurately represent their position to the court and counsel. I did not deem it necessary for them to be here today as all of this is very emotional for them."

"I understand. As I am sure *you* understand it is your duty to convey whatever offer is made here today to them before you reject it. Are we on the same page?"

"Yes, your Honor."

"Let's proceed then." The judge flipped pages from a file. He seemed to have every motion, deposition, and order that had been issued. He finally pulled out what appeared to be the original complaint and the motion to dismiss and gave the rest to his law secretary.

"I see your clients are asking for three million dollars in compensatory damages and a change in policy for the Carlane County Jail. Is that correct, Ms. Parker?"

"That's correct, your Honor. One million for each wrongful death and a change in policy to prevent future unwarranted deaths resulting from withholding medicine. There is no debating that our country has an opioid epidemic. Ignoring the treatment plan and prescriptions for people with opioid use disorder can be a death sentence. As you can see from our papers, your Honor, we believe the requested change in policy also has constitutional implications. Withholding medicine from these inmates is tantamount to denying diabetics the insulin they need to survive while they're incarcerated. Our constitution has already ruled that to be cruel and inhumane treatment. We believe we can obtain the same ruling here."

The judge seemed to find Angela's statement interesting, but said, "That is quite a boast Ms. Parker. However, that is not what we are here to discuss today. If I can read between the lines, I would say your clients will not negotiate on the change in policy but will accept a lower amount in damages. Is that correct?"

John looked for facial expressions that might indicate the judge's thoughts. Nothing so far. John was glad, though, to see the judge searching for flexibility in her position. He knew his turn was coming.

Angela responded, "That's correct, your Honor. For them, the change in policy is more important than the money. They want to save lives. However, they are not prepared to waive damages completely."

"And have you discussed this with opposing counsel? It seems to me there is room for settlement here, and you may not need this court in order to make that happen."

"As your Honor is aware, both sides have recently changed counsel. Although I did get a chance to speak with Mr. Tylor, he was adamant that his client would not accept a change in policy. So I thought it prudent to come before your Honor today to put our position on the record. My clients are being more than reasonable, your Honor, but the other side is not willing to even consider our suggestions." Angela looked at John, perhaps expecting him to correct her.

Alright. Exaggeration. He had not been adamant. She was now trying to bait him into an emotional reaction. He knew the game.

No longer looking happy, the judge said, "What is going on, Mr. Tylor? Is it true your client is not willing to settle or to show any flexibility in the negotiations?"

"Your Honor, as my predecessors have maintained all along, this is a frivolous lawsuit. There is no basis under the law to force my client to implement a change in policy. And with due respect, that's not the purview of this court either. The pending lawsuit does not meet the requirements for proximate cause or negligence under any view of the facts. And that's without considering the governmental immunities that support my clients' position. I cannot, in good conscience, advise my client to accept settlement terms that would not be imposed upon them at trial."

Sheriff Mason looked pleased at what John said. In fact, John had said it mostly for his benefit. He knew that the judge would be less pleased.

"Mr. Tylor." The judge paused for effect. "I know you are new to the case. However, you should have read all the prior motions as well as my decisions on this case. You seem to be arguing for dismissal of this case once again and ignoring my prior rulings. I have already considered those arguments and deemed them unavailing. Having heard nothing new from you, Mr. Tylor, and seeing no flexibility on your side, I see that we are all wasting our time here. I will set this case for trial in thirty days and begin jury selection. Do you have anything to add?"

John knew going to trial had been a possible and, in fact, a likely outcome. However, hearing Judge Foley say it made it coldly real, like a doctor informing you of a condition that you already suspected you had. Sheriff Mason looked outraged. John had to create an opportunity to still get to a settlement and avoid trial. He wished he would have had more time last night and this morning to prepare a response.

"Understood, your Honor. Since the court has deemed the legal arguments unavailing, then we will indeed consider the proposed settlement with the proviso that there be *no* damages whatsoever and *no* acceptance of wrongdoing on the part of my clients. Moreover, we respectfully request that should there eventually be a settlement, the record and any settlement terms be sealed." John hoped this would provoke an explosive response from Angela.

She stood, nearly toppling her chair. "That's outrageous, your Honor. They want to prevent the public from finding out about any settlement *should* there be one, simply as conditions to negotiate."

"I agree with Ms. Parker that your proposed conditions are stringent for you to only *consider* the change in policy. But at the same time, Ms. Parker, you need to discuss these conditions with your clients. If what they want at the end of the day is the change in policy, they may not care who knows about it. Please make sure you discuss it with them."

"I will, your Honor, but keeping this quiet is a ploy on the defendant's part because he is up for re-election this year."

The judge smirked at the sheriff and said, "Sheriff Mason. I trust your campaign planning is going well?"

"Couldn't be better, Judge. How's yours going?"

The judge smirked again and ignored the question. "Anything to add, Ms. Parker?"

"No, your Honor."

"I will clarify where we stand for purposes of the record. If the plaintiffs agree to waive all damages and forego requiring any admission of wrongdoing, and if they agree to seal the record, if and when it is settled, the defendants will agree to consider and discuss between the parties a change in policy. Am I correct, counselors?"

"That's correct, your Honor," said John immediately, afraid that the sheriff would interject or attempt to derail the progress he had just made.

"I will convey this to my clients, your Honor," said Angela.

"Wonderful. I believe this negotiation has potential, but it will now be up to you to make it happen. I will still proceed to set up the trial. So, you have thirty days to come to terms and give me a settlement agreement I can approve. If that happens, I will cancel the trial. Thirty days, that is it. Understood?"

"Your Honor, if I may?" interjected John.

Judge Foley nodded to him.

"For these negotiations to work, we need to be assured that the plaintiffs and their counsel will not discuss this with the media even now. Would your Honor consider issuing a protective order preventing both parties from discussing the case with any third parties even now?"

"I think that is a good idea, Mr. Tylor. I will issue such an order." He gestured to his clerk to start preparing the order.

"But, your Honor," began Angela.

"There is no reason for the media to be involved at this point, Ms. Parker. And since it was *your* clients who demanded a jury trial, there is no reason to taint the jury pool. The order will be issued today and last until trial."

"Understood, your Honor," said Angela. She seemed to struggle to hide her anger.

"Anything else from either side?" asked the judge.

Both attorneys declined.

"The parties are dismissed," said the court officer on the judge's right.

John followed the sheriff as he stormed out of the courtroom. Angela looked at John and said, "I'll be in touch."

Sheriff Mason grabbed John by the shoulder. "I told you that I'm not changing the policy. Now, this thing is going to trail? In thirty goddamn days? I can't believe this!"

"The trial is scheduled, but we can still work out a settlement. The judge wanted to put time pressure on us. We have one month to work something out. I mentioned that this could happen. You and I need to sit down and discuss our options. I have some recommendations that I'd like to review with you. How about I come to your office tomorrow morning?" John didn't yet have recommendations. He would need to have them by then.

"You do that. I have to get back to work now. Real work. I have a county to police." He walked off.

John expected Sheriff Mason to call Jackie right away to complain about today's events. He knew that she'd be stewing until he could give her his own perspective. But now, he needed to head home to call rehab centers.

CHAPTER THIRTY-FOUR

Camille left her apartment in good time to get to Mio Posto. The late morning sun was bright, and Granville Street was becoming busy with shoppers and professionals heading out for an early lunch to beat the crowds. She saw a homeless young man looking in a garbage container for food and asked if he might like something from Starbucks. She stepped into the coffee shop, ordered a Bountiful Blueberry Muffin and a cup of water to go and gave them to him.

She arrived at the restaurant as they were opening. A middle-aged woman walked in behind her, dressed in jeans, casual shoes, a yellow top, and a rumpled blue blazer. Since she was the only other customer in the restaurant, Camille greeted her and asked if she was Peggy Morton. It was indeed her. Camille was surprised that she didn't look more professional. Ms. Morton asked Camille if she remembered the instructions, and Camille confirmed.

Robert walked in with the girls. Upon seeing Camille and the supervisor, he left without a word. The girls ran to Camille shouting, "Mommy!" The three hugged in the large entrance, and Camille kissed their faces. She wanted to hug them forever, but she had to wipe away her tears.

"Are we gonna eat in the piano room?" asked Rosalie.

"Yes, we are," said Camille, trying to match her older child's excitement.

"Yay!" the girls yelled in unison.

"Are you gonna sing a song?" asked Mia.

"Maybe. We'll see. I want to see how *your* playing is coming along. Have you been practicing?"

The girls looked at each other, then Rosalie answered on behalf of both. "Kind of. Not every day."

"Well, I brought some music books. You can play for me." Camille looked at Ms. Morton, then back at her girls. "I want to introduce you to someone. This is Ms. Morton."

"Hello, children. I'm here to make sure you have a safe visit today."

By the looks on the girls' faces, Ms. Morton had already frightened them with that comment.

"Is she your friend?" asked Mia.

"She'll help with our visit today. Maybe Daddy told you about it?"

"He said you take drugs, so we can't be alone with you," said Rosalie.

"Well, that's not really true. Anyway, please say hello to Ms. Morton."

"Hello, Ms. Morton," said the girls.

"Hello, Rosalie. Hello, Mia," Ms. Morton's smile was so forced, it looked like it hurt.

The restaurant hostess gestured for them to follow her.

"Is Adam here?" asked Rosalie as they walked to the room.

The hostess answered. "No, he's off today." The girls groaned.

The rectangular table had eight seats. Camille and the girls sat at one end of the table, and Ms. Morton sat at the other. Camille noticed a smell of grilled beef.

The hostess moved two plates of bite-size pieces of grilled filet to the girls. "Compliments of Adam. His custom with your girls caught on with the other cooks. Your server will be here soon," said the hostess, as she left.

The girls devoured the flavorful morsels. Rosalie and Mia looked like they hadn't bathed for several days. Their hair was dirty and uncombed, and their clothes appeared wrinkled and stained. They ordered hamburgers and fries, and Camille ordered a small chicken salad. Ms. Morton said she'd just have water.

"Alright, so let's hear your scales," said Camille. "You first, Rosalie."

Rosalie moved to the piano, sat at the bench, and played her scales with enthusiasm, if not precision. Camille gave her some instructions and pointers. "Ah, much better," she said, after Rosalie played again. They did that a few more times, then Camille pulled a songbook out of her bag. She opened it to Rosalie's favorite song, *All About That Bass* by Meghan Trainor. Rosalie loved the upbeat nature of the song, and the chords were simple for her: A, B minor, and E.

Camille and Rosalie drifted from teacher/student to co-players. Camille added a few chords of her own, and both started singing the rhythmic song. Even Mia jumped in with her little voice. The three voices belting out "I'm all 'bout that bass, 'bout that bass, no treble," filled the room with excitement, fun, and energy.

It was Mia's turn. She played a simple scale, then her favorite song, *Twinkle, Twinkle, Little Star*.

"I wish you could live at home, Mommy," said Mia. "Then we could do this all the time."

"I know, but this is still fun, right?"

"I guess."

Their food arrived. Camille had instilled a custom of speaking French during meals. So, they all naturally fell into that routine. "La nourriture est là. Mangeons," said Camille.

Ms. Morton interjected, "You can't do that. I need to understand what you're saying. And since we live in America, I speak English." She looked at Rosalie and said, "What did your mother just say?"

With a quivering lip and a weak voice, Rosalie said, "The food is here. Let's eat."

Camille felt like picking up one of the hamburgers and shoving it into Ms. Morton's long face. She was astounded that she would make her girls feel bad about speaking another language.

She knew she needed to avoid crossing the supervisor, but it was also important that her girls not witness her apologize for speaking French, reinforcing the shame that Ms. Morton made them feel. "That's okay. Girls, let's speak English for today so Ms. Morton can understand us."

The mood had changed from upbeat and happy to somber and intimidating, with both girls fighting tears and not enjoying their food. Camille wanted to change the mood back. First, she offered Ms. Morton some fries, which she accepted. Then Camille said, "Girls, I bought you each a pretty new dress. I know how much you both love dresses. After we eat, you can try them on, okay?"

"Yes," they both said, gaining back some energy.

After the girls had had enough of the burgers, the waiter came by and they ordered brownies and vanilla ice cream.

"Let's go try on the dresses while we wait for the desserts," said Camille as she led the girls to the restroom. Ms. Morton followed.

"Mia, you're first." Camille reached into her bag and pulled out a girl's sleeveless summer dress, with horizontal stripes of blue, green, yellow, and red.

"It's like a rainbow!" Mia shouted.

"I know you love rainbows," answered Camille. She removed Mia's wrinkled dress and replaced it with the new one. "It fits you perfectly."

Mia jumped up and down and said, "I wanna see it in the mirror!"

Camille stepped behind her, put a hand on each side of her chest, lifted her small body onto the sink counter and kept her hands on her so she didn't fall. Mia could now see her full body in the mirror.

"I love my rainbow dress!" she shouted.

Camille put her down and looked at Rosalie. The mood had improved. Rosalie was waiting to see what was in the bag for her. Camille pulled out a navy blue, cold-shoulder tunic shirt-dress with a flowing design and ruffled sleeves.

"Oh, that's so cool!" said Rosalie.

"Take off your dress and put this one on," Camille said.

"Can I go in there?" Rosalie asked, pointing to the stall. While five-year-old Mia was fine removing her dress in front of a stranger, seven-year-old Rosalie preferred privacy.

She walked into the stall and closed the door. After a few seconds, the stall door creaked open on its own because Rosalie hadn't latched it properly. She had started to remove her old dress and her legs were visible. Camille noticed that she had two bruises on her left leg. Ms. Morton appeared to notice them as well. Rosalie closed the door, latched it properly then came out a few seconds later, looking embarrassed and wearing the old dress. "I'll try the new one on at home," she said sheepishly.

"It looked like there were some bruises on your leg. Why don't you let me see?" said Camille.

"I just fell when I was riding my bike," said Rosalie as she glanced at Mia.

"Okay." Camille didn't want to embarrass her further. "Well, are you sure you don't want to try on your new dress?"

"No, it'll fit. I'll put it on at home."

"Okay."

Mia's new dress revealed more of her arms than her old one and Camille noticed they were dirty. She cleaned them with a wet paper towel from the bathroom. In a playful tone, she asked, "Are you girls taking baths at night or in the morning?"

"I haven't had a bath in a long time!" boasted Mia.

"Usually at night," said Rosalie.

As they made their way back to the room, Camille considered what to do with all this information. The girls had not been practicing piano or taking baths, and it looked like Robert had not been giving them clean clothes. She'd witnessed these things before. But now bruises?

CHAPTER THIRTY-FIVE

Camille, the girls, and Ms. Morton arrived back in the room as the waiter was delivering the desserts. Camille told the girls that she wanted to speak with Ms. Morton for a minute, and the adults stepped just outside the room.

"Ms. Morton, yesterday, Rosalie complained that her father had been mean to her, and today I see bruises on her leg. I'm concerned."

"Obviously, I'll include the bruises in my report, but she said they came from falling off her bike."

"She didn't tell me before that she fell. Something doesn't feel right. I know my Rosalie."

"That doesn't mean anything to me. Like I said, I'll include it in my report."

"What if her father hit her? What if the girls are in danger?"

"Did he ever hit the girls when you lived with him?"

"I don't believe so."

"Did he ever hit you when you lived with him?"

"No."

"Then why would you attribute the bruises to him?"

"Well, he does have a temper. He has hit other people."

"Look, I have no evidence to suggest that your husband is beating the girls. In fact, I understand that the girls were with you recently for an unsupervised visit. So, for all I know, the bruises could have been caused by you."

"I would never do that. You saw how I interact with them."

"Yes, very nice display. I've been doing this a long time Ms. Simard, and I know that most parents can put on a good show for the supervisor. I'm not saying you hit your daughter, but I am saying that I would have more reason to suspect you than your ex-husband."

"How can you say that? Rosalie was trying to hide the bruises from me." Camille was careful to not let her tone pass from upset to angry.

"You're the one whom the judge requires to have a supervisor, not your ex-husband. You're the one who abuses drugs. That is very dangerous when children are involved."

Camille thought the conversation had become too confrontational. Ms. Morton carried certain views about Camille based on her drug history. Perhaps that was to be expected in her line of work. Perhaps she had seen horrible situations of child neglect and endangerment resulting from drug use.

"Okay. Well, thank you for including the situation in your report. I would ask you to also please note how the children looked – their clothes are dirty, their hair is tangled, and they haven't bathed in a few days. By the way, thank you again for arranging your schedule to be here with us today."

"You're welcome," answered Ms. Morton with no expression.

They walked back into the room. As Camille cleaned the brownie and ice cream off her daughters' faces, she thought more about what she'd witnessed. Her intuition was that the bruises were caused by

Robert. Perhaps his girlfriend moving in caused extra stress. Camille also knew that, given her drug history, her word carried less weight than his. She had to protect her girls, but she needed evidence.

She thought of the app that Adam had shown Gabby. Might that work? If Robert discovered she installed it on Rosalie's phone, he'd be furious with Camille. She looked at her girls' faces and decided to proceed.

"Rosalie, let me see your phone," said Camille. "Please practice your scales with Mia for a minute."

"I need to see any changes you make to her phone," said the supervisor.

"Of course."

Ms. Morton moved to sit next to her. Camille couldn't remember the name of the app, so she entered "call police" in the app search field and found it. The description said that if you touch and hold the home button for two seconds, it calls police, and your location is provided through the phone's GPS. It also starts recording audio. She downloaded the app, opened it, and completed a profile for Rosalie. The instructions noted that if you called by mistake, you could cancel before it went through. She tried it. A message came up saying "Police will be contacted in 5 seconds." Below the message was a button to cancel. The number in the button changed to four, then to three as it counted down. Camille hit the cancel button.

She showed it to Rosalie and had her practice a few times, even practicing while the phone was in her pocket. They cancelled the call each time.

"I don't want to get in trouble," said Rosalie.

"Many parents put this app on their kids' phones when they can't be with them," said Camille. "It keeps them safe."

The inspector remained silent.

Camille brought the girls back to the entrance where Robert was already waiting. She hugged Mia and whispered, "I love you." She hugged Rosalie and whispered, "If you ever feel in danger, touch that button."

Robert grabbed a hand from each girl, sneered at Camille, and left.

Camille felt sick, which was probably due to the bruises she'd seen and to her taking only half a strip of Suboxone that morning. She worried that the sickness would get worse.

CHAPTER THIRTY-SIX

Camille started walking home. The air was warm with a breeze. She stopped at the park across the street from Mio Posto and sat on a bench facing the street.

She longed to feel better. She remembered how, as a young child, a rare hug from her mother could make her troubles go away. She yearned for that feeling. She still knew where to find opioids downtown from her relapse six months ago. Within an hour, she'd be able to buy an OxyContin or a Percocet or heroin. She was shocked that these thoughts entered her mind. She closed her eyes and gripped her wristband.

She saw someone familiar walking on the sidewalk but couldn't yet make out who it was. Eventually, she saw that it was Gabby, who seemed to be looking around nervously.

"Gabby!"

Gabby didn't hear her name. Camille tried again, louder.

"Oh. Hi, Camille."

"You don't look good, my friend," said Camille.

"Yeah, it's been a rough couple of days." She continued to look around but also looked at Camille and said, "You don't seem to be in the best of spirits, yourself."

"I've had a bad day too. Let's grab something at Starbucks. It sounds like we both need to talk," Camille said.

"Well, as usual, I have no money, but if you're buying, I'd love a tea. Also, can we go somewhere with more privacy?"

Camille suggested they go back to the piano room at Mio Posto. They arrived, and each ordered a large green tea. Camille mustered a pained smile and said, "Remember when we would 'advise like guys'?"

"Yes, I remember. Although, our problems were much smaller back then."

Several years ago, Gabby and Camille were meeting over tea and overheard a conversation between two men at the next table. One guy would describe a problem, and the other guy would immediately give his friend advice. Then the reverse would happen. It seemed that men were incapable of just listening and providing the other person a sounding board. Gabby, ever the wordsmith, had said, "Hey, let's advise like guys." They tried it, and although they didn't plan to have many conversations in such a dry manner, they thought it had some merit in certain situations.

"Well, shall we?" asked Camille.

"You go first," offered Gabby as she took the first sip of her tea and put her hands around the warmth of her cup.

Camille told her about the situation with her doctor and the fact that she could only get an appointment with a new doctor thirty days out.

"It sounds like this medicine is harder to get than *illegal* drugs."

Camille smiled. "It sure is. Adam warned me about that. Anyway, I might need to make a two-week supply last for a month, or longer. I'm starting to go through withdrawal from taking only half. I'm having urges. I haven't had them this severely in months."

Gabby looked like she was preparing her thoughts. "Camille, there's no medicine where you can cut a doctor's prescribed dosage in half and not have ramifications. Why don't you just reduce it by twenty percent, stay there for a couple of days, then another twenty percent, and stay there for a couple of days? Eventually, you'll get to less than half, but if you're going down more gradually, you may be less sick."

"I suppose you're right." Camille worried about running out completely, but she agreed that the fifty percent drop was too much for now, especially with everything she had going on.

"Once we finish our tea, just go home and take more."

"Your turn," said Camille.

Gabby adjusted in her seat. She told Camille about helping the police arrest Base and their requirement for two more arrests – of dealers, runners, or users.

"It sounds to me like you need to finish doing what the cops want, but you should also get an agreement in writing. Maybe that lawyer guy we met the other night could help. They sometimes take on cases for free. I think it is called pro bonus or something."

"Pro bono." Gabby interjected.

Ever the teacher. "And you probably know where to find other dealers. Just repeat what you did with Base. Regarding turning in users, I guess it depends on your survival instincts on one hand and your ethics on the other."

"Finding other dealers here in Terrace is not easy, but I do like your suggestion of seeing if that John guy can help me with documenting things." Gabby reached into her bag and pulled out John's card. "I kept this because I thought I'd use it as a bookmark" She looked at it. "I'll wait outside the Harris Clark building tomorrow morning and see if I can catch him going in. You're up."

Camille told her about the visitation hearing and the home inspection, which she suspected she failed because of the front door lock.

"Why don't you just fix the front door yourself?" asked Gabby.

"The lock may need to be changed, and I'd have to get new keys for all the tenants. I bet I'd be breaking some law if I did it myself. Then I'd really be screwed."

"Maybe. But maybe it's something simple."

"True. It's worth checking. But even if I fix it, the inspection is already done."

"Girl, you're at the most important moment of your life! You need to stop thinking of problems and start thinking of solutions. You need to survive!"

Camille had never seen that level of passion from Gabby. She saw in Gabby's eyes a fighting spirit. Perhaps she'd developed it on the street. Camille suddenly realized how difficult it must be for a middle-aged woman to survive on the street. She found her spirit and aggression contagious.

Gabby continued. "How can you get the inspection redone? Maybe the inspector hasn't filed her report yet."

"The inspector seemed like a nice person, and the only issue she mentioned was the front door. Maybe if I fix it or get it fixed, find out where her office is, go there, and appeal to her sense of empathy and motherhood, she'd consider checking it out again," said Camille.

"Now you're talking. I know it's a long shot, but what other options do you have?"

"You're right. It's a tall order to get it turned around, but there's nothing to lose in trying." Camille took another sip of her tea while she enjoyed the bit of extra confidence she felt. "So, what's your next problem, besides trying to avoid a long prison sentence?" asked Camille.

Gabby told her about the dealer yelling out her name when he got arrested. "They probably know that the cops expect me to help with more arrests. I think they're trying to kill me."

Camille drew her brows together. "Um, do you really think they'd do that? Facing a murder charge is a much bigger deal than facing drug charges."

"I thought that too. I thought maybe I've read too many thrillers. But yesterday, I went to the library and googled "confidential informant killed." It happens. A recent university graduate in Florida was killed. There was a twenty-year-old kid in North Dakota, and even a guy in Illinois last year. These were people with families. I imagine it's less risky to kill a homeless person with no family support. They could easily slip fentanyl into any package of heroin I buy from them."

"Can you stay away from heroin? Maybe now is a good time to try to quit. You said you've done it before." Camille grabbed Gabby's right hand with both of her own hands. "Plus, using as often as you do will kill you one day. You can only beat the odds so many times. You know that."

"Yes, I've been thinking that now is indeed a good time. Except these cops want me working with them, not vomiting and having diarrhea somewhere. Then we always finish too late for me to get into a church for the night." Gabby told her about sleeping in Chicago last night.

"It sounds like you're unsafe on the street. The only thing I can think of is to keep a low profile. Keep hiding. How about I help you out for the next few days by paying for a hotel? With my current legal battles, including home inspections, you know that I can't have you stay at my place."

"Of course. I wouldn't want to compromise your situation. I would never forgive myself."

"There's the Homestay Hotel about two blocks away. I'm sure it's only about sixty bucks a night," said Camille.

"I hate to have you pay for a hotel, but I think I need to accept your kind offer. I *will* repay you one day."

"Don't worry about it. With your language skills, maybe one day, you'll get clean, write a book about your adventures, and take me on a vacation off the profits. A nice vacation for covering a couple of hotel nights sounds like a good deal to me."

Camille took out her phone and used it to book and pay for a room for three nights at the Homestay. "Done," she said

"Thanks, Camille. I guess it's your turn."

Camille considered telling her about the bruises she saw on Rosalie, but she was starting to feel even more withdrawal symptoms, and she was worried about getting everything done for the home inspection issue. "We've each done two," she said, clutching at her stomach. You need to get checked into the hotel, and I have a lock to fix." Camille had no idea how she was going to fix the lock, but she knew she had to get it done.

CHAPTER THIRTY-SEVEN

Camille made the short walk to her apartment. Across the street, a construction crew worked on a building renovation project. The front door of her building was closed and locked this time. She went to her apartment, picked up the half-strip of Suboxone, tore it in half again, and put the quarter piece under her tongue.

She returned to the front door, opened and closed it several times and saw that it locked about half the time. It seemed the deadbolt had become misaligned. She wondered if there were some type of metal file to enlarge the opening that the deadbolt went into. She walked across the street and approached the trio of construction workers sitting on a planter wall, on break. One looked to be her age. He had thick dark hair, green eyes and perhaps a week's worth of facial fuzz. She greeted them, looking more at the one her age.

"Hello yourself," said one of them, a balding middle-aged guy. "We enjoyed watching you play with your door."

"Actually, that's what I wanted to talk to you guys about. Do any of you have a …" She imagined what it must be called, "file for metal?"

She ended the question looking at the green-eyed man.

"I have … in my toolbox," he said with a Spanish accent. "Do you need … lend one?"

The middle-aged man looked at him and said, "Why do you think she came over here, Santiago? And the word is borrow, not lend. What size do you need, sweetheart?"

She smiled at the guy her age and said, "Just bring a couple of different sizes."

"Hear that, Taco? She likes different sizes," said the older man.

The green-eyed man went into the building and came out with several metal files.

"I help you to …" he said, seeming to search for more English words but not finding them.

"Sure. Thank you," she said. They crossed the street. "My name's Camille."

"I am Rodrigo."

"Pleased to meet you. That other guy called you Santiago."

"He call me lots of things. He also call me Taco. He think because I speak Spanish, I eat tacos. He call me Santiago, because Santiago is my hometown. In Chile. I come to USA for year to see the country and learn speak English."

"Interesting. English is my second language too."

She showed him what she thought was the problem, and he agreed. He took the file that fit best in the opening in the metal. He filed all sides of the opening with rapid, short strokes.

After a couple of minutes, they tried the door. It seemed to lock more frequently now, but still not all the time. Camille asked for the file, then did exactly what he had done, while he rested his arms. Then he did it again for another minute.

They tried the door ten times. Each time, the lock held. "I can't believe it!" Camille said. She shook Rodrigo's hand vigorously with both of her hands and yelled, "Thank you! Thank you!"

"De nada," he said. He gave her an air kiss like people do in South America and said, "Goodbye, Camille."

As he began to walk away, she called out to him. "Wait…" He turned around to her. She was going to suggest they exchange phone numbers but everything else on her plate flooded her thoughts. Dating would be her last priority. "Thanks again."

He stepped back toward her, and said, "I work here for more weeks. You know, maybe we take coffee one day."

"Yes, perhaps."

Back in her apartment, Camille called Jerry to get some advice on handling the inspection situation, but she didn't reach him. She turned her attention to locating the home inspector. After several google searches, she found a map with pins indicating where all the Child Services offices were. There were many. She decided she'd call each nearby office and ask for Laticia Rivers. If she located her, she'd end the call, and drive there, hoping to see her in person.

She called the first number, but they knew of no Laticia Rivers. She dialed the second one.

"This is the Department of Child and Family Services. Is this an emergency?"

"Uh no. May I speak with Laticia Rivers?"

"Just a moment."

I found her! Although she had planned to hang up once she knew which office the inspector worked in, she decided to wait to see if Laticia Rivers answered to know if she was in or not.

A voice on the phone said, "This is Laticia Rivers."

Oh! She's *there!* As soon as she heard her voice, her phone beeped with a new incoming call, displaying "Jerry Murphy" on her screen. She was desperate to speak with Jerry and knew she may not get another opportunity. She more desperately wanted to avoid speaking with Ms. Rivers on the phone, knowing that would remove her in-person opportunity. She often hit the wrong button on her phone, even when calm. Her phone dinged again, seeming irate that she hadn't made her choice.

"Hello?" she heard Ms. Rivers say again.

Camille settled herself enough to see that the result of pushing one of the buttons should be to answer Jerry Murphy and end the call with Laticia Rivers. She held her breath and touched that button. She didn't say anything. Just waited.

"Hello? Camille?" came Jerry's voice. She succeeded. Or did she? What if she connected all three parties? She kept silent, studied her phone, and pressed end. She didn't want to take a chance. She pressed end again, and once she knew there were no parties on the line, she called Jerry back. Thankfully, he answered.

"Hey, girl. I just tried calling you."

Camille told Jerry about not passing the home inspection, her subsequent repair of the front door, and wanting to visit the inspector.

"I'd advise against that, Camille."

"I thought you might. I just want to know if I would be breaking the law if I showed up unannounced at her office."

"Well, you could be seen as trying to influence a court officer. She could become angry and write an even harsher report, or she might even charge you with trespassing."

"How likely is it that one of those things would happen?"

"Unlikely, but it *could* happen. Don't do it."

Camille valued Jerry's legal advice. They ended the call and Camille began pacing, trying to decide whether to follow her new instincts or the guidance of her lawyer.

CHAPTER THIRTY-EIGHT

Adam tapped his fingers on the steering wheel, excited to be within one mile of the lake house. The air outside smelled fresh and felt dry through the half-open windows as the car left behind a cloud of dust from the gravel road. In the backseat were their bags with additional clothes, the cooler with the steaks and vegetables, and a wrinkled Subway bag, containing the garbage from lunch that Brooke had purchased for them.

Suddenly, Adam pulled the car slightly right onto the small shoulder and stopped. "Shit. Look at that." He pointed a little ahead, at the edge where the road met the trees, at a small injured rabbit immobile and a large black raven walking toward it. Adam and Brooke got out. "Get outa here!" he yelled at the predator, forcing it to move its large wingspan and take a position on a branch a short distance away. The rabbit tried to move but couldn't.

"What can we do? He's gonna get torn apart by that freakin' raven!" said Adam.

"I don't know much about nature, but I think this is normal. We could keep the bird away for a bit, but I think that would only be buying the rabbit some time."

Adam paused for a few seconds, then reluctantly said, "Yeah, I suppose." He and Brooke stayed by the rabbit for a moment then got back in the car.

A couple of minutes later, Adam turned right onto a small hill that was the start of the lake house driveway. As the car slowly moved, the scene unveiled itself. First, the cloudless blue sky before the car reached the top of the small hill. As the car leveled – the beautiful, still lake. Finally, the flood of maple, pine, birch, and cedar trees as they drove closer. The driveway was on the right side of the lake house, so as they parked, they enjoyed an unobstructed view of the blue water.

"My God," Brooke muttered. "This *is* beautiful."

Short cement posts supported the long single-story building with pine-colored wooden siding.

"My parents bought this place from my grandmother a couple of years ago, after my grandfather passed away. My aunts and uncles have the lake houses on the next two lots, so they were happy that we bought this one. It's got a lot of memories." Adam beamed.

"I can imagine."

"I'll show you around outside." They walked toward the wooden deck that flanked the driveway side of the cottage and wrapped around to cover the span of the lake side.

"What was he like?" asked Brooke.

"Who?"

"Your grandfather."

"Oh. Well, he was the coolest guy in the world. I'll tell you about him, but first let me show you around."

They reached the center of the weather-beaten deck facing the water and paused to take in the sights. They could see all the way to the shore on the other side of the lake, about a mile and a half away. There were only two or three motorboats out on the water. One of them was towing a wakeboarder in a neon green life vest. A man and a woman rode on a pair of paddle boards.

"My grandfather took down a few trees to get this view," explained Adam.

Looking at the ground from the edge of the deck, a drop of about eight feet, Brooke noticed a small animal with black and white stripes on its back. It was running, stopping, then running again.

"It's a chipmunk," said Adam.

"I know. Well, at least I thought that's what it was."

"My grandfather used to make us laugh by playing a prank on the chipmunks. You know those peanuts in a shell you can buy in a big bag?"

"Yeah."

"When we were kids, we'd give them to the chipmunks. Eventually, they'd take them right out of our hand and even walk across our laps to get one."

"That sounds so cute. Not just the chipmunk but picturing you as a young boy."

"Well, my grandfather would get a fishing rod, remove anything dangerous like hooks and stuff and tie a peanut on the end of the line. He'd drop the peanut to the ground from the deck. Soon a chipmunk would come and grab it. Grandpa would then start to 'reel him in' – only one or two feet off the ground, of course. We'd be in stitches watching the chipmunk suspended in midair with its little legs moving. Grandpa explained that the chipmunk's sense of survival told him to not let go of the peanut, no matter what. It was true. The chipmunk would get lifted to danger rather than give up the peanut.

Grandpa would then let the chipmunk down gently."

"That sounds hysterical! I can just picture it."

"Yeah, he had a huge sense of humor. Let's walk down to the lake." He took her left hand with his right. She didn't resist. In fact, she seemed pleased. There were about a fifty steps. It could have been a hundred miles for all Adam cared, given the thrill of holding her hand.

Several seagulls glided above the water in the distance. Brooke and Adam could hear an occasional call of a loon on the lake.

The stairs flowed into a platform, then a final set of about fifteen stairs to the rocky shore.

"Why does this last set of stairs look newer than the other ones?" asked Brooke.

"My dad and brother built them earlier this spring. The old ones weren't safe anymore."

"Didn't you help?"

"No, they did it during the long weekend when I wasn't available." Adam immediately thought his answer was too loose but was relieved when she didn't ask why he wasn't available, since jail may not have been a great answer.

They were close enough to the water now that they could see a few rolling waves that had been created by the wake of a distant motorboat. The swells rocked the dock before announcing their arrival on shore.

Adam and Brooke reached the shore and strolled across the ten-foot walkway to the dock. At the edge of the dock, Brooke reached down and felt the water.

"How is it?" Adam asked.

"Well, it's cooler than this hot air, but it's definitely swimmable."

"Nice."

Brooke looked at the fishing rods that were stored under the platform. "Do you guys go fishing?"

"Yeah. Well, we usually just fish off the dock. I used to get so excited when I caught a fish. My grandfather did too, especially when I caught a good-size one." Adam held his hands about fourteen inches apart. "I'd yell to him upstairs, 'Grandpa, I caught one!' He'd walk out onto the deck, see me hold up the prize, give me a giant smile, and congratulate me."

"That sounds pretty fun. Did you eat the fish too?"

"Yeah, the big ones. My dad taught me how to clean them. I guess he learned from my grandfather. And my grandmother would cook them. She'd coat them with flour and fry them in butter. So damn delicious. Now I cook them like she did. The most fun was when we had a big crowd here, and I'd catch enough to feed everyone. A fish fry."

Brooke looked at him with her captivating eyes. "You talk about it as if it's all in the past."

Adam thought about all the rehabs he had attended, the charges, the court cases, the sicknesses he'd been through – all of which had kept him away from here. In a way, the lake house was indeed part of his life before addiction.

"I guess I just don't get around to coming here much anymore."

"What's kept you so busy?

"Ah, just school and work and stuff. Come on, I'll show you the inside."

They walked back up the stairs, again holding hands. Her hand felt soft, dry, and feminine. Adam wanted to never let go.

On the way up, he pointed to the center part of the lake house. "That was the original building. My grandfather added on at both sides.

Apparently, he built his first house himself, so he knew how to build."

"It sounds like your grandfather was quite a man. This place seems to be the essence of him."

"Yeah, I miss him. He was my hero. My dad says he wishes he would have spent more time with him and gotten to know him better when he was alive."

"I think that's a common regret when a parent dies."

"I suppose. I don't think I'll have that regret. My father and I spend a ton of time together."

"That's awesome. Adam."

"Anyway, let's get our day of fun started. How 'bout we go in, get changed, and go for a boat ride? Maybe when we're on the lake, you can tell me about *your* family."

CHAPTER THIRTY-NINE

Adam unlocked and opened the front sliding door. He smiled and breathed in the familiarity of the inviting interior. The dark wooden floors, well-used pieces of furniture, and pictures with scenes of outdoors brought a flood of positive memories, like coming back to your childhood home. He showed Brooke where the bedrooms and bathrooms were, and they each went to separate bedrooms to change clothes.

Adam put on blue swimming shorts and his sleeveless red Jimmy Butler Bulls jersey. He applied his mother's makeup to his track marks before going to the family room.

Brooke emerged wearing a teal green cover-up that showed most of her legs. Only two buttons were done, revealing a white bikini underneath and a sexy belly button ring. She was wearing black sandals and a white sun hat. He silently thanked God for her, his freedom, and his sobriety.

"Wow," said Adam.

"Shut up," she said playfully.

The powerful urge to kiss her was counterbalanced by his shyness to do so. He wondered if he should just walk up to her and do it, or ask for permission, or forget the whole thing. He decided to waste time talking.

"So, we keep our boat at a dock in a calm harbor. We can walk there. It takes about two minutes. Are you okay to walk on the gravel road in your sandals?"

"Um, yes."

"Can I kiss you?" The words flowed out almost involuntarily.

"Wow. Talk about random!"

He put his right hand on her back and his left hand on her shoulder. They kissed for several seconds. Then several more seconds. Then more.

"Like I said in the restaurant, sometimes you wait too long to do the right thing," she said.

Adam wondered if she was implying that more than kissing would be okay. He wanted to, but he questioned if it was fair to her to go further without revealing his situation. He thought he might tell her during the afternoon.

"Alright. I'll work on that." He grabbed the boat key and took her hand.

After their short walk to the harbor, Adam removed the speedboat covers. He hopped in, extended his hand to Brooke, and guided her to the front passenger seat. He started the engine and untied the ropes.

"Alright. Ready to see the lake?"

"Absolutely," she said.

Adam drove the boat to the other side of the lake, steered through a narrow channel to another, larger part, across it, then to a river, at the end of which was a small but fast waterfall coming into the river. He put the boat in neutral and spoke loudly to be heard over the noise of the engine and the roar of the waterfall. “This is where the water comes in to feed the lake.”

“Cool. I guess it’s the fast current that’s making the boat move away from the falls, even though we’re in neutral?” asked Brooke, speaking as loudly as Adam.

“Yeah. When I was a teenager, I’d come here with my cousins. We’d get close to the waterfall, one guy would stay in the boat, and a bunch of us would jump in the water and pop up about fifty feet away. I’m not sure how dangerous it was, but we sure never told our parents.”

“Sounds like normal teenagers – doing dangerous stuff your parents wouldn’t want you to do.”

“Yeah, I guess.”

He put the boat in forward, steered it away from the waterfall, and then gave it full throttle to start the trip back. While driving, he saw Brooke close her eyes, tilt her head toward the sun and soak in the rays. He admired her. He admired every little thing about her.

He skillfully maneuvered the boat to the dock in front of the lake house, cut the engine, jumped out, tied the boat to the dock, then extended his hand to help Brooke out.

“That was amazing,” she said.

“Yeah, it’s definitely my happy place. When I’m here, I don’t have urge—”

Blood rushed to his face. He had become so comfortable talking to her that he’d forgotten he couldn’t be open.

“Sorry, I thought I saw someone on the deck upstairs, and it startled me. I was just saying that when I’m here, I don’t have urgent things to look after.”

Brooke looked a little confused. He wondered if now might be as good a time as any to tell her. However, he didn’t know how to do it. He'd gone over the talk a thousand times in his head but couldn't bring himself to externalize it. Instead, he said, "How 'bout we lie on the dock and listen to the waves?"

"Sounds good. Do you have sunblock on?"

"Nah, I don't use that stuff. But thanks for asking … *Mom*." Adam walked to the shore to get two chaise lounges that were stored under the platform. He placed them on the dock, then ran upstairs to grab a couple of beach towels and water bottles. He took his seat and shifted the conversation away from himself. "So, I know you have two big and protective brothers. What do they do?" he began.

"They're both soldiers. My oldest brother served in Iraq."

"Cool. What did your parents think of that? Did you consider the military?"

"I thought about it, because I always wanted to contribute. My parents discouraged it. They said they risked losing my brothers and didn't want to risk losing me too."

"Makes sense. How did you decide to study radiography?"

"I wanted to work in medicine. We couldn't afford medical school, so that wasn't an option. A few years ago, my father was in a car accident. At the hospital, I saw the radiography technician take images. We talked about the field and about all the technology involved. I got interested, and that was that."

"It sounds pretty cool. Your classes plus your job must keep you freakin' busy."

"Yes, I like being busy. I also do some volunteer work with my dog."

"What volunteer work?"

"I take her to nursing homes. It's called pet therapy. Most of the residents love her. They like having Daisy do simple things like shake, roll over, and fetch a ball. The visits make *me* feel good too."

"It's pretty cool that you do that."

They sat comfortably without talking for several minutes. Waves from the wake of another far-away boat swayed the dock. They could hear only the water and occasional creeks of the dock. The air smelled fresh, and the sun doused their skin.

After a while, Adam opened his eyes and looked at Brooke. "Should we jump in?"

She smiled without opening her eyes. "I was thinking the same thing."

They stood up slowly, sluggish from the sun.

"It's deep off the end of the dock, so you can dive in, jump in, whatever you wanna do," said Adam.

Brooke removed her cover-up, revealing a fit body. Adam felt his body begin to respond, so he dove into the water. Brooke followed.

"This is exquisite," she said in the water after tossing back her wet hair.

"I know. It feels so good after that sun. Let's swim to my aunt's dock over there." The dock in front of his aunt's lake house was about two hundred yards away. It was a swim Adam had done a million times.

A devilish grin crept across Brooke's face. "Race you!"

Adam was a good swimmer, but Brooke was better. They reached the other dock, returned, then swam for about another twenty minutes.

Back on the dock, they laid on their towels and let the sun and breeze dry them. Brooke reached for her phone. "Four o'clock already."

"Yeah, let's head upstairs. I'm going to make you a great dinner."

Inside the lake house, Adam spotted the bottles of Canadian Club whiskey, Jack Daniels bourbon, and red wine on the counter and suspected Brooke saw them too. In fact, she probably noticed them earlier and may have been wondering why he hadn't offered her a drink all afternoon.

He decided to tackle that subject after they changed out of their swimsuits.

CHAPTER FORTY

Camille had wasted time deciding whether or not to make the risky trip to the home inspector's office. If she waited any longer, it would be too late to see her. She thought again about the look in Gabby's eyes when Gabby told her to focus on solutions, not problems. She got into her car.

She'd arrive around four-thirty. She hoped the inspector would still be there. On the way, she thought more about Gabby and said a prayer for her, hoping that she could get through her predicament. Camille couldn't imagine the pressure and danger of turning in drug dealers or the scenario of spending many years in prison. She hoped that Gabby could someday be in recovery, like Adam and herself.

The building directory indicated Child Services was in Office 308. Camille examined the security desk and staff that were guarding access to the elevators. They looked impenetrable. She bided her time, hoping the security staff would become busier with more visitors. After a few minutes, a large group of important-looking people came in. She thought that if she got in front of them, the guards would be eager to dispense with her to deal with the group.

She scurried to the security desk and spoke to the youngest security guard.

"I'm Camille Simard. I'm here to see Laticia Rivers."

"Do you have an appointment with her?"

"Yes." The fact that Laticia Rivers didn't know about the appointment was not relevant.

He called her number. No answer. The security guard looked at his colleagues who now needed help processing the large group of people.

"She may be in the conference room and not able to answer her phone," Camille said.

The young man hung up the phone and said, "Spell your name, please." He typed it in then reached down and pulled out a large sticker with her name printed on it and the words "Access to 3rd Floor."

Camille went up and saw a sign on door 308: Illinois Department of Child and Family Services. Inside, a large glass wall separated a small waiting area from a set of offices. It appeared that the people working in this office seldom had visitors. There was an open window in the glass wall and a person sitting working on the other side of it. She finally looked up at Camille and said, "Can I help you?"

"Yes, I'm here to see Laticia Rivers."

"Do you have an appointment?"

"No, but I was hoping to see her regarding a matter with my daughters." Camille hoped that Ms. Rivers might be curious about what the matter was and agree to see her.

"What's your name?"

"Camille Simard."

The attendant called Ms. Rivers, spoke to her for a few seconds, and then said, "Go through that door and keep to the right. She's in room D."

Camille followed the instructions. Laticia Rivers was standing in the door of her office, looking curious.

"Ms. Simard, this is highly unusual."

"I realize that, Ms. Rivers. I just wanted you to know that I fixed the front door."

"How did you get the superintendent to finally fix it?"

"I fixed it myself."

"It seems you have a habit of taking matters into your own hands – fixing the door, then showing up here unannounced."

Although Ms. Rivers was being stern, Camille detected a speck of a smile and hoped that Ms. Rivers was more impressed than angry with her determination.

"Please, I know that it's inappropriate for me to come here, but I had the impression that with the exception of the front door, the inspection was good. I also had the impression that I could speak to you mother-to-mother. Please, if you have not yet filed your report, could you come by and take another look?"

"Well, as I said, this is highly unusual."

"I wanted to let you know also, that during the supervised visit with my girls this morning, I saw bruises on my daughter Rosalie's leg."

"Did the supervisor see the bruises?"

"Yes, but I think she believed Rosalie's story that she fell off her bike. I suspect there's more to it. Mother's instinct, I guess."

"I'll contact the supervisor after you leave to see what she says. As for the inspection report, its status is confidential. Your coming here is ill-advised. I suggest you not undertake such a stunt again."

Camille thanked her and left, wondering if her visit would have a positive or negative impact. She'd find out at the next hearing.

CHAPTER FORTY-ONE

John had spent the afternoon calling rehab centers. They all described their programs and said the next step would be to do a phone assessment with Daniel. Daniel was not yet willing to do so, saying he'd just stop on his own. There had been several heated arguments with no conclusion. John finally left for the office. He had earlier sent Jackie a text suggesting they meet near the end of the day, and she had replied, saying the sooner the better.

He parked in the partner lot and walked to Jackie's office.

"A trial in thirty days? What the hell, John?"

"I see you got Sheriff Mason's perspective."

"Have you forgotten that he's the client here? And I must say, when you and I spoke earlier, it did sound like you had not sufficiently prepared. I guess I'm not surprised at the outcome. Personally, I'm not sure where the old John is."

"What do you mean by that?"

"The old John would have used the forty-eight hours since getting the case to devour the material, prepare unbeatable and overwhelming arguments, spend the night practicing and rehearsing the arguments, and kill the settlement conference. Kill it. Not let it go to trial."

He countered, "I believe I'll be able to settle the case before trial. I created an opening to do that. I just need some one-on-one time with the sheriff. I'm meeting with him tomorrow morning. I also got the judge to issue a protective order preventing Angela from talking to the media for now."

"Yes but going to trial is disappointing. You let us down, John."

"Like I said, we still have the option to settle before trial. This case has more nuances than you and I expected. The families' claim has some legitimacy that's not so easy to dismiss." He ended the conversation and returned to his office, fuming. He still couldn't believe that Jackie was his superior. However, he focused on the case and considered his next steps. He wondered if any more post-incarceration deaths had occurred recently. If so, those families might also join the lawsuit, making the problem worse. He opened his computer and touched the icon for the Harry system.

"Awaiting instructions," said the voice.

"Give me a list of people who were released from Carlane County Jail in the last two years."

"Researching … Here is the document."

A long Excel sheet listing names, offences, and release dates appeared on his computer.

"Give me a verbal summary of this list," ordered John.

"The list contains 6,811 names. Eighty-two percent of the offenses are possession of a controlled substance."

"How many of these people died within ten days of being released?"

"Researching." The system paused for a couple of seconds, then said, "Forty-seven. Highlighted."

"How many of these deaths were caused by an overdose?"

"Cause of death information is available on thirty-nine of these deaths. The Carlane County Coroner reports overdose as the cause of death for thirty-six."

"What was the cause of death for the other three?"

"Two deaths were suicide, and one death was homicide."

"For the thirty-six overdose deaths, how many of these people were taking medicine for their addiction prior to incarceration."

"Researching." A circle spun on John's computer. "That information is not available."

"You can bet that some of them were in fact taking medicine," John said.

"I'm afraid I don't understand your instruction."

John sometimes forgot that he was talking to a computer.

He knew that Angela would eventually find out about the thirty-six overdose deaths. It would take her longer because her small firm would not have the technology that Harris Clark had, but she would eventually get the list. She would have her staff call the families of each, determine who among the thirty-six was on addiction medicine before incarceration, and invite them to also file lawsuits. This thing could grow. Getting to a settlement was becoming urgent.

John glanced through the long list of people who had been released in the last two years. The list was sorted by date of release, with the most recent releases at the top. He was surprised to see a familiar name: Adam Lambert. He had no idea that Adam had just been released from jail. He liked Adam when he had met him Tuesday night and now realized why Adam said he was no longer on Suboxone.

He researched Adam's police and court records:

- *Arrested for possession of a controlled substance a year ago. Probation for twelve months.*
- *Arrested for possession again five months ago, violating his probation.*
- *Pled guilty to two felony counts of possession. Released for time served.*

Not a favorable outcome, having a felony record, John thought. However, he imagined that after that amount of time in jail, anyone would be eager to get out and might accept a deal like that.

He realized that Adam was in the same situation as the people whose families were suing – he'd gone into jail on addiction medicine and had been released without it. He was at risk. John wanted to reach him, although he wasn't sure what he'd say if he did. He called Mio Posto, but Adam wasn't there.

John shifted his mind back to the case to determine a path to settlement.

CHAPTER FORTY-TWO

Adam connected his phone to Bluetooth speakers and instructed it to shuffle songs from Lil Wayne, Eminem, and Red Hot Chili Peppers. He smiled when Brooke looked at his list and complimented him on his choice of music. He offered her a drink, not sure what he'd do if she accepted and if she suggested he have one also.

"No thanks. I'll probably have a drink when we eat."

Relieved, Adam told her he was going out back to start a fire for dinner.

"Don't you have a grill?"

"Yeah, but steaks are better cooked over hardwood coals."

Brooke took a seat out back and watched him. He picked up an axe and a piece of dried cedar and split it into small pieces of kindling. He crumbled up some newspaper and placed the kindling on top of it. He ignited the paper, which ignited the kindling. When it was in full flame, he set slightly bigger sticks of wood, repeating the process with bigger pieces until large pieces of hardwood were in full flame.

"It's interesting how a fire can get bigger and bigger so fast," said Brooke.

"Yeah. It's nice, but horrible if it gets out of control. Often there are fire bans, but we're okay today. That wood will be beautiful coals in about a half an hour. Let's go back inside. I'll whip up a few things and keep an eye on the fire from the kitchen window.

"Can I help you in the kitchen?"

"Nah, it's a one-person job."

"Okay. Then maybe I'll read a few pages of one of my textbooks on my phone while I enjoy the view." She sat in the family room, and Adam brought her a large glass of ice water.

Adam removed the T-bone steaks from the fridge to let them get to room temperature. He removed two large potatoes, washed them, wrapped them in tin foil, and went outside to put them on a cooking grate above the fire, positioning them on the sides to avoid the direct flame.

Back in the kitchen, he was in his element. A twenty-minute fury involving multiple frying pans, spices, jalapeños, cheeses, butter, olive oil, fresh vegetables, and a serious game-face produced three delectable dishes: a simmering frying pan containing buttered balsamic mushrooms, another containing roasted parmesan broccoli, and a third dish in the oven. Pots, dishes, knives, sauces, and vegetable peelings covered the counters, stove, and sink.

Brooke arose from the sofa. "It sure smells good in here." She spotted the delicacies waiting in the pans. "Those look amazing." Adam enjoyed the compliment, and he anticipated she'd be even more impressed once she tasted everything. He was thrilled to be working side by side with her as they cleaned the kitchen.

He poured a fresh bag of nachos into a large bowl, opened the oven, and removed a small but beautiful serving of Buffalo-style jalapeño dip. "A little appetizer for us," he said.

She took a nacho, scooped some of the dip, let it cool for a minute, then tried it. "Wow. This is incredible."

Adam tried it and proudly agreed.

"I guess I'll have that drink now," she said, smiling.

Adam was sure to not hesitate. "Great, we have cold beer, some red wine, and whiskey."

"What are *you* going to have?" she asked.

"Well, I'll be driving right after dinner, so I better not." He felt himself beginning to blush, so he jumped up and went to the kitchen.

"I'll still feel safe if you have just one," said Brooke.

Adam knew she'd feel awkward drinking alone. He opened the fridge and saw a container of iced tea.

"Okay. Hey, you know what would be great with that dip?"

"What?"

"Iced tea and bourbon, with tons of ice."

"Sounds good, if it's easy to make. I don't want you missing this beautiful dip while it's hot."

"It'll be less than a minute."

Adam took out two large glasses and put them on the counter in a spot where Brooke couldn't see them. He put ice into both, poured bourbon into one, poured iced tea into both, and stirred them. He saw only a slight difference in color between the two and hoped it wouldn't be enough for her to notice.

He picked them up then paused. In his short time with Brooke, he hadn't revealed his situation, but he also hadn't outright deceived her. He thought about the many times he had deceived people to use drugs – telling his parents he was going to work when he was really going to buy drugs, calling in sick to work, hiding drugs throughout his home.

He brought the two glasses to the table and admitted, "I didn't put bourbon in mine."

"It's really okay if you have one drink."

"Actually … I don't drink," he said with a nonchalant tone.

"Really … Oh. I didn't know."

He decided to offer a casual explanation. "I used to drink, but I decided to stop for a while."

"That's cool. Often, when I drink, I don't even feel like it, and I do it just to not be out of place." She grabbed her glass, walked to the kitchen and dumped the liquid into the sink, holding the ice back with a spoon. "I'll have what you're having." She poured herself straight iced tea.

"You didn't have to do that."

"I know, but I'd rather enjoy the beautiful nature and this wonderful food with a clear mind."

They savored the appetizer for several minutes. Adam felt like the mood had become a little awkward, but not overly so. "I think it's time to cook the steaks," he said. He grabbed them and a steel spatula and headed to the fire pit.

The wood had transformed into a set of embers with only small bits of flame remaining. Adam wiped the grate with olive oil-soaked paper towel. "I think we're good to go." He laid the T-bones on the grate then took the opportunity to light a cigarette. After a while, he put the almost cooked steaks onto a plate, covered them with tin foil wrapped tightly around the plate's edges and said, "They cook a bit more after you take them off, and if you keep them wrapped, they keep their juices."

"Sounds like you know your stuff. Maybe you should be a chef!"

They chuckled and went inside to enjoy the meal and each other's company.

"I think this is about the best meal I've ever had," Brooke said once they were finished.

They sat at the table, the dirty dishes still in front of them, and talked for about a half an hour. Adam felt like they could have talked for a million more hours and not run out of things to say.

Once they were finished cleaning, Brooke looked at him and smiled. "I'm going to freshen up a bit, and I'll be right back." She headed to the restroom.

Adam walked to the other restroom and brushed his teeth. Brooke was probably doing the same. They came out and sat next to each other on the couch. Adam put his arm around her.

"You sure know how to show a girl a good time. Today was spectacular. Thank you."

"I can't believe I was able to spend a day with you," said Adam.

They leaned toward each other and started kissing. They continued making out on the couch, and it became clear to Adam that things could progress as much as he wanted.

"Do you have protection?" she whispered.

Adam did have a condom in his pocket. He wanted to say yes, but he also felt it would be deceitful to go that distance without her knowing about his condition. "I'm afraid not. I guess I don't plan ahead very well."

"You're right. That's okay. We'll plan for the next time we come here."

"For sure," Adam said, excited that there would be a next time.

He realized though, that she'd probably change her mind about a next time, once she knew his situation. He had to do tell her at some point. He was tired of not being fully honest with her. It was eating away at him. On the other hand, he was enjoying these few days of normal more than he could have ever imagined.

Maybe during the ride home. Yes, definitely during the ride home.

CHAPTER FORTY-THREE

Adam held the door for Brooke as she got into the car. They talked, listened to music, and discussed each other's future careers. In recent years, Adam seldom thought about his future since he was focused on surviving the present, so he enjoyed someone else imagining it for him.

"I see you with four or five quaint restaurants. You're the talk of the town because your food is so amazing," said Brooke.

Adam liked the vision. "That would be cool. I've been tryin' to get my father to go into business with me in a small restaurant."

"What style would these five restaurants be?" asked Brooke.

"Girl, I don't know! You're the one who created this dream."

"I may have voiced it, but I bet it's *your* dream."

"Okay, I'll tell you about one idea. A restaurant with a nice bar atmosphere but with top-notch food, like really high-end bar food. Thick gourmet burgers, special pizza with the finest and coolest cheeses, cauliflower bites spiced so you can't get enough, poutine like they make in Quebec."

"I'd go," Brooke said.

Adam started talking with even more excitement. "A lot of people who like going to nice restaurants may like getting that quality food in a fun bar atmosphere. People like meeting other people when they eat. Why should they have to eat greasy crap when they do that? Oh, and I'd serve really cool cocktails. I'll need your friends to sample them for me."

Brooke chuckled. "Would you serve that dip you made for me?"

"A feature attraction," he said as he started to laugh, giddy from imagining a future and from having Brooke listen to him.

"I'll *definitely* go," she said.

"My turn. Let's see. I see you becoming a radiology technician, like you're planning, working for five years, saving your money, then goin' to med school to become a radiologist doctor. Oh, and having three kids while you're doin' all that."

"I'm tired from just thinking of it."

"Does it sound good, though?"

"That would be a nice future, yes."

They eventually stopped their game and just enjoyed each other's presence. Adam continued to try to muster the nerve to tell her.

"Why don't we stop at your house before you take me home? I'd love to meet your father, and I wouldn't mind seeing your mother again. I want to thank them."

"Sure." Adam decided that he wouldn't tell her before they stopped at his house.

They pulled into the driveway, walked through the front door, and down the hall to the family room. His parents were sitting on the couch – his mother watching a movie, his father half-watching it and half-working on his computer. Sharon was wearing jeans, white socks, and a black top. David was in shorts and an old T-shirt that had not yet dried from his recent workout on the elliptical in the basement. They stood up.

"Hello, Brooke," said Sharon.

"Hello, Sharon." She looked at David, and said, "Hello, Mr. Lambert, I'm Brooke."

David shook her hand. "Nice to meet you, Brooke. We've heard a lot about you in the last two days."

"Adam told me a lot about you both as well."

Sharon jumped in, "Sorry for our appearance. We weren't expecting company."

"You look great," Brooke said to Sharon.

"I was referring to my husband!" Sharon said as she smiled and tugged his sweaty T-shirt. "Can I get you a drink or a tea or anything to eat?"

"Oh, no thanks. I'm still full from Adam's spectacular cooking. I just wanted to stop in and say thank you for letting us use your lake house today."

"You're welcome. It's there to enjoy. I just don't know how Adam managed to get such a pretty girl to go with him," said David, grinning.

They talked about the lake house and its history for a few more minutes. Sharon seemed as enamored with Brooke as she had been earlier that morning. David also seemed to like her. Adam was thrilled that something in his life was impressing his parents. It was a feeling he hadn't had for years.

He hated to break the mood, but said, "I need to get Brooke home."

All four walked to the front door. Brooke walked out before Adam. David gave Adam a pat on the back and a squeeze of the shoulder.

During the drive to Brooke's apartment, Adam strained again to gather the courage to tell her that he was an addict and a felon. He came close several times. She deserved to know. However, the relationship would almost certainly be over. He had never had a relationship like this. When he was with her, hours seemed like minutes. He felt like a different, better person. He *was* a better person.

They reached her apartment, and he stopped the car. "I'm looking forward to seeing you again," he said. He struggled to think of the right words to tell her. He realized the words didn't matter. Whatever words he used, the message would be the same, and it would be a grenade on their new relationship. His heart pounded, and he labored with shortness of breath. She was bound to see these physical signs of stress if he didn't do something.

He couldn't do it. He reached in to kiss her. They kissed for a few minutes, until she said, "Thank you so much for such an amazing day."

"I work tomorrow afternoon. Do you want to do something at night?" Adam asked.

"I'd love to, but *I* work tomorrow night," she answered.

"Alright, How 'bout Saturday morning brunch?"

"Yes, that sounds great." She looked at him deep in the eyes and said, "I'll miss you till then." The moment made him think there really was a God.

Adam started to drive home and noticed how two extreme and opposite feelings can exist at the same time. He was elated that he was clean and was falling in love. These were things he wanted more than anything in the world. But his secret was tormenting him.

CHAPTER FORTY-FOUR

Adam again spotted his old drug dealer a few blocks from Brooke's place, and his heroin brain immediately responded. It launched hostilities and transformed his mind into a battleground – Adam against the voice of his heroin brain.

Voice: *Holy shit. There's your guy. Your old guy!*

Adam: *Shut up. No!*

Voice: *You still got thirty-five dollars.* He's *right here!*

He forced the car past his old dealer. After three blocks, he turned around and gravitated back. He stopped short at a small strip plaza that contained two businesses still open: a yoga studio and Steichman's drug store. The other businesses were closed – a meat store, a diner, a jewelry store, and a hair salon.

His heroin brain did some math. *Okay, you see the probation officer in twelve days. You'll be tested then and randomly tested any day after that. The stuff's not detectable after ten days. So, you can do it today and be clean when you go. You won't go to the state pen.*

Adam wished the arithmetic would have shown that he was too close to his drug test date.

He rubbed his face, started the car, and continued to drive in the direction of the dealer. His head felt ready to explode as the battle in his mind continued to rage. He remembered seeing a Mariano's grocery store nearby. He stopped there with only a few minutes before the closing time of nine-thirty and grabbed two T-bone steaks, each a little over fourteen dollars. Together, they'd be approximately thirty dollars, which would leave him without enough money to buy a hit. He fought his urges while he compelled himself into line at the cashier.

Three people in front of him were waiting to pay. He'd be the last customer to check out. The voice was screaming. *Just leave now. Leave the steaks here, keep your money, walk out, and go get the stuff!*

He tapped his legs nervously and cracked his knuckles. The wait for his turn to pay was an eternity. Finally, he reached the cashier and forced his hands to place the steaks on the belt.

"That'll be 14.75," said the cashier.

"Wait. What? Did you get both of them?"

"Yes, didn't you see the sticker on them? There's a big sign in the meat department saying the items with a red star are two for one. You'd best use them or freeze them by tomorrow," she said.

"Can you take the red sticker off and charge me the full price?" he asked, only half-joking.

The cashier chuckled. "It's the first time I've gotten *that* request."

He paid and looked at the twenty dollars still in his wallet.

"Can I buy two more?" he asked.

"Sir, we're closed," said a manager nearby, holding keys and ready to lock the doors as soon as Adam left.

It's *destiny*, said the voice.

Adam drove to the end of the parking lot. Turning right would take him home. Left was toward the dealer. He gripped the steering wheel so hard the leather that wrapped it became loose. He turned left.

"Damn. Been a while, boy," began the dealer.

"Yeah."

"How many?"

"Your stuff is still clean, right?"

"Damn right, boy. My slogan is 'Not a speck of fentanyl.'"

"I need just one bag. You got any rigs?"

Adam's stomach roiled, and his hands shook as he passed the twenty-dollar bill. The dealer handed over a stamp-sized bag of heroin, then reached into the pocket of his baggy shorts and pulled out a small paper bag that contained a packaged insulin syringe and other paraphernalia. He put something else into the paper bag, but Adam couldn't see what it was.

"Good to have you back. There's a welcome back bonus in there for you."

Adam had no idea what the guy was talking about, but he also wanted to leave as soon as possible. He drove back to the plaza and tried to find a somewhat secluded place to park. Several people, mostly women, were parking their cars and walking into the yoga studio with smiles, cell phones, and brightly-colored yoga pants. The best he could find was a spot directly in front of the drug store, with an empty spot next to him on the driver side. There wasn't much light, but inside the bag, he could see a syringe and a spoon. He took a cigarette out of his pack and broke off the filter.

He needed some water to mix the heroin in the spoon. He also needed better light and more privacy. He could get these things inside the store. He sat motionless, trying to muster the energy to throw the heroin and rig into the garbage and leave. He grabbed the seat of the car with both hands and squeezed it as hard as he could while he grinded his teeth.

Finally, he walked into Steichman's, bought a bottle of water, and asked where the restroom was. Although he was in a hurry, he took note of his surroundings to ensure he didn't recognize anyone. On the way to the restroom, he walked by a large man wearing a Steichman's vest. Under the vest was a white shirt whose lower buttons seemed ready to pop as his hairy gut tried to escape. He wore a soiled red tie that started at the top with a huge wrinkled knot and ended ten inches above his hidden belt. The man must have been the manager because he was scolding another employee. Several aisles away, Adam got a glimpse of a young woman, also in a Steichman's vest. She wore glasses, and had her blonde hair tied back. She was putting bottles of shampoo on shelves.

Adam locked the door of the stall in the men's room and removed his shoe and sock from his left foot. His foot wouldn't leave visible evidence. He took out the baggie, the spoon, and his lighter and placed them on paper towels he'd laid on the floor.

He didn't want to go through with this, and he did want to at the same time. The battle with the heroin voice had continued ravaging his brain ever since he'd driven past his dealer. It was getting stronger.

Voice: *This is the right decision. Just once. No one will know. There'll be no harm done.*

But Adam knew there was harm. There was *always* harm – to him, to his family, and now to his relationship with Brooke. He thought about the many friends who'd died. He thought about Gabby, who nearly perished.

Voice: *No one will know. You love it. It is part of you.*

Adam knew the risk of getting arrested – of breaking probation a third time. He'd end up in the pen for sure. And with all that entails.

Voice: *It is your oxygen. You know that. Quit pussying around and get it over with, so you don't have to think about it anymore. You're tormenting yourself. You deserve some peace.*

Adam clenched his fists. Then he clenched them harder. His fingernails nearly pierced the skin of his palms. He yelled out, "No! Not today. Not today. Fuck you, heroin!"

He threw the baggie into the toilet, but he couldn't find the lever to flush it. Apparently, it was one of those toilets with a sensor that detects body heat and automatically flushes when the person walks away. He looked for the button that overrides the toilet sensor but couldn't find it. He tried to move toward the toilet then away, hoping to trigger it, but it wouldn't flush.

Someone entered the rest room. "Hello!" the man bellowed.

"Yo. Occupied," Adam responded.

The paraphernalia was probably visible under the stall door, so Adam quickly picked it up. His bare foot was probably visible also.

"This is the manager. I heard some commotion. What the hell's going on?"

Adam tried to match the man's commanding voice. "I'm taking a shit. Leave me alone."

He stuffed his sock into his pocket along with everything else he'd picked up, and he shoved his bare foot into the shoe. He was desperate to get out but didn't want to leave anything incriminating behind. The bag of heroin with his fingerprints was still in the toilet. Frantic to get it to flush, he pulled down his pants and underwear, sat on the toilet, then got up. Finally, the baggie swooshed out of his life.

"I'll be damned if I let some goddamn junkie shoot up in *my* store," shouted the man.

"I'm just going to the bathroom. Leave me alone."

Adam heard the man touch three numbers on his phone. "Yeah. This is Steichman's Pharma on Malton Street. My emergency is there's a sonofabitch disrobing in my restroom and shooting heroin."

Adam turned the knob to unlock the stall door and went to open it. The door was supposed to open outward from the stall, but it wouldn't move. The manager was holding it shut.

"You're not leaving 'til you're in handcuffs, punk. The cops are on their way." The man went back to talking into the phone, "Yeah, my address is …"

Adam had to escape. The heroin was gone, but he still had the rig and it could not be flushed. If he was still there when the police arrived, he'd be sent to the state penitentiary for breaking his probation yet again. There was absolutely no way he'd let that happen. It seemed that the man had put his phone on speaker and had placed it on the floor, so he could use both of his hands to hold the door closed.

Adam yelled, "He's restraining me against my will!"

The 911 operator said, "Sir, are you restraining the perpetrator?"

"Goddam right I am. The cops better get here fast, or I'll deal with this lowlife myself."

"Sir, please do not engage with the perpetrator. He could be armed and dangerous. You're endangering yourself, your staff, and your customers. Please stand down immediately."

"And let this piece of shit get away?"

"Sir, please stand down immediately."

The man continued to hold the door. Adam backed away from it as far as he could, and with the adrenaline-induced strength, he charged at the door with his shoulder, blasting it open and pushing the man to the floor.

Like a wild animal out of its cage, Adam was out of the bathroom in an instant. The manager almost reached him again as Adam exited the front door. The man stood in the entrance and yelled, "Tell all your junkie friends that they're not welcome here, you dope-fiend douche bag!"

Adam realized that if he got into his car, the man would write down his license plate, and the police would be at his home within an hour. So, he ran past it. He stopped and couldn't help issuing a small act of defiance. "Your mother needs to teach you how to tie a tie!"

Adam ran far enough away that he'd no longer look suspicious, but he kept running. It felt good. It was helping him deal with the adrenaline that had been released as a result of the two scares – being arrested and relapsing. The first scare was not over yet. The second scare never would be.

He ran for another ten minutes and was drenched in sweat. He turned around and hoped that by the time he got back to the store, the police would have been there, taken statements and left. His watch showed a few minutes before ten, when the store would close.

Approaching Steichman's, he stayed on the other side of the street. He could see inside the lit store but sensed that people in the store couldn't see him. The manager come to the front door, locked it from the inside, then disappeared back into the aisles. The lights went out. Adam now had a chance to get to his car and escape. He hit the unlock button, opened the driver door and started getting in. He saw two employees leaving the store – the young woman he had gotten a glimpse of previously and some other guy.

The interior car light was designed to stay on until the engine started. Adam was the only illuminated thing in the dark parking lot, like a spotlight on an actor in a theater. He saw the woman and man look at him. She looked familiar, but he couldn't place it. He hid his face with his left hand and pressed the start button with his right. The light went off. He clutched the steering wheel, backed up, and geared forward.

Driving by the woman and man, he continued to cover his face as best he could. The woman looked at him like she knew him.

He continued driving, thinking about what had happened, more specifically, what had happened before the manager entered the bathroom. He had a massive urge to use, the needle was full, yet he didn't use. Once again, he'd won the battle! He clutched the steering wheel and yelled at the top of his lungs. "I beat you! I fuckin' beat you, you heroin motherfucker shit!"

He savored the victory. But not for long, He now remembered where he'd previously seen the girl from the drug store.

CHAPTER FORTY-FIVE

Gabby was in the business center on the fifth floor of the Homestay hotel. She'd been using the computer to find message boards and Instagram or Facebook posts about drug buying and selling in the hopes of finding another dealer in Terrace. She had once heard that joining Facebook support groups for addicts sometimes generated friend requests from fake and temporary accounts that were actually drug dealers. She joined several groups, hoping to lure such requests.

Since her conversation with Camille, she'd thought a lot about how to help the police make two more arrests. She had decided that she wouldn't expose other users. She'd spend the rest of her life in jail, rather than inflict more pain on other addicts. She would try to find another dealer and make a purchase with the officers watching. However, she wasn't having much luck finding one on social media, at least not yet. She planned to ask Jenkins and Gray for more time when she met up with them. Surely that was reasonable. More time would hopefully also enable her to connect with John and request his help.

She had checked into the hotel earlier and had administered the hit that she purchased in Chicago the night before and had left her bag with her things in the room. As she rode the elevator down to the second floor, she was looking forward to a few minutes of rest before having to meet the officers. She was also thinking about what to say to John tomorrow. She wondered what case he was working on that had prompted him to want to meet with her and Adam.

At the door of her room, she searched her pockets for the room key. Two rooms down, she saw a girl, probably about seventeen, in a short skirt knocking on the room door. A middle-aged abdominous man opened the door, confirmed the girl's name, and welcomed her inside. Gabby knew about human trafficking from living on the streets, and this girl looked like she may have been a victim. Gabby planned to call the front desk and report the situation as soon as she was inside her own room. However, her key card wouldn't work.

She went to the front desk, waited for the attendant to finish checking in a guest, and said, "Hello, ma'am. My key's not working."

"Oh. Our apologies. Which room are you in?"

"211."

The woman looked at her computer. "Are you Ms. Jones?"

"Yes."

"One moment." The women picked up her phone, waited a second, and said into the phone, "211 is here."

"Ms. Jones, there's a problem with your room. We'll be able to explain in just a minute."

Gabby had an inkling of what was transpiring.

An employee walked into the reception area from one of the hotel hallways. He stood on Gabby's side of the front desk.

The attendant behind the desk said, "Ms. Jones, our staff went into your room to restock the mini-bar and—"

"I didn't use anything from the mini-bar."

"Yes, but we don't know that until we go in and check. Our staff found drug paraphernalia in your room." The woman waited for a reaction, but Gabby didn't give her one. "So, I'm afraid we need to evict you."

"Why?"

The woman looked down at Gabby. "I just told you. Because we found drug paraphernalia in your room."

"Why does that mean you must evict me?"

"Well, obviously, we don't allow drug use in our hotel."

"I didn't hurt anyone or put anyone at risk."

"It's illegal," said the woman.

"Where's my bag?" asked Gabby.

"I have it behind the counter. Obviously, we needed to go through it to see if there were more drugs or anything else dangerous on our property."

"Those are my personal things. Please give me my bag."

The woman looked at the other employee, hesitated, and then passed Gabby her bag.

"If you don't allow illegal activities, you better go up to 213. Mr. Potbelly is in there having, well, probably *trying* to have, sex with an underage prostitute."

"You don't know that. It seems you're trying to change the subject. The police are on their way here to arrest you."

The male employee spoke up, "Why'd you tell her that? Now she'll leave before they get here – especially since you returned her bag. Plus they said we can't restrain her."

Gabby wondered if this man had ever had an original thought in his life. He and the front desk woman argued while Gabby dashed out the door and saw the police arriving. As the police exited their car, she yelled, "Officers, there's some drug addict at the front desk arguing with the staff."

"We know, ma'am. That's why we're here."

"Also, please check out room 213. There may be a trafficking victim in there."

"Who are you?" asked one of the officers.

"I'm a guest at the hotel. I'm late for work. Remember, 213."

"Thank you, ma'am," one of them said as they hurried inside.

Perfect. Her hope that the police were in too much of a hurry to ask for her name or for more details came true. She also hoped that they would enter room 213 and rescue that girl.

She darted down a side street, and as she gained some distance from the hotel, she wondered if the police might try to contact Camille since she paid for the room. She concluded that it was unlikely that the police would go to that length for just a possession charge, especially when there was no longer evidence in the room.

She was back on the streets. She had to get arrests for Jenkins and Gray. Base and his colleagues knew what she was doing and that she was a threat to them. She felt like a bleeding fish in a school of sharks.

CHAPTER FORTY-SIX

Gabby was making her way toward the meeting place. The many advantaged people who made Granville Street busy during the day were less plentiful this late in the evening. About four blocks from her destination, she felt a tap on her shoulder from behind. Terrified, she considered fleeing, but she probably wouldn't be able to outrun whoever it was.

She turned around and saw the guy Base had spoken to just before the police arrested him. He was wearing the same grey hoodie as the night before. This close, Gabby could make out the tattoos. They were all in black ink. The one on his neck was a large spider web. The one on his forehead was four large capital letters *EWMN*, and one was a teardrop on the left side of his face.

He was smoking a cigarette. A few steps behind him stood another guy, younger and bigger – perhaps an extra set of hands if needed.

"Hey," said the inked guy.

"Hey," she responded.

"You Gabby?"

Gabby turned away from him. "I have somewhere to go."

"No problem. Just a sec. Don't be afraid of me."

"What do you want? Who are you?"

He wouldn't give her his name. She decided to think of him as Ink.

"I want to thank you," he said.

"Oh, really? Okay. You're welcome." She started to walk away.

Ink gripped her shoulder. "Hang on. For serious. I want to thank you."

"For what? I don't know you."

"For getting that bastard, Base, arrested. That son bitch was bad news. We was all afraid of him. Even his supplier."

"I don't know what you're talking about. You look like a guy that people could be afraid of, yourself."

"Me? Nah. I'm gentle like a dove." He put his arms out and moved his hands up and down from the wrists.

"Why are people afraid of Base?"

"That son bitch kill a guy in Chicago last year. Kill him just 'cause he was sellin' too close to his territory and wouldn't relocate. That guy he kill had a family."

"Okay, well again, I have to go." Gabby stepped away once more.

Ink grabbed her shoulder more tightly. "Now you gotta stop being so rude. I'm talking to you nice, and you bein' all rude. Pissin' me off."

She took it as a threat. She was concerned about getting to the police on time, but this guy was a more immediate and dangerous problem. She forced a half-smile and said, "I suppose you're right."

"That's better. Anyway, I suppose you lookin' for a new dealer."

"I don't need any right now."

"C'mon. You people always need some right now." Ink looked at the other guy, and they both laughed.

"I have no money."

"I want to give you a gift ... for getting that bastard off the street. If you like it, maybe you start buying from me. But you don't gotta. It's just a gift." He handed her a baggie.

She had to take it. She put it in her pocket. "Thank you. I'll use it tomorrow. I already used today."

"Use it now."

She felt her face twitching with fear, and she started thinking of ways to get out of the situation. "I used just a few hours ago. This would be too much. I only use once a day."

Ink shook his head and tsked at her. "So much bullshit. You people can always use a top-up. I want you to see how good this shit is." He pointed to a narrow walkway between the two buildings they were in front of. "Just step over there and do the hit."

His eagerness convinced her that the bag was laced with fentanyl or anything else that could be fatal. This was not a gift. It was a murder weapon. There were no witnesses nearby, so if she refused to use, he and his associate would probably find another way to deal with her. While she hesitated, she looked Ink over and spotted something inside the left pocket of his hoodie. She couldn't make it out for certain, but it looked like a gun. Now she worried that if she ran, she'd receive a bullet in her back. Ink's partner walked around her so that she was now between them. There was no escape.

"Okay, I suppose I could use a top-up. Let me get my rig." She reached into her bag, yanked out her hand, and pelted pepper spray into Ink's eyes. He screamed, put his hands to his face, and fell to the ground. The other guy grabbed her left arm with both of his hands, and she pivoted and doused his eyes. He howled even louder than Ink and buckled over.

Still on the ground, Ink moved his left hand from his eyes toward the pocket that contained the gun. Gabby drove every pound of her body weight through the heel of her hard leather shoe into the back of Ink's hand causing blood, another scream, and probably broken bones. She got the gun, threw it into her bag, ran down the alley, and emerged on the other side of the block.

She rushed to the spot where she was to meet Jenkins and Gray and arrived with her heart pounding. She was ten minutes late, and they weren't there. Probably just as well, since she was carrying a gun. By now, there was probably a warrant out for her arrest.

She needed to get off the streets, fast. Ink and his sidekick wouldn't be incapacitated for long and would do everything they could to ferret her out. One of them was probably at the train station by now in case she went there. She thought of the vacant retail spot she'd used before. If there weren't any security dogs guarding it, she'd be safe there.

She ran to the place, knocked on the window of the back door, and listened. No barking. Some time ago, another homeless addict had shown her how to get in. She looked around and found the piece of lead pipe he had used. She held the pipe horizontally and placed the left end of it on the left side of the doorjamb and lowered the right end of it until it rested on the other side. It was slightly larger than the width of the door. She hit the right end of the pipe several times with a large rock. Each hit lowered that end of the the pipe, making it more level, and expanding the doorjamb slightly. After several hits, the doorjamb had expanded sufficiently that it separated from the short deadbolt. With the door open, she knocked out the pipe, walked in, and relocked the door from the inside.

She flicked her lighter on to break the total darkness. She opened her bag with one hand and held the lighter above it. She picked up the gun and studied how to use it, holding it in the shooting position and feeling the trigger with her index finger. She heard movement outside and extinguished the lighter.

"Let's go," said a man's gruff voice outside. "C'mon. Over here."

A key was being inserted into the door. She kept the extinguished lighter in one hand, continued to hold the gun in the other, and pointed it toward the floor a few feet in front of her. Perhaps the noise of a gunshot would scare away whoever was coming in. The deadbolt turned, the door opened, and the killer bark of an angry dog filled the room. She flicked the lighter on and saw a large German Shepherd charging at her and almost upon her. She released the lighter and fired the gun to scare him and his owner.

The dog yelped. The man yelled, "Holy shit!" He ran back to his truck and sped away.

She flicked the lighter back on and was sickened to see that she had injured the dog's left front paw. The injury did not appear life-threatening, but the dog was still yelping and was immobile. Police would be there soon. She hoped they would provide care to the dog as she grabbed her bag and ran out the door, crying for the animal.

She'd be safer downtown, but she'd have to risk being spotted at the train station. She ran the half-mile to the Terrace East station, constantly looking over her shoulders. When she arrived, she looked around for Ink, his sidekick or any other dangerous people. She saw that the next train headed to Chicago was in twenty minutes, so she waited in a cubicle in the rest room, then scurried on at the last minute.

She made it safely to Union, receiving a fine on the way there for not having a ticket. She planned to survive the night, then take Camille's advice and see if she could find John in the morning to help with her informant situation. She found a parking garage where she figured she could get an hour or so of sleep before being asked to go somewhere else.

Before laying down, she knelt and prayed. "Dear God, please help that innocent animal."

CHAPTER FORTY-SEVEN

Adam was at home in the basement watching television. No-one else used the basement much, so he felt like it was his place and enjoyed the relative privacy. His parents were asleep upstairs in their bedroom.

He was trying to regain some calm after the episode at the drug store, and after his realization that the girl he saw may have been Brooke's friend, Kate. When he'd met her in Mio Posto and at Havana's, she hadn't been wearing glasses and her hair had been down. He wasn't totally sure, though, and since an hour had now gone by and he hadn't heard from Brooke, maybe the girl he saw wasn't Kate, after all. He certainly hoped so.

His phone rang, showing Brooke's name. He was nervous about why she may be calling, but he still looked forward to hearing her voice. He inserted his earphones and pressed answer.

"Hey, Brooke."

Her voice carried concern. "Adam? Are you okay?"

"Yes. Of course. Why? Sup?"

"Kate's here. She works at Steichman's."

He crumpled into the leather couch. "Yeah?"

"Well, she said there was a huge scene there tonight. Some criminal came into the store, took his clothes off in the bathroom, and started to shoot up. The manager went in to see what was going on, and the guy attacked him and ran out of the store. The police came with sirens on and questioned people."

Adam didn't know what to say.

Brooke continued. "I felt horrible that she and everyone in the store went through that and had been in danger. Then she told me the guy was you!"

Adam's new life had come crashing down. He still wasn't sure what to say. "Uh …"

She added, "I told her no way. We've been discussing it for the last half-hour."

"Brooke, how 'bout I come to your place and explain."

"What do you mean? Were you the guy or not? Are you a heroin addict?"

Adam took a deep breath. "Yes." He was terrified about where their relationship would go now. But he also felt a tinge of relief from the burden of hiding his secret.

"Oh my God!" she yelled.

"I'm coming over."

"No. Don't do that. My God. I've been seeing a heroin addict!"

"I wanted to tell you, but I was afraid you'd have this reaction. And I know. It's a normal reaction. Brooke, I've been clean for five months, I go to NA meetings. I'm starting another outpatient program on Monday. Yes, I almost relapsed today, but I didn't. I beat it."

"Are you violent?"

"No! The guy wouldn't let me leave, and the police were coming. I had to push the door open, and it knocked him over."

"I knew this relationship was going too fast," said Brooke.

"What do you mean? Let me come over there."

"No. Kate's afraid of you."

Adam thought more about everything she had said. "Wait. Did Kate speak to the police about me?"

"No. She didn't recognize you until she saw you in your car, and the other employee pointed you out as the guy who came into the store. The police were gone by then."

"Okay." At least he was safe from the police.

"Are you a criminal?"

"Brooke, having this condition is a crime. Yes, I was arrested twice for possession."

"Are you a convict?"

"Yes. I served time in jail for the possession charges. I'm a felon."

"My God!"

"Brooke, I'm more than my addiction."

"Adam, I really liked you, and I really had a good time with you, but I didn't know this. I'll need some time to think about this."

"Brooke, everything is fine. Yes, I have a drug disorder. I don't blame you for feelin' the way you do. I understand it, and that's why I was struggling to find the right time to tell you. Let's at least meet tomorrow and talk. I'll go to CC, and we'll meet for coffee after your first morning class."

"I don't know. I have a lab in the morning, then a class, then workshops at two-thirty. I might have a break at nine because sometimes we finish the lab early, but—"

"I'll be there at nine. If you're not out, I'll wait 'til two-thirty. I don't work until the evening. Maybe we can take the bus back together."

"You might be waiting a long time."

"I'm okay to wait."

"Well, okay, see you tomorrow."

"Okay. Thanks, Brooke. I'm sorry."

He hung up and covered his face with his hands. His chest felt heavy from the pain he had caused Brooke. He also thought about the pain he had caused everyone close to him for so long. Brooke was just the latest example. The degree of regret seemed insurmountable, but he was determined to get through it. He went to bed, hoping to get some sleep before the early morning.

FRIDAY

CHAPTER FORTY-EIGHT

Camille had worked well into the night creating a resume, searching online for job opportunities, and applying to several. She got up after only a short sleep and got ready for the day. She planned to make a series of calls to contacts, but she knew she wouldn't be able to reach anyone until after nine.

Since she had time, she sat at the piano to work on her daughters' song. She always enjoyed glancing outside occasionally to watch life on the street, especially the morning hustle on the portion of Granville Street that she could see. People walking to work, people going in and out of coffee shops, and, unfortunately, the occasional homeless person getting up to find survival for the day.

After playing the melody for one particular lyric, she grabbed a pencil and adjusted the rhythmic flow of the phrase to reveal the beauty of the words. Just above the top of the sheet music, her line of vision outside showed a woman getting out of a parked car. As the woman approached, she recognized Laticia Rivers.

Camille dashed out of her apartment, locked the door behind her, and went down one and a half flights of stairs until she was close enough to hear activities at the front door. She heard the door being pushed, pulled, and shaken. Then silence. Then more pushing, pulling, and shaking. Then more silence.

Camille jumped down the remaining flight of stairs and went outside as Laticia Rivers was walking away.

"Hello, Ms. Rivers," she shouted.

The home inspector turned around to face her. "Oh, hello, Camille."

"It's like Fort Knox, no?"

"I suppose it is. Congratulations."

Laticia Rivers walked toward her. "Since you're out here, there's some information I should share with you. You'll be receiving a call from Child Services today to communicate the status of your daughters."

"What do you mean?"

"I heard this information from Peggy Morton." The memory of the visitation supervisor sent chills through her. "I had previously called her to discuss the bruises, so she called me to let me know about these developments."

"What developments? What are you talking about?"

"Well, this morning, the police responded to an emergency call that had been placed by an app on your daughter's phone. When they arrived, the home was quiet, but they entered and reviewed the recorded audio on the app. There was enough evidence for Child Services to remove the girls."

"Evidence of what?"

"Your suspicions were accurate. It appears that your ex-husband hit your older daughter."

"Oh my God … Can I go see them?"

"You'll need to call your lawyer about that. I understand your judge allowed one supervised visit only."

"My poor girls. Mes filles! They must be so frightened. I shouldn't have let things get to this point. Thank you for telling me, and for coming back."

"You're welcome."

Laticia Rivers crossed the street to her car, and Camille returned to her apartment. She sat at the table and dialed Jerry Murphy. To her surprise, he answered.

"Jerry, my girls are with Child Services. I need to see them. I'm going to go find them."

"Camille, you know that's not possible. You were allowed one visit, regardless of the circumstances. There must have been good cause to remove them, so they're safer than they were with your ex-husband."

Camille's body was limp, and her voice was shaky. "They need me. They need to see me."

"Yes, they do. So, you need to make that happen at the Tuesday hearing. The best thing you can do for them now is to get a job. Your termination will be news to the judge, and not good news. He'll interpret it as your fault, regardless of the circumstances."

"Getting a job between now and Tuesday will be impossible."

"You need to do the impossible. I'll see you Tuesday."

Camille paced back and forth in the living room and imagined how uncomfortable her little girls must be in a stranger's home. She took a series of quick breaths to calm herself down. She thought about what Jerry said. Getting a job was the best thing she could do for her girls. While she had a couple of leads, she had nothing that could get her an offer before Tuesday. She *had* to figure out a way.

CHAPTER FORTY-NINE

Gabby took the train back to Terrace early Friday morning. The passengers near her seemed disturbed at her state of appearance. She got off at Terrace East, surveyed her surroundings and began walking west toward Harris Clark. The boutique stores were not yet open, and most of the people sleeping on the street were not yet awake. She continued looking ahead, to the sides, and behind for danger. She stopped at a McDonald's restroom to clean up as well as she could. The ten-minute walk felt like hours.

She found a discreet spot near the Harris Clark building to hide and wait. After some time, she saw him. She took a few quick steps, then touched the back of his suit jacket. "Hey, John Tylor."

He looked surprised and didn't recognize her. He also looked perplexed at her condition.

"It's Gabby."

"Oh. Yes, of course. Hello, Gabby. What a surprise to see you. Is everything okay?"

"I'm glad you remember me, John. I'm in desperate need of some legal help, and I thought of you. Do you have a minute to talk?"

"Uh, yes. Come up to my office."

"I have no money to pay you, of course."

He waved her off. "I've actually been looking for some pro bono work, so maybe you have something for me."

The office building was as fancy inside as it was outside. She ran her fingers through her hair to try to tame it and tugged on the bottom of her shirt as if that might remove the wrinkles. As they walked off the elevator on the fifth floor, a well-dressed receptionist greeted John, and he asked her to please send two coffees to his office.

John's office was a moderate size, but it had a nice desk with a plush leather chair and two guest chairs. Piles of neatly-stacked papers occupied a small portion of his desk.

"Sorry about the clutter. I'm working on a case, and I've got less than a month to make magic happen. I wasn't expecting any clients today, but I'm happy to have one."

"I'm sorry for taking up your time."

"Not at all. I must tell you though, that I'm not a criminal lawyer, so we may need to get someone else involved. You told me a bit about your situation the other night. It appears there have been some developments since then?" John removed the red and blue pens from his shirt pocket and opened his notebook.

"Well, I'm in a predicament, I can tell you that. I think I might have a way out. But maybe my plan is as unrealistic as the novels I read."

John chuckled. "Please start at the beginning then you can tell me what you have in mind."

She told him everything.

"You've had quite an ordeal. It's amazing you've been able to fight through it."

"I guess I'm more successful at fighting men trying to kill me than I am at fighting addiction."

John smiled. "Perhaps. You said you have some thoughts on how to get out of this?"

"Yes. The cops want arrests. I believe someone tried to kill me. Wouldn't the police be more interested in an attempted murder charge than drug arrests?"

"I would think so."

"Well, I have the evidence for attempted murder. I have the baggie of heroin that Ink gave me and the gun that he was carrying. Do you want to see them?"

"Not right now. You ... you have the gun in your bag?"

"Yes." It dawned on Gabby how dumb it was for her to walk into an office with a loaded gun. Outrageous things had become normal to her.

John picked up his phone and asked his assistant to come in. She was an older woman with a kind face and professional look. John explained the situation, and within minutes, a security guard came into John's office. Wearing latex gloves, the guard opened Gabby's bag, saw the gun, and left it there. He put the bag in the corner of the office and stood in front of it. John stepped out of the office to consult some other people, and his assistant dropped off two new cups of coffee plus some pastries and some fruit.

Gabby began to question if she should really trust John. Maybe he stepped out to call the police. Why did he leave her in his office with a security guard?

He returned about twenty minutes later. "So, I spoke with one of our criminal lawyers, and she and I called the district attorney's office. They're sending someone over to speak to us right now."

Gabby gripped the armchair and said, "Why are they coming here?

"They're sending over a lab technician to take the evidence and a police officer to take your statement. If everything you said is confirmed by the evidence, they may offer us a favorable plea bargain. I doubt you'll be able to avoid jail altogether though. We'll get all the agreements in writing."

Gabby shook his hand and held his forearm with her other hand. "I can't thank you enough."

"You came up with a good strategy. Maybe you should think about becoming a criminal defense attorney."

"It does look like a good community," she said. "Are addicts allowed to be attorneys?"

He smiled. "Maybe you can use this incident as a catalyst to get clean."

"I wish it were that easy," she muttered.

They walked together to a conference room and Gabby sat down. John told her to make herself comfortable and that he'd be back once the officers arrived.

Through the large conference room window, Gabby observed the well-dressed, contented people walking by with apparently important things to do. They were all members of the firm, much like she had been a member of the school when she was healthy. She missed being part of something.

John and the security guard entered the conference room. Two uniformed officers arrived, introduced themselves, and introduced the plain clothed person as a crime scene investigation agent. The security guard put Gabby's bag on the table then left. John motioned for everyone to sit.

The CSI agent remained standing and pulled some latex gloves and evidence pouches from her case. She removed the gun from Gabby's bag, careful to not point it at anyone. "It's loaded," she said, then removed the bullets. She placed the gun and bullets into an evidence pouch and labelled it. She did the same with the baggie of drugs. She pulled out a fingerprint kit, took Gabby's fingerprints, then excused herself from the room.

The two uniformed police officers stayed behind with John and Gabby. One officer pulled out a notepad and the other started a recording device.

When the interview concluded, the lead officer stepped out of the room to make a call. When he returned, he said, "The baggie that Ms. Jones provided to us was indeed a lethal mixture of heroin and fentanyl. Those men would probably have killed her if she hadn't gotten away. The gun has her fingerprints and another set, which may match those of this Ink guy."

"What's the next step, officer?" asked John.

"We'll need Ms. Jones to accompany officers to find this guy. Jenkins and Gray have been informed of these developments and will take Ms. Jones in an unmarked car to try to find him. Once he's arrested and we can confirm the fingerprints, you can speak to the DA's office again to finalize the plea agreement. We'll seek no further participation from Ms. Jones, but she must be available for a police lineup and willing to testify at trial."

Gabby and John both started to speak. John asked her to start.

"Shouldn't we finalize the agreement *before* I help them get Ink?"

"I was about to say the same thing. Officers, I'll put everything down on paper and get all parties to sign. It shouldn't take long."

"That's fine, sir," said one of the officers.

"Also, when do you want Ms. Jones to go with Officers Jenkins and Gray?" asked John.

"As soon as she wraps up here. They agreed to start their shift early to deal with this. Terrace cops don't often get the opportunity to work on an attempted homicide."

"Thank you for your time, officers. I'll walk you out," said John. He looked at Gabby. "Give me a few minutes to call the DA's office to confirm and document the details."

Alone in the conference room, she thought about having to go out on the streets to find Ink. Her leg muscles tightened.

John came back some time later and told her that it was all set up. If they arrested Ink tonight, Gabby and John would be going to court on Tuesday to present their plea agreement.

"Okay. By the way, what about the trespassing I did last night and the dog situation?" Gabby asked.

"I know you feel bad about the dog. I'm sure the police found him soon after and got him the care he needed. And it's unlikely the police will investigate it deeply enough to tie it to you."

"Okay. I pray for that poor animal."

"I know. Something else I discussed with the DA's office and the police is your safety until we go to court on Tuesday," said John.

"I've been contemplating that myself," said Gabby. "Even if Ink gets arrested, there are others who will be out to get me. Plus, I'm still an addict. I'm going to need heroin in a few hours."

"While you were waiting, my assistant called a number of hospitals to see if one could take you in for detoxing."

"Well, you probably didn't find any, right?"

"Indeed. The police need you alive to testify on Tuesday, so they want you to be in custody when they pick you up to go look for Ink. Hopefully, you'll find him this afternoon. After that, you'll be transported to Carlane County Jail."

"Detoxing there will be heinous. Adam told me they don't give you anything other than aspirin," said Gabby.

"I know. But you'll be safer there than on the streets."

"What if we don't find Ink?"

"Then they'll look for him themselves. Based on your description, including possibly a broken hand, he should be easy to identify. They'll eventually find him, but they'll still need you to testify. The deal will hold, but you'll be in jail until they find him."

"Let's hope we find him this afternoon," she said.

"Yes, if that happens, the next time you see me will be in court on Tuesday.

"I can't thank you enough."

John told her to wait in the conference room. While she was concerned about the jail experience, she was grateful that it would be only at the county jail, and the time served would probably not be extensive.

She looked through the conference room door and saw Jenkins and Gray approaching.

CHAPTER FIFTY

Gabby was eager to get the identification over with. As she and the officers took the elevator down and walked to the car, she no longer felt like a criminal in their presence. She felt like a teammate.

The Chevrolet Malibu was inconspicuous. Jenkins got into the driver's seat, while Gray rode shotgun, and Gabby got into the back. She didn't find it so uncomfortable without handcuffs. She saw some sort of camera hooked up near the dashboard, and it appeared to be recording.

Gray cleared his throat and spoke, addressing the device directly and over-pronouncing his words. "This is Officer Gray of the Terrace Police precinct. With me are Officer Jenkins of the same precinct and cooperating witness, Ms. Gabby Jones."

Jenkins smiled at Gray's discomfort with being recorded. "Dude, just talk normally," she said.

"What do you mean? I *am* talking normally."

"You're talking like a goof, e-nnun-ci-a-ting every syllable."

"Well excuse me. I've never used one of these things. Stupid technology shit."

Gabby interjected, “Officers, I think it’s still recording.”

“Shit!” yelled Gray.

“That was recorded too,” said Jenkins as she laughed out loud.

Gray remained silent for a second, then with somewhat more normal diction, said, “Ms. Jones, please state your name for the recording and acknowledge your understanding of what is supposed to happen today as well as your consent for this recording?”

Gabby complied, Jenkins started driving, and Gray asked Gabby questions.

“Had you seen this Ink person before the incident where he gave you drugs?”

“Yes, a couple of times. I saw him the day you arrested Base. He spoke to Base just before you arrested him.”

“And when else?”

“I saw him once sitting at one of the outside tables at Rosi’s Char House. I was heading to Savior Church to sleep. I think these dealers like to sit outside, so the occasional customer or runner can walk up to them and pick up their order.”

“Why are you sure it was him?”

“His tattoos are noticeable. Neck, forehead and cheek. And they’re all in black ink.”

As they drove to the first location, Gabby wanted to be sure the people outside couldn’t see her through the tinted windows, so she conducted several experiments waving, smiling, or mocking passers-by or people in other cars. None responded, so she was satisfied.

Jenkins spoke for the recording. “We’re approaching the location where the witness last saw the suspect.”

“I don’t have to get out of the car, right?” confirmed Gabby.

"Right," said Jenkins. "You're safe. Just keep your eyes open and see if you recognize anyone."

She looked out the window, trying to stay low in her seat. A few people walked past but no one she recognized. After a few minutes of waiting, Gabby said, "I think the only reason he was here last night was because he was following me."

"Yes, you're probably right," said Jenkins. "Let's try the area around the church and around Rosi's."

As they drove by the restaurant, Gabby looked at the people sitting at the outdoor tables. "The two guys sitting at the middle table – one of them looks like him."

"What makes you think that? Can you see tattoos?" By now, they were past the restaurant. "No, that guy with the scarf and hat could be him. He was the same size and shape, and his left hand was under the table."

Jenkins said, "We'll need a positive ID, not just size and shape. But it's pretty strange for someone to be wearing a scarf and hat in this weather. If it is Ink, he probably suspects we're looking for him."

"We can't drive by a second time," said Jenkins, talking to Gray. "I'll go around and park across from the restaurant a short way down the street, maybe in front of that Lapis Lazuli store."

Gray gave Gabby binoculars, and she surveyed the people at the tables. After about ten minutes, the guy stood up. Although his hat and scarf covered the forehead and neck tattoos, Gabby was able to make out the teardrop tattoo on his cheekbone, and his left hand looked injured.

"That's him," she said.

Gray took photographs.

"Are you sure?" asked Jenkins.

"Yes."

Ink had stepped away from the tables and was preparing to light a cigarette on the sidewalk.

Jenkins called for backup. "We're arresting the suspect now."

The officers checked their weapons.

"Stay in the car, Gabby. Don't get out for any reason," ordered Jenkins.

"That's my plan!" she answered.

"Let's go," said Jenkins.

Ink noticed the officers but did not run. Gabby couldn't hear them, but she saw Jenkins showing Ink her badge and Gray holding his gun in his holster. A squad car appeared, and two uniformed officers stepped out to help with the arrest. The people in the restaurant drifted toward the front window to watch the officers lead Ink to the back seat of the squad car. Jenkins and Gray returned to the Chevrolet, congratulated themselves and Gabby, then drove Gabby to Carlane County Jail.

A day earlier, she faced death or a long prison sentence. Fortunately, those threats had atrophied. She was massively relieved. She now had a new concern – withdrawal in jail.

CHAPTER FIFTY-ONE

Camille had spent the morning calling colleagues, then musical theater organizations where she heard there may be an opening, then just cold calls to other venues. Of the people she reached, only one said they might have an opportunity, but the potential need was three months out.

She ordered a chicken harvest salad at Corner Bakery and ate it in the restaurant, interrupted several times by current and former Academy students, sometimes with friends, sometimes with parents, stopping to say hello. Their admiration was a welcome boost in the midst of her situation.

She returned to her apartment, sat at the kitchen table and thought about what to do. Her phone rang. She didn't feel like talking to anyone, but when she saw that it was Adam, she answered.

"Adam. How are you?"

"Okay. Some shit happened last night that I'll tell you about. I'm in a coffee shop with a bunch of people around right now."

Camille's concern shifted from her own problems to Adam. "Did you relapse?"

"No. I came close though. There's a meeting tomorrow morning. I'm calling to see if you're goin'?"

"Yes, I'll go. Are you going to one tonight?"

"No. I'm working tonight."

"Do you want to get together and talk?"

"No, I'm okay. We'll talk tomorrow morning. How are *you* doing?" he asked.

"I've had much better weeks too. I'm trying to find a new job as soon as possible, but I don't have any good opportunities yet."

"You should get into theater therapy for addicts."

Camille chuckled. "Yes, if there were such a thing."

"There is. Two of the rehabs I went to had it. The rehab tries to get people to learn about their strengths and to feel good about themselves by performing or being in a show."

"Really?"

"It never worked though. One rehab had the counselors try to direct a show. It was pretty stupid 'cause they didn't know much about theater. Then the other place, they brought in theater teachers, but nobody listened to them because those people knew nothing about addiction and couldn't relate to the patients."

"Actually, you may be on to something, Adam."

"Anyway, see you tomorrow."

"Yes. It'll be good to catch up."

Camille stood and started pacing again. Her mind was racing. At university, she had studied the therapeutic benefits of musical theater. She had seen musical theater boost self-confidence, empathy, and concentration as well as provide an emotional outlet. All qualities that could benefit addicts. Given the opioid epidemic, surely, this was needed.

She envisioned a business approach. She could start a new program, where they put on a show in a rehab center. Patients who are interested would be the performers and stagehands. She could provide this to teen and young adult centers. The parents or patients would pay a small tuition and cover the costs of basic costumes. The participants would receive training, education, and self-discovery. Most rehab centers have a small auditorium or other gathering place. Those could be used for shows and rehearsals. There wouldn't have to be any set construction, lighting, or microphones, so the costs would be minimal.

This idea, though, wouldn't get her a job by Monday. Perhaps, Cindy would be interested in the concept. A program like this would broaden Academy's reach, expand their brand, and play a role in addressing the national opioid epidemic.

Camille had tried to reach Cindy several times since Broadway Frank fired her on Wednesday. She tried again.

Cindy answered with an upbeat tone. "Camille, I got back into cell phone coverage about a half an hour ago, and I just got off the phone with Frank. It seems he and I had a miscommunication about what a break for you meant."

Camille stood while she talked. "Yes, that was bizarre. But I'm not calling you to get my old job back. I have a proposition for you."

She told Cindy about her idea. Cindy liked it and suggested a few adjustments to the business approach. Never one to delay making a decision, she said, "Okay, we haven't taken you off the payroll yet. I'd like you to stay with us and get the program going. I'm excited about Academy playing a role in this crisis, small as it may be."

"Something else," said Camille. "This will be near and dear to my heart. I want more responsibility and some ownership in this new program. I'm willing to take a salary reduction, in order to become a minority shareholder in an Academy subsidiary that will provide this service, like maybe twenty percent."

There was a pause on the phone. Camille could hear Cindy's kids telling her it was time to get going. "That might work. We can figure out the details later. I also need you to help out the new director. I heard he's struggling. He'll continue running the rehearsals and directing, but I'll tell Frank that you're going to be an advisor, and any important decisions must have your input. He won't like it, but that's the way it's going to be. We need to fix that show immediately."

"I'm happy to help."

"I also told him that when I'm back next week, I better see the kids smiling and laughing. That's what Academy is about."

"I agree."

"I'm looking forward to the new program and to getting Annie back on track."

"Thank you, Cindy."

"One more thing," Cindy continued. "You may not want to hear this, but in the spirit of openness, I should tell you. One of the parents called me and complained that Academy had employed a director with an opioid disorder. The parent was concerned about the safety of the children and the security of her property. I told her that safety is our number one priority and that I can vouch that no staff member presents a risk. I told her that we are inclusive when it comes to casting and when it comes to employees, and that perhaps there are less inclusive theater organizations where she may feel more comfortable."

Camille thanked her, said goodbye, and slumped into her cozy chair. She recalled telling Jerry that it would be impossible to get a job by Tuesday. She had done the impossible. She sent a text to Adam, expressing how grateful she was for his suggestion.

CHAPTER FIFTY-TWO

Adam sipped his fourth coffee at Carlane College. He'd managed to get there by nine, but Brooke's lab must not have finished early. He'd spent the hours talking to the occasional person he knew from his courses there, checking Facebook on his phone, and just waiting. His phone dinged, and he read the text from Camille. He smiled and sent a note back congratulating her on getting back into Academy.

Being at the college, and having a lot of time to kill, he thought about the courses that had been interrupted when he was arrested. He'd been enjoying CULIN2205 *International Cuisine* because it taught not only how to make the foods from places like India, France, or Mexico, but also some culture and history. What a cool way to learn about a country. That course also reminded him of when he and his dad would get an apartment in the city where his father was working, and they'd try different ethnic restaurants. They called it research for Adam's career. His favorite food, once he discovered it at a restaurant in Seattle, was Greek. The loud spices, fresh ingredients, and unique dishes like moussaka and baklava thrilled him. Greek was soon toppled, though, by Peruvian. Adam loved the way they covered thick pieces of fish with creamy, rich and brightly colored sauces. Then, Peruvian was eventually replaced with Indian, and in particular, the buffet at New Asian House, in Edmonton. They'd walk in, and within minutes, Adam would be savoring a full plate of chicken masala, beef vindaloo, and garlic naan.

The other course interrupted was CULIN2000 *Food Laws and Regulations*. That course sucked, but Adam had done a lot of work to get through half of it. He was bummed that he'd have to start both courses over next term.

At two-thirty, Brooke walked in. Adam was as excited to see her as he had been the previous times. In fact, it was nice to see her and not have to hide a part of himself. He felt like he had shed a hundred pounds of body armor. Brooke had only a small smile on her face. "Sorry I couldn't meet earlier," she said.

"No problem."

"Shall we walk to the bus?" she asked. She was warm and pleasant.

"Sure. Well … we have some time. How 'bout we go outside and sit for a bit?" He tossed the rest of his coffee into the garbage.

The CC campus contained several modern buildings, and a well-maintained, albeit plain, grounds area. No rolling hills or big old trees, just cement paths bordering areas of grass with a few modest patches of hardy geraniums. They sat on a bench, and Brooke placed her pretty hands on her lap. Adam supposed he wouldn't be holding them anytime soon. Maybe never again.

"I'm … not quite sure how to start this conversation," Brooke said.

"My name is Adam, and I'm an addict," Adam replied, with mock enthusiasm. Brooke smirked a little, but it faded quickly. His did as well. "I've been an opioid addict for three years. I'm committed to my recovery. I've gone to seven rehabs, I go to meetings, and I'm starting another outpatient program on Monday." He told her about his charges, his jail time, his release terms, and his status as a felon.

Brooke looked at him as if she might find a physical sign of his addiction. "You're quite a different person than I thought."

"I'm not a different person, Brooke. But I do have a disorder. I'm so sorry that I didn't tell you."

She shook her head and stared straight ahead. Adam wished he could see her captivating brown eyes. "I had no idea about any of this."

"I know." He took a deep breath. "I'm very sorry. I used you. I used you to feel normal for a few days. Well, to feel more than normal. I had no idea how wonderful life could be until I met you."

"Yes, it's been a nice few days," she stated. She finally turned to face him. "Do you have diseases like AIDS or Hepatitis?"

The question hurt, but Adam understood why she'd ask it. "No. I never shared needles."

"Do you steal?"

"In some of my bad days, I stole things and sold them to get money for heroin. That's behind me."

"How do you know it's behind you? Are you high right now?"

The reality was that he couldn't be certain it was behind him. "No. I haven't used since I went to jail."

She looked back at the ground. "I almost slept with you."

"That's why I didn't push it. Even though I sure wanted to."

They sat in silence for a few seconds. He wanted to look at her but followed her lead and looked forward.

"I understand that for addicts, using drugs is the most important thing in the world. Is it the most important thing for you?" Brooke asked.

"No, *not* using is the most important thing for me."

Brooke looked at him and said, "We've known each other for less than a week, but I think I was falling in love with you."

Once again, he experienced simultaneous positive and negative emotions. Hearing her say she was falling in love with him made the world a beautiful place. But her describing it in the past tense made his heart bleed. "I *know* I was falling in love with you."

Their eyes met, then they got up and walked toward the bus.

"Brooke, I'm not surprised at your reaction. I'd feel the same way if I were you. Again, I'm very sorry that I didn't tell you."

"I can understand how carrying this secret must have been difficult for you. Maybe we should take a couple of days to think about things."

Adam was happy she didn't say she never wanted to see him again. Maybe she was too kind a person to say it right now. "I guess. How 'bout I call you Sunday night? Maybe we can get coffee or something again."

"That sounds fine."

"Great." He wasn't sure if they'd date again. One thing was certain, though. Their relationship would never be the same. Maybe it would evolve to friends. Maybe, after a while, they'd never see each other again. Or maybe they could now grow their relationship to its fullest based on truth and honesty.

They walked to the bus, boarded, and continued to talk, although about other topics. Adam got off to catch another bus to Mio Posto. He knew he'd have to push himself to get through his shift at work.

CHAPTER FIFTY-THREE

Adam's job today was prep, which included washing, peeling, and chopping vegetables; weighing and mixing ingredients; and cleaning. Prep was lower pressure than cooking because you didn't have situations where you had to get multiple perfect entrées out in a short time. Today was a good day to enjoy the lower pressure.

Prep also gave him time to think. Most of his thoughts were positive. He reflected on his near relapse and was proud that he beat it. He'd never let it get that far again. He'd never buy drugs and get into a position where he had to use will power. He went through every moment he had spent with Brooke and wondered how many years of sobriety it would take for her to consider him normal. Many. But he was young. He had time.

David picked him up after his shift at eight-thirty.

"How are things going with Brooke?" his father asked on the way home.

"Well, I'm not sure what's going to happen. She knows I'm an addict."

"Oh. You told her?"

"No … she … found out. I almost relapsed and her friend saw me and—"

"You almost relapsed?! What do you mean?" David pulled over and stopped the car.

Adam told David about the previous night. Since he was embarrassed, he kept it short.

"Why didn't you tell me?"

Adam wasn't sure if his father's tone was anger, despair, disappointment, or love. It seemed it was all of that. "How could I tell you?"

"You just do. I know you're going to have urges. Tell me when you have them. Tell me if you think you're going to have them. Shit, if you're home and you actually relapse, tell me as you're injecting, so I can come and keep you alive. Just tell me!"

"The good news is I beat it, Dad. I beat that filthy piece of shit!"

"You're right. I'm proud of you. And now you know you can beat it. Remember how to do it. By the way, I keep calling your lawyer to find out where you're supposed to get the Vivitrol, but he talks in circles, then I demand a name to call. I call that person, and they don't know a thing, then the cycle repeats. I can't wait till you see your PO. Hopefully, he'll explain it."

"Yeah, that'll be good," said Adam.

"So, are you upset that things are uncertain with Brooke?"

"Yes I am. It sucks. But I guess it was bound to happen. She had to know sooner or later."

"I know you really liked her. I'm sorry, man."

"Yeah." Adam looked out the window, hoping to end the conversation.

He got home and had a long bath, interrupted a couple of times by a knock on the outside of the door, and a shout from his mother, "Are you okay in there?" His parents knew that when he relapsed at home, it was usually in the bathtub.

His phone vibrated on the side of the tub. A text from his friend Josh was on the screen. He hadn't seen him since he'd been out of jail, although they'd texted a few times. He dried his fingers on a towel and swiped his phone open.

how u doin, read the text from Josh.

ight. think my gurl breakin up w me

sucks man. did u least get sum

dude it wasn like that. I really liked her. she found out my past

u always looken for love. forget it

she was one in million

wanna hang 2nite

no. stayin clean

just come over n chill

im not doin shit no more

np. I wont either

ight maybe. later

later

He got out of the tub, put on shorts and a T-shirt, and went to the kitchen. His father was working at the table on his computer.

"Sup, Dad?"

David kept typing and said, "Just working on a slide deck I have to present tomorrow morning."

"Tomorrow's Saturday."

"I know. We're working through the weekend because we're replanning the project. There's a presentation to the board Monday morning."

"Wanna take a break? We can go to the club, and I can beat you in a game of pickleball."

David stopped typing and looked up. "That sounds pretty good, actually. We haven't done that for a long time. Except *I* would beat *you*."

"Sure, Dad. You can always hope."

David paused, like he was considering it. "Hmm, I better keep working on this stupid deck." He looked back at his computer.

"No problem."

David's eyes went back to Adam. "Are you having urges?"

"No. I'm okay."

David adjusted in his seat. "Are you sure? Remember what I said."

"I know. I'm fine."

"Okay. Maybe this weekend we can go. I'll need a break at some point," said David.

"Yeah, Sunday?"

"Sure, that'll work. I really look forward to it."

"Where's Mom?"

David's eyes returned to his computer. "Running some errands. She'll be back soon."

Adam went to the basement and turned on the TV. After a few minutes, he received another text from Josh.

Whatup, said the text.

not much. You? answered Adam.

Watchin a movie. cmon over

ight

Adam went upstairs. "Dad, I'm goin' to Josh's."

David looked up. "You sure that's a good idea?"

"We're not gonna do anything."

"I don't know if you should go there."

"I just wanna get out for a bit."

"Okay. Come home in an hour, okay?"

Adam walked two blocks to Josh's. They'd been friends for only a few years, but it was comforting to see him. Josh lived with his parents, who were out. He was holding a beer when he greeted Adam at the front door.

"Hey man, c'mon in. I'm watching *The Revenant*." After a few steps toward the den, Josh added, "Denny's coming over too."

Shit. Josh was an occasional user, but Denny always had something going – usually painkillers. Adam and Josh had just sat down when the doorbell rang. When Josh opened the door, Denny spotted Adam and yelled out, "Hey A-Dam. They let you out?"

Josh offered them beers. Denny accepted. Adam didn't.

"What the hell? You can't have a beer with your buddies anymore?" said Denny.

"Shut up, Denny," Josh said.

They sat in the den, and while the movie was still on pause, Denny pulled an Altoids container from his pocket, popped it open, and bragged, "Dudes, I brought some Oxies." Josh and Adam both declined. Denny pushed harder, and Josh agreed to take one.

"Adam, you gotta take one too."

"Nah, I got no money."

"Don't worry about it," said Denny. "You can owe me one."

"Nah, I'm stayin' sober."

Denny's face looked angry. "Don't judge us, dude!"

"I'm not." Adam wanted to leave, but he'd been there for only five minutes and wasn't sure how to leave without it being awkward. After a few minutes, he held his phone where the others couldn't see it and texted his father, *call me. just listen.*

His phone rang.

"Hey Dad … Oh … Well, I just got here, but I guess … Shit."

David interjected, "Is everything okay?"

Adam continued. "Alright, I guess. I'll be there soon." He ended the call.

"My dad's computer crashed, and he's worried he lost some important file or some shit. He asked me to help him. I gotta go." On the walk home, he thought about the Oxies at Josh's place. He didn't plan to hang with Josh again anytime soon.

CHAPTER FIFTY-FOUR

Adam got back home just before eleven o'clock. David was at the kitchen table shutting down his computer and Sharon was upstairs having a bath.

"What was that text and call all about?" asked David.

"Denny came over. He's a goof." Adam rolled his shoulders as if his shirt were causing him discomfort. "That's why I wanted to leave."

"Why is he a goof?"

"He wanted me to take an Oxy."

"You didn't, did you?"

"No, of course not."

"Are you feeling like you might relapse?"

"No, I'm okay. I'm goin' to the basement to watch some TV."

"Okay. I'm going to bed because I have that meeting tomorrow morning"

"Yeah. Good luck with your presentation tomorrow."

"Thanks. I'm looking forward to playing pickleball with you on Sunday," said David.

"Me too."

"I love you, Adam, never forget that," said David.

"Love you too."

Adam gave David his phone then went to the basement, turned on the large-screen TV, and found *Ted 2* on Netflix. About thirty minutes into the movie, he felt cool from the air conditioning, so he went upstairs to get a hoodie.

Back in the basement, he threw on the hoodie. Touching the outside of it, he felt something in the pocket. He reached in and found a paper bag. He'd inadvertently grabbed the same hoodie from the previous night. He looked in the paper bag and saw all the paraphernalia. At the bottom of the bag rested a baggie of heroin. He was confused because he had flushed the baggie down the toilet yesterday. Then he remembered the dealer saying that he was putting a "welcome back bonus" in the bag.

His heroin brain woke up. It started fighting for control again, voicing its opinions. Adam put everything back in the bag, placed it on the floor and tried to focus on watching the rest of the movie. He no longer found it amusing. In fact, he couldn't concentrate on it at all. He just sat on the couch staring blankly ahead while the scenes went by and the battle raged in his brain. When the movie was over, he removed the hoodie, left it in the basement, and stepped outside for a cigarette.

Back inside, he went upstairs to his bedroom, being careful not to wake his parents. He wished he was tired, but he was too restless to sleep. He didn't want to be near the heroin or the rig.

To kill time until he felt tired, and while his normal brain and his heroin brain continued to fight it out, he looked through his room. Everything still looked somewhat fresh since he had been home only five days. He started by looking out the window and saw the house next door. A family with two boys lived there. The boys often played basketball with each other in the driveway, reminding Adam of himself and Carter when they were younger. Adam sometimes looked at them and longed for the world as it was before his addiction.

The twisted screen in the window reminded him of years ago, when he would occasionally smoke weed late at night. He'd open the window, twist out the screen, and blow the smoke outside. Back then, the marijuana helped calm him enough that he could go to sleep.

He turned to the left of the window and looked at the pictures on the wall. His favorite was of him at around fifteen standing with his aunts at the lake house. He smiled. He was always comfortable with his aunts. With them, there was no judging, no lectures, no expectations that he couldn't meet – just kind words, butter tarts, and sometimes a raspberry pie.

To the left of the pictures was a framed copy of the first verse of the serenity prayer. He read it to himself.

Continuing his counter-clockwise journey, he stepped into his closet. He was grateful for his mother helping him to buy nice clothes. He looked at the contents of the shelves and saw a stack of seven notebooks – one for each rehab program he'd completed. He thumbed through a couple of them, thinking of all the work he had done, all the notes he had made, all the promises he had made to himself, his counselors, and his family. "Asshole," he mumbled, angry at himself for not keeping any of those promises.

To the left of his closet was his desk and computer. He turned on his computer and went to Facebook to see if there were any new pictures of Brooke. Many of his Facebook contacts were online chatting about getting and using drugs. He shut it down.

He looked at the shelves on the third wall of the bedroom. They were filled with his trophies for tennis, soccer, and basketball. There was also a sculpture of a snowmobile, made out of nuts and bolts and other miscellaneous hardware. He remembered thinking how cool it was when his father had bought it for him. He also remembered the many wonderful snowmobile trips he'd gone on with his father.

The internal battle with his heroin had raged for several hours. None of these beautiful keepsakes could silence the enemy. He was worn out. Depleted.

He went downstairs to the main floor, then to the basement. He reached into the bag and removed the contents. He emptied about half of the heroin into the toilet, knowing that his resistance was low and that he had no medicine to protect him. He might be losing this battle, but he had no intention of losing the war.

Sitting on the toilet seat, he held his lighter below the bent spoon that contained the heroin mixture. He tied off his arm with a shoelace to cut off blood circulation and make whatever meager veins that remained on his forearm more receptive to the needle. He didn't have as much concern about leaving a mark on his arm as he did the previous night. He held the syringe between his index finger and middle finger and inserted it into his arm. A burnt smell lingered in the silent room.

Adam's face was solemn as this was a solemn task. His lips were pressed together, and his body was tense. His thumb started to gently push on the syringe plunger to move the fluid from the syringe into his bloodstream. His mouth, face, and entire body started to loosen. He saw the bent spoon, lighter and empty baggie on floor.

He continued pushing. Fifty percent done; seventy-five percent done; done. He pulled the empty syringe out of his vein. The enemy rushed through his body, and he now belonged to it. He tried to stand up but fell to his knees. He tried to crawl out of the bathroom, but everything went black.

SATURDAY / SUNDAY

CHAPTER FIFTY-FIVE

"David!" David woke up suddenly and saw Sharon standing beside the bed, frantic. Her arms were extended away from her body about halfway between vertical and horizontal. Her face exuded fear and emergency. It was three in the morning.

"I checked on Adam. He's unconscious. I can't wake him up!" She turned and began running downstairs.

David jumped out of bed and followed. "Where is he?" David asked, halfway down the stairs to the main level.

"He's in the basement. Don't even come down. Just stop at the phone in the kitchen and call 911."

David dialed.

"This is 911. What is your emergency?"

"My son ..." David was not even sure what to say. "... he's unconscious in the basement."

"Is he breathing?"

"I don't know. I'm not beside him."

"Okay. Are you at 614 Elm Street, Parkdale?"

"Yes."

"Responders are on their way. Are you on a portable phone?"

"No."

"I need you to find a portable phone and go to him."

David scurried and eventually found one in the living room. "Okay, I'm on a portable." He ran to the basement.

"Sir, what position is he in?"

"He's facing down."

"Please turn him over onto his back."

David pulled him out of the bathroom doorway and turned him over. "Okay, he's on his back."

"Is he breathing?"

"I don't think so. He has vomit in his mouth."

"I need you to scoop the vomit out of his mouth with your fingers."

David scooped out as much as he could. "I did it."

"Okay, I need you to give him mouth-to-mouth resuscitation. Do you know how to do that?"

"No."

"Pinch his nostrils, cover his mouth with yours …"

David heard the first responders walk in the door and rush downstairs. He stood up and stepped aside. The police had arrived before the paramedics. They pulled a Narcan container out of a bag and tried to administer it. One of them said that the Narcan package was defective. They started looking for another one. The paramedics arrived, and they administered Narcan, but to no avail. They pounded furiously on Adam's chest.

One of the police officers took David aside and started asking questions. "Where was Adam last night? What did he do? When did you last see him?" David answered a couple of questions, then requested they conduct the interview later, and not while paramedics were working on resuscitating his son. He realized that he was still in his underwear, but had no intention of leaving his son. He walked back to be near Adam. They were still pounding on his chest.

After several minutes, one of the paramedics said, "Let's take him out." The responders put Adam on a stretcher, carried him upstairs, and put him into an ambulance.

David trailed them as far as the front door. "Should we follow you to the hospital?" he asked one of the paramedics.

"Yes." The paramedic sounded optimistic. It gave David hope.

David and Sharon went upstairs to get dressed. When they came back downstairs, several police officers were still there. One of them was standing at the stairway to the basement, blocking it.

David looked outside and saw that the ambulance was still in the driveway. "Why haven't they taken him to the hospital yet?" he asked.

After a pause, one of the officers said, "They'll work on him in the ambulance first, then take him."

Another officer said that some of them would stay in the house.

During the two-minute drive to the hospital, David talked about the dramatic actions he would take to help Adam if he survived this incident, if they would have one more chance. He would move Adam away, perhaps to another country, or maybe he'd go live with him at the lake house.

At the hospital, David announced themselves to the attendant at the front desk. The young man nodded, picked up the phone, and said, "The parents are here." He then told David and Sharon that someone would be out shortly.

In the waiting room, David thought about all the signs that indicated the outcome was not going to be good. Adam had not regained consciousness in the home; the paramedics didn't bring him to the hospital as soon as he was in the ambulance; a police officer was guarding the stairs to the basement as if it were a crime scene; even the way the attendant at the hospital said, "the parents are here" sounded foreboding. Still, hope trumped logic, and he waited for someone to come out and say his beloved boy was alive – that David had that one more chance to help him. He couldn't bear the thought of losing him. He had known for years that death was a possible outcome of Adam's disease. However, knowing and seeing were completely different things. *Just one more chance. Dear God, please. One more chance. I beg you.*

After a couple of minutes, two women came through the locked door into the waiting room. One was in her mid-forties, wearing a white doctor's smock. Behind her was a younger woman who seemed to be an assistant or a student. The woman with the doctor's smock sat in a chair facing David and Sharon. The other person remained standing behind her.

"I'm Dr. Chen," said the doctor.

Both Sharon and David eked out a greeting. Dr. Chen proceeded to ask them questions about Adam and his lifestyle. David didn't understand why she was doing this, and after a couple of questions, said, "Why are you asking us questions? Can you just tell us. Is he alive?"

Dr. Chen looked offended. She shook her head and said, "No."

Sharon gasped, started crying, and said, "No! My boy! No!"

David held Sharon's hand and remained silent.

Sharon said, "Can we see him?"

"Yes, you can see him if you want to," answered the doctor.

David looked at Sharon and said, "I don't need to see him, but I'll go with you if you want to go."

Sharon looked at no one in particular, and said decisively, "I want to see him."

The doctor guided them into a room where Adam's body was lying on a gurney. She left.

David looked for a final time at his cherished son. His handsome face. His eyelids covering his gentle eyes. His broad shoulders, thick chest, and strong legs. He thought to himself, *How could I have let him die?*

Sharon hugged Adam's body and wept. "My beautiful boy. My beautiful boy."

CHAPTER FIFTY-SIX

David opened the car door for Sharon. The drive home was silent. At home, they found several police officers still there. One of them offered David and Sharon his condolences. He suggested the officers search the house and remove any drugs or paraphernalia, and David agreed. Two officers searched Adam's bedroom and the basement while a third continued standing at the top of the basement stairway.

"I'd like to ask you a few questions," said a fourth officer. It was the same person who had started asking David questions in the basement while the paramedics were banging on Adam's chest. David thought about the officer's statement. There was no offer of condolences or any recognition of David and Sharon's feelings, just "I'd like to ask you a few questions."

David said that he and Sharon weren't in condition to answer many questions but would try for a couple of minutes.

"When someone dies from overdose, it is a drug-induced homicide. We have to investigate." The officer started asking again about the events of last night – who Adam had been with, where he had been, etc.

David's loathing of this person grew with each question. He saw him personifying everything wrong with the so-called war on drugs and about how the laws were designed to maximize the harm inflicted on addicts, as if that would cure their disease. The war on drugs was really a war on drug-addicted people. Adam had been one of its refugees and now was one of its casualties.

After a couple of minutes, David suggested to the officer they stop and resume some other time. The officer wrapped up by saying, "Well, we'll need to ask more questions. We'll need his phone and his Facebook account. The lieutenant will be coming by later to get those things and some more information."

That officer left, and the two officers searching the basement and Adam's room completed their task. They didn't find anything other than the syringe and paraphernalia in the basement. They left, as did the officer who had been blocking access to the basement staircase.

David and Sharon were alone.

Daylight was starting to emerge outside for everyone else. David looked at his phone and saw the time was a few minutes after five. He and Sharon decided to wait until about seven to call Meghan and Carter.

David pushed back most of the tears. "My boy," he cried as a few escaped. "I let him die. I let him die. He needed me, and I wasn't there. I was in bed. I let him die."

Sharon rubbed his back. "We can't blame ourselves."

She went upstairs to put away things. David headed to the basement to begin the gruesome clean up. He picked up his son's vomit with a cloth, rinsed the cloth in the sink, then did it again several times. There was dirt to clean up from the responders who had come in. He vacuumed it.

Shortly before seven, David and Sharon knew it was time to make some calls. David placed the call to Meghan.

"Hey, Dad!" she answered in her regular happy voice.

"Hi, Meghan. Are you at home?"

"Yes, I'm just getting ready for work." David could sense her happiness at her state of life – recently married, both spouses working, living in a vibrant big city, and taking in everything it had to offer.

"I have some bad news, Meghan."

Her voice changed, and she uttered a fearful, "What?"

"Adam passed away last night."

David heard a pitiful cry then a soft, "No." Then more crying. "He overdosed?"

"Yes."

More crying. "We're coming over," she said.

Carter was next. Carter had just returned to the apartment he shared with a roommate at the University of Wisconsin two days earlier. He'd gone early to get settled before classes, which were to start on Wednesday next week.

David dialed. No answer. He called again. No answer. He called again.

"Hello," Carter answered in a groggy voice.

"Hi, Carter. It's Dad."

"Hey, Dad."

"Where are you?" asked David

"I was in bed sleeping."

"Carter, I need you to wake up fully."

The grogginess disappeared from his voice and was replaced with concern. "What?"

"Adam passed away last night."

"Oh, God … Oh my God." Another soft cry that seemed to last an eternity.

"What happened?"

"He overdosed."

"He was clean for so long. Why did he relapse? Couldn't they rescue him? Couldn't they give him Narcan?"

"We found him too late, Carter. I'm sorry." David thought about how close Adam and Carter had been. He keeled over in pain, held the phone away to keep Carter from hearing, and mumbled, "I'm sorry I didn't keep him alive for you." He gathered enough strength to bring the phone back to his mouth and ear, and heard whimpers of, "My brother ... My big brother."

David waited.

"Do you think he suffered?" asked Carter.

David hadn't yet thought of that question. "I don't think so."

"I'll get the next bus home," Carter said.

"Don't rush. Pack properly and come as soon as you can, without rushing."

"Okay, I'll see you soon, Dad."

"Okay."

"I love you, Dad"

"I love you too."

"Tell Mom I love her."

"I will."

A little later, David called his mother, who lived in Buffalo, New York. David's sister answered the phone. David had what was now becoming a familiar conversation. His sister was devastated. She said she'd let their mother and their siblings know.

Sharon called her mother and had a similar conversation.

David and Sharon called a few close friends, including Camille, who wept and prayed.

After they hung up, Sharon said, "What about Brooke?"

"I don't even know her number." David picked up Adam's phone, which they had previously moved from their bedroom to the kitchen counter, and they found Brooke's number. David sent her a text from his own phone, *This is Adam*'s *father. Please call me when you get a chance.*

David's phone rang immediately.

"Hello, Mr. Lambert, this is Brooke." She sounded concerned.

"Hello, Brooke."

"Is everything okay?"

"I'm afraid not, Brooke. Um, I don't know you very well, but I think you would want to know this. Adam passed away last night."

"Oh my God. Wait, is this a sick prank? Is this really Mr. Lambert, or someone who stole Adam's phone?"

"Brooke, this is David Lambert. You came by the other night, after you and Adam spent the afternoon at the lake house. You said you had early classes the next day."

"Oh no! What happened?"

"I believe you know that Adam suffered from opioid use disorder."

"Yes, I did know."

"Last night, he relapsed."

"Oh my God. Maybe … maybe it's my fault!"

"Don't think that for a second, Brooke. I must tell you, the last few days of his life were his happiest. He couldn't stop talking about you. He wouldn't stop looking at your picture. Thank you for giving my son a few happy days. I think he had a chance to fall in love before he died. You gave him that."

She was now crying. David waited.

"Can I come over and see you guys today?"

"Of course. Come by whenever you're ready."

CHAPTER FIFTY-SEVEN

John thought again about reaching Adam Saturday morning. Hoping to find a contact number or even an address, he googled "Adam Lambert", but that yielded no useful information. He checked the jail records to see when he entered jail, which also would be the arrest date and learned that it was March 22, 2016. He went to the Terrace News website. It was a weekly paper, and the first publication date after Adam's arrest date was Saturday, March 26. After sifting through short articles in the police beat report about a stolen bicycle and a twenty-year-old caught with alcohol, John found it. "Police arrested Adam Lambert, 24, of the 600 block of Elm Street in Parkdale, on one count of possession of a controlled substance."

"Harry, search for an address: Adam Lambert in the 600 block of Elm Street, Parkdale, Illinois."

"614 Elm Street."

"Send it to my phone."

John drove to the address. He saw several cars in the driveway and on the street. Apparently, the family was having company. He rang the doorbell, and a man in his mid-fifties with a solemn face opened the front door. John could see visitors inside and thought one of them looked familiar.

"Hello, sir. My name is John Tylor. You must be Mr. Lambert."

"Yes, is there something I can do for you?"

"I met your son Adam a few days ago at an NA meeting."

"Oh. Okay. Thank you for coming by."

John was confused at the response. The woman who looked familiar walked to the front door. She also looked sad.

"Hello, John, I'm Camille. We met Wednesday at the NA meeting."

"Yes, of course, Camille. Hello."

"It's kind of you to come by," said Camille. "How did you find out?"

"I'm sorry. I'm afraid I'm not sure what you're referring to. Is everything okay here?"

David covered his mouth with his right hand. Camille motioned to John, and said, "Let's talk outside for a minute."

David looked at John and said with a shaky voice, "Feel free to come in afterward."

Outside, Camille looked like she was gathering up the energy to continue. "Adam passed away last night."

John breathed in quickly. "Oh no. An overdose?"

Camille nodded.

John explained the research he had done, how he found out about Adam, and his conclusion about Adam being in danger. "I was coming here to check on him. I wasn't even sure what I was going to say when I saw him."

"He got out on Monday. He was working on getting his life in order. He had his job back, was about to start an outpatient program, and he was seeing a girl."

John shook his head. So much potential, gone. "I still can't understand it."

"What do you mean?"

"Why did he do it? He had everything going for him, and he knew the risk, yet he used again." He stopped when he saw Camille's horrified face. "I'm sorry. I know that was insensitive. I just feel so horrible for him."

"John, Adam was fighting it every minute of every day since he was released. Last night, he lost the fight for one of those moments."

"I wish I would have gotten here yesterday, but, I suppose I didn't have any information he didn't already know."

"Why don't you come in for a few minutes? The relatives will be coming in for the funeral, but most aren't here yet. Adam's older sister is here. His younger brother is on his way. And there are a couple of friends of the family. Like me."

"Just for a minute." John did not want to intrude on a gathering of loved ones, but he wanted to express his condolences.

"Before we go in," Camille began. "Did Gabby reach you yesterday?"

John told her about the interaction that he had with Gabby, the fact that she was now in jail and would likely get a decent outcome on Tuesday.

"Will you let her know about Adam?" Camille asked.

"Yes, I don't think I'll be able to reach her until Tuesday, since she's detoxing in the medical unit." For a second, John thought about when to tell Gabby. Perhaps waiting until after her court appearance would be best, even though she wouldn't be happy about him withholding the information.

John followed Camille into the house. He saw the piano on the right. The cover was on the keys. The dining room table on the left was barren. Walking down the hall toward the kitchen and family room at the back of the house, John felt even deeper sorrow as he saw the family pictures that included Adam.

The people in the family room were silent. Camille introduced John to Sharon and David, then to Meghan, then to the two other friends.

John shook Sharon's and David's hands and said, "My deepest condolences. I cannot imagine."

"Thank you," said Sharon. She looked numb, as if her mind and body were not yet allowing the pain to fully enter. She and David continued standing together.

David thanked John and paused before continuing. "It's odd. I never anticipated how widespread the pain would be. Adam has fifteen aunts and uncles. They're all devastated. He has two living grandmothers. I don't know if they can bear the pain. I haven't even counted how many cousins he had, but he adored them all. Most are older than him, and he looked up to them. They're in grief. Neighbors have been stopping by, shocked. Even people who just met him, like you, feel something."

John looked at him and said, "Yes I do. I was very impressed with Adam. I realize that nobody will feel the pain as much as you and Sharon."

"You said you met Adam at an NA meeting?" David asked.

"Yes." John anticipated the next question.

"Do you have substance use disorder?"

"I do not, Mr. Lambert. I'm working on a legal case that involves addicts."

Sharon said, "Well, I hope you do well for them. Do you know that Adam is the fourth person within two blocks of here to die of this in the last two years?

John was embarrassed that Sharon thought he was doing something to help addicts. "I am very sorry to hear that," he said.

David spoke up. "I tell you who should be sued. That jail that wouldn't let Adam have his medicine. The medicine kept him alive, and they took it away from him."

John needed to leave. First, he was a stranger to this shattered family and was certain they would prefer to be with their loved ones. Second, based on what David had just said, if he and Sharon found out that other families were actually suing, they could end up joining the class action suit. John would be speaking with the opposing party. Most importantly, he felt disingenuous being in their home while representing the organization that David just complained about.

He shook their hands again. "Mr. and Mrs. Lambert, I am so very sorry for your loss. I apologize for intruding. I'll see myself out."

Sharon thanked him for coming by. David covered his face with his left hand and nodded.

CHAPTER FIFTY-EIGHT

John drove home and thought about the devastation he had just witnessed, how it would get worse for David and Sharon as the situation sunk in further, and how it would last a lifetime. He thought about Sharon's comments that Adam was one of four people within two blocks who had perished. John knew the national statistics, but Sharon's statement about four people within two blocks was more powerful. It made the epidemic local and real. And Adam had given it a face.

The pain he saw firsthand and Camille's explanations convinced him that Sheriff Mason's policy was flawed. He now wished he were representing the other side. Adam's death convinced him that the policy had to change.

He arrived home before noon. Velinda and Daniel were out. He sat in his study at his oak desk surrounded by shelves full of all manner of books. He positioned a single sheet of paper in landscape orientation in front of him. He took blue and red pens out of the drawer. On the left half of the page at the top, he wrote in blue, "What the Sheriff Wants Most." Below it, he drew a large circle, and inside the circle, he wrote, "Get re-elected." On the top right half of the page he wrote, "What the Families Want Most." He drew a circle below it and inside wrote, "Change the Policy." He added, "Save lives," and underlined it in red.

He stared at the separated circles and tried to imagine them overlapping like a Venn diagram with some common ground. What if changing the policy actually helped the sheriff get re-elected? There was a growing recognition in the country of the epidemic and of the toll it was taking on families. Public opinion was starting to shift, only slightly but shift nonetheless, to consider addicts as sick instead of as criminals. Perhaps Sheriff Mason could be seen as progressive. His image as tough had been carefully cultivated over the years, and it was secure. Might tough *and* progressive be even more appealing to voters? He knew that he would have to bring convincing evidence that a policy change would help the sheriff's election campaign.

"Harry, I need to create new research based on an opinion survey."

"Please tell me the opinion survey question."

"Quote. Some opioid-addicted people take doctor-prescribed medicine for their addiction. Do you believe jails should allow these people to continue taking their medicine while incarcerated. Question mark. End quote." John watched his words appear on his computer for verification.

"This appears to be a Yes/No question. Please verify," said the Harry system.

"Correct."

"What are the demographics and location for the survey?"

"Five hundred adults within one twenty-five miles of Terrace, Illinois," John answered.

"Are there any other specifications?"

"No."

"By when do you need the results?"

"This Monday at four p.m."

"This survey will require twelve phone researchers to work between now and the completion time. The cost will be 4,200 dollars. Do you wish to proceed?"

"Yes. Send the results to my legal assistants and me."

"They will be sent."

He called Angela Parker.

"This is Angela."

"Angela. John Tylor."

"John, is it a habit of yours to call opposing counsel on Saturdays?" She didn't wait for an answer. "Are you calling to say your client is ready to change the policy and pay restitution?"

"Angela, the ball was in your court to check with your clients on whether or not they would forego restitution."

"I will, but that question will have a better answer if your client is willing to change the policy," she jabbed.

"If my client agreed to change the policy on condition that your clients drop compensatory damages completely, would they go for that?"

"I doubt it. There has to be at least some compensatory damages."

John raised his voice. "Damn it, Angela, you and I both know that he won't agree to compensatory damages. The families want the goddamn policy changed. Do your part – drop the compensatory, and I'll do my part – change the policy. We'll have a settlement and lives will be saved."

"Whoa." Her shock sounded genuine. "Where did that come from?"

"Plus, if we get to a settlement, we'll lift the restriction on media coverage. You can talk to the press as much as you want."

"Let me talk to my clients. By the way, as you can imagine, my staff has been researching to find any other deaths that occurred shortly after leaving jail and if they had similar circumstances. If we don't settle, it's likely that we will find more families to join the suit. Plus, if new deaths occur going forward, obviously, I will approach those families also."

Apparently, Angela thought she could scare him into a settlement. He was glad that he was miles ahead of her. Angela would soon learn of Adam's passing and would approach David and Sharon to join the suit.

He paused before responding. "Fine. This is a one-time offer. I'm seeing my client Tuesday morning, so you need to give me the answer by end of day Monday. If your answer is 'yes', we'll have a settlement, and you can get media coverage. If the answer is 'no', we both know you'll lose in court, and your loss will also be public."

"I like this newer, stronger John. Maybe we should work together sometime."

John rolled his eyes. "Let's just get this done."

Now he had to convince the sheriff.

CHAPTER FIFTY-NINE

David wanted to have the funeral as soon as possible. So did Sharon. On Saturday afternoon, they drove to the Methodist church where they occasionally went to Sunday service. Meghan and Carter joined them. Reverend Wood was in his office, which contained four cushioned chairs in addition to his own desk chair. He was in his mid-forties and spoke with a confident voice and had an engaging disposition. He invited everyone to sit and wheeled his chair to the front of his desk to complete a circle.

"We were hoping that we could have a service for him as soon as possible," said Sharon.

"Of course." He opened a book that contained handwritten schedules. "We could do it Tuesday."

"Is Monday possible?" asked David.

Reverend Wood turned a page backward and said, "We can do that. Two o'clock?"

"Yes, that would be good," answered David.

The reverend said, "I know it's a devastating time for you right now. Do you feel you're in a position to tell me a bit about Adam, so I can prepare for the service?" He hadn't met Adam, because the family had only started going to the church occasionally while Adam was in jail.

"Tell me what he liked, didn't like, what he did, anything like that."

Sharon started. "I think he would have liked you, Reverend Wood. I wish he would have had a stronger interest in religion."

David told the reverend about all the outdoor sports that Adam loved to do, and how he and Adam spent so much time together skiing, fishing, boating, and playing racket sports. David thought about how those moments were among the best of his own life. He couldn't imagine even heaven, if there was one, being better than those moments.

"He liked Lil Wayne," said Meghan.

The reverend smiled.

"He also loved watching *Shameless*, *Empire*, and *Entourage*," said Carter.

"Did you spend a lot of time with him?" Reverend Wood asked Carter.

"Yeah, when we were younger, we were always together. We skateboarded, played basketball on the driveway, went to the community pool, played football with my dad—"

Sharon interjected, "I remember I used to get comments from the neighbors about how nice it was to see two boys playing outside so much, while many other boys were inside playing video games."

Meghan added, "When they were young, they called each other 'best bro'. How appropriate for two brothers who were best friends."

"What about you, Sharon?" asked the reverend. "What can you tell me?

"He always liked listening to me play the piano. Often, I'd have piano students early on Saturday or Sunday mornings after Adam worked late the night before. He never complained about piano playing. In fact, occasionally he'd tell me how much he enjoyed it."

After the better part of an hour, Reverend Wood said, "I know we haven't even scratched the surface of things you'd like to remember about Adam. Some bereaved families find that writing things down can help the grieving process."

David said, "Yes, I've actually been thinking about that."

"Also, if you have anything that Adam has written, either recently or as a young child, please bring it to me. That will help me get to know him."

They wrapped up and returned home. David told his family that he was going upstairs to lie down for a few minutes. He lay on the bed, and Adam's death continued to sink in.

Adam was gone. His future killed. The world's future with him in it deleted.

The fishing trips that he and David would have had were gone. As were the snowmobile trips not yet taken. The times that Adam would have hung out at the lake house with his family were gone. The times that Adam would have beat David in tennis, basketball, or pickleball were gone. The playful teasing Adam would have done with Carter and Meghan was gone.

Gone was the help that Adam would have provided to strangers in need. Gone were the additional little jokes he would have made, brightening people's lives. Gone were the fun times that he and friends would have had for the next sixty years.

The thousands of meals that Adam would have made for his family and others were gone. The new recipes he would have created were gone. The training he would have provided to young cooks when he was older was gone.

The children that Adam would have had were gone before they were conceived. Their children too. And their children. The smiles they would have generated, the inventions they would have made, the music they would have created, the love they would have given and received. Gone.

All gone. David realized that when you're older and have grown kids, your future isn't the rest of your *own* life. Your future is that which would be lived by your children, and their children. A big piece of that future was now severed.

He crossed his arms and pressed them into his stomach, almost as if he had to keep it from blowing apart. He walked into the ensuite bathroom and fell to the floor on his side, hands still pressed into his stomach with a physical and mental pain so severe, he didn't know how he'd get through the next seconds or minutes. He couldn't come to terms with the fact that he let his son die.

He forced himself to get up off the floor. He couldn't stand, so he sat on the tiled surface that surrounded the bathtub. He kept trying to figure out how he let it happen. He needed to talk. He sent Sharon a text asking her to come upstairs.

Sharon came up immediately and asked if he was okay.

"I knew he was sick last night. I knew he was going to relapse. I knew he was at risk. I knew he was vulnerable, and I went to bed. I fucking went to bed! I let him die!"

Sharon, alarmed at David's state and intensity, said, "David, you have a job. You have to provide for your family. Of course you went to bed."

David was shaking almost beyond control. "I'm his father. I should have protected him. What good is a father if he doesn't protect his children?"

"He was an adult, David. You have two other children who need you now. You've got to be strong. You've got to be strong *for them*. There's nothing you can do for Adam now."

Her words were true. He also knew that his guilt would haunt him for the rest of his life.

For the next many hours, during the stronger moments, David dealt with the gruesome tasks that needed to be done when someone dies. Tasks that are a thousand times more gruesome when it's your twenty-four-year-old son who perished. David searched for a place to have Adam's body cremated. He pondered the oddity of using Yelp to find a satisfactory crematorium. He met with them and made the arrangements.

He searched for organizations to direct donations to. He spoke with several and decided on two: Shatterproof was a national organization focused on ending the devastation that addiction causes. David liked their focus on addressing stigma and changing laws. Hope-for-Healing was a local organization focused on harm reduction. He could see their efforts helping in the immediate community.

Sharon did more hosting than David. She had more friends in the area who came by.

Meghan and Carter put their hearts and souls into preparing portions of the funeral service. They found pictures of Adam, selected the best ones, and took them to a shop to get them printed onto large foam boards to be displayed at the funeral. They reviewed hours of old video footage of Adam to select a few seconds to show. They contacted musical friends who were willing to use their talents to honor Adam at the funeral. And they prepared a heartfelt eulogy.

With the house being full of guests, by Sunday afternoon, David needed to replenish things like Diet Coke, Kleenex, and ice. He drove to Walgreens and parked next to a car he recognized as belonging to one of Adam's old friends. He looked forward to saying hi if he ran into him. Inside the store, as he was searching for Kleenex, David overheard voices one aisle over, in the liquor section. They were the voices of a couple of Adam's old friends. David changed his mind about seeing them when he heard what they were saying.

"Yeah, he sure became a fuckup. Wouldn't leave that shit alone."

"I know. We all moved on, but he wouldn't."

"I'm not going to his funeral. Why should I go to a funeral of someone who caused his own death?"

These were friends who had tried all the same drugs that Adam had, but who had not become addicted. He decided to avoid them – in the store and, hopefully, for the rest of his life.

MONDAY

CHAPTER SIXTY

David was pleased to have all of his and Sharon's siblings, nieces, and nephews at the funeral. All had to travel, some from long distances involving multiple flights. Many of David's and Sharon's friends came, and many of Adam's old friends came, although not the ones David had overheard in Walgreens the previous day. There were friends from middle school and high school, who were now young men and women who'd recently graduated from college and were now in their first jobs. There were also more recent friends – young people who were not attending their first opioid overdose funeral.

John Tylor was there, looking somber. Camille was there, forcing a strong face. Brooke came and could not keep back her tears. David asked her to sit with the family, but she said she'd rather stay at the back. She probably wanted to be near the door in case she couldn't control her tears and needed to step out.

There were also people who were only casual acquaintances – classmates and their parents from as long ago as second grade, a bank teller who only knew Adam from the bank and who had always remarked to David and Sharon how polite he was. Several people from Mio Posto came.

After most people had taken their seats, David and Sharon were still standing in the lobby when a stranger approached them. He was a large man about thirty with a worn face and dressed in a dark suit and tie.

"Mr. and Mrs. Lambert, my name is Al Kott. You don't know me, but I served time at Carlane County Jail with Adam. I heard the news yesterday, just a few hours before I was released, myself."

David smiled slightly and said, "Al, thank you for coming."

"That was very kind of you," said Sharon.

"I gotta tell you, Adam was well-liked by everyone there, truly. He had this incredible sense of humor and kept us laughing. He was a real competitor on the basketball court. He often made food for the guys." The man smiled. "Mr. and Mrs. Lambert, he made our time there better. He really did. The world was better with him in it."

"Thank you very much," said David.

"I gotta tell you also. He was real serious about his recovery. The jail offered meetings five times a week. He went to every one. He used to tell us that he couldn't wait to get out and begin his new, sober life. Most of us guys there fought the same demons he did, and he inspired us."

David was warmed by the words of this complete stranger who knew Adam, perhaps as well as anyone. He was enormously grateful for his perspective.

David was also concerned about Al's safety, having learned that he was just released and an addict. "Are you going to be okay having just gotten out?" he asked.

"Yes, sir." He pointed to a man a generation older than himself, standing near the door. "That's my father. He's driving me to rehab right after the service. I actually wasn't sure whether I should go or not, but when I heard about Adam, I decided I was definitely going."

"Glad to hear that. Thanks again, Al." David hugged him and patted him on the back. "Let's get into the sanctuary."

Reverend Wood welcomed everyone, then began in his captivating voice. "I did not have a chance to meet Adam. But I got to know him over the last few days from talking with his family. They also shared with me things that Adam had written over the years. These included poems from school, notes, and goals from rehab programs. I'd like to share with you a poem that Adam wrote in sixth grade.

"At the beautiful lake,
Together with my whole family,
Away from all of my troubles,
Through the beautiful trails,
Underneath the dark blue sky,
Inside playing cards,
At the restaurant with the best chicken wings,
I am happy."

Reverend Wood paused for a few seconds of silence then mentioned how the first three lines captured Adam's love of nature, his love of family and the fact that even at the age of eleven, he felt struggles.

He then proceeded to deliver a beautiful speech that incorporated almost everything he had heard from the family two days earlier. Several family members also spoke, conveying their love, and telling some humorous anecdotes about him. Meghan and Carter's musical friends performed several touching songs.

The service finished, and the family went home to begin their new life.

TUESDAY

CHAPTER SIXTY-ONE

John drove to the sheriff's office Tuesday morning. Angela Parker had called on Monday to say that the families would accept his deal. He now had to convince the sheriff.

"I'm here to see the sheriff," he announced to the officer at the security desk – the same woman who was there the last time.

She grinned. "Sheriff Mason?"

"There's only one," he responded with a smile.

She laughed. "Please follow me, Mr. Tylor."

Sheriff Mason was in the waiting area outside his office speaking with a man who appeared to be in his sixties and was wearing a loud, tan suit. He told the man to wait then motioned John to follow him into his office. They sat at his round conference table, and the sheriff's assistant brought them coffee. The framed poster of Joe Arpaio's quotes was no longer in the office.

Sheriff Mason took a noisy sip of black coffee from his large mug. He looked John in the eye and said, "So, young man, how are you going to finally make this thing go away?"

John looked him back in the eye. He'd had enough condescension.

"Sheriff Mason, I am not your employee or your son or anything else that would allow you to address me as 'young man.'" He paused. When Sheriff Mason was about to say something, John interrupted and added, "I am your legal counsel, and you are my client. I will address you as Sheriff Mason, and you will address me as Mr. Tylor. Alternatively, we can address each other using first names."

John waited to see if Sheriff Mason would yell and throw him out of his office, or if he'd respect John's requirement to be treated as an equal.

The sheriff let out a hearty laugh. "Jackie told me you had brains. Glad to see you got balls too." He chuckled some more. "How about in my office, you call me Peter, and I'll call you John. In your office, you make the call."

"That will work."

"So. John, what advice do you have for me?"

"I'll answer your question, but please allow me to give you some background first."

"Okay."

"When I initially heard about this case, I thought it had no merit. However, I now believe there is a chance, albeit a small one, that the families could win at trial."

Peter's civility toward John remained, but his calm was short-lived. "What the hell? Jackie told me we'd win at trial, if it ever got there."

John continued with confidence and precision. "My professional opinion is that we would *likely* win. However, there is a possibility of losing."

"This new perspective pisses me off. Alright, give it to me straight."

"There were two main reasons why I originally thought the families could not win at trial – something called proximate cause, and something called deliberate indifference."

"Okay. I'm familiar with those terms, but give me your perspective."

"As you know, proximate cause means the plaintiffs would have to prove that your decision to have a policy to deny the medicine actually *caused* the deaths."

"These people went out, injected, and overdosed. We didn't inject them. So we should be good there."

"You didn't inject them, but the plaintiffs may argue that denial of their medicine made a relapse more likely – in fact almost certain – and that the relapse was more likely to be fatal." John paused to let Peter digest that statement.

He continued. "They could argue that without their medicine, many people with opioid use disorder are bound to relapse – that their brain disorder causes the relapse, as sure as someone with epilepsy has a brain disorder that causes a seizure."

"That would be crap. Seizures are involuntary. Taking drugs is not."

"Maybe. Maybe not. I've spent time with addicts over the last week. I've learned that sometimes, for addicts who have a severe case, nothing can deter them from using, even the likelihood of death. So, is relapse really voluntary or is the addict sometimes simply less powerful than his addiction? Angela would try to convince the jury the latter is the case and that removing their medicine makes a relapse foreseeable."

Peter tapped the table with his fingers. "The deaths occurred after they left the jail. These people were safe in my jail."

"She'll say the inmates were safe in your jail because there was no heroin in your jail, but that you could have predicted that once the person was exposed to the elements without their medicine – exposed to a world where heroin is plentiful and easy to obtain – there was a high probability that they would relapse."

"One thing's not adding up. These people were obviously relapsing while they were on the medicine before they were incarcerated. That's why they ended up here. Police found them in possession."

"Angela may have doctors explain that while relapse can happen, even while on the medicine, the probability of a relapse occurring is significantly less while on the medicine, and the relapse is much less likely to be fatal."

"I suppose a jury with a bunch of liberals could believe anything, other than a person is responsible for his own behavior."

"Again, my responsibility is to provide you this information. That's it for proximate cause. A jury could be swayed that your policy caused the deaths."

Peter cracked his knuckles and said, "Alright. I can't wait to hear about deliberate indifference."

John's posture remained strong. "Although you, your police, and many public officials are protected by immunities so you can perform your jobs, if plaintiffs can argue that your decision or actions showed deliberate indifference to a serious medical need, then there could be liability."

"How the hell could they show that? We provide medical care whenever it's needed, and when we know about it." He returned to drumming his fingers on the table.

"They would have to show two things – first, that the deceased had a serious medical need. Unfortunately, that is easily proved, since doctors had already prescribed medicine."

"The doctors prescribed a narcotic! John, I'm not as unread as you may think on these matters. I know about these medications and why they're prescribed."

"I understand. The plaintiffs could use that knowledge against you to prove the second item. Angela will argue that you *knew* denying the medicine would create a risk of serious harm by releasing the inmates to the elements without their doctor-prescribed medicine to protect them. Remember also that part of the suit is for the pain and suffering that the inmates went through withdrawing from their medicine in your jail. Angela may also argue that you knew the inmates would go through that pain and suffering."

Peter leaned back and said, "Alright, so winning at trial is likely, but no longer certain, does that sum it up?"

"Yes."

"Got it."

"There is something else to consider."

"More bad news?"

"More information to consider. If we do not settle soon, this suit will grow. Angela Parker will find other families who lost a loved one under similar circumstances. In fact, there was a death just last Friday of someone who was released last Monday. It appears that it was a similar case."

"How do you know that?"

"I am one of the best lawyers in the city. It is my job to know that."

Peter seemed to appreciate John's swagger. "Who died?" he asked.

"Adam Lambert, from Parkdale."

Peter searched his memory. "Adam Lambert … I don't know many of the inmates, but I think I know who that guy was. He was that kid who went to all the drug counseling meetings, and he was always making food for people, playing basketball or playing cards. One of those quiet, popular types, I guess. He died?"

"Yes. You can be sure that Angela will learn of that, contact the family, and try to get them to join the suit. She is probably compiling a list of anyone who was released from the jail in the last few years and who died shortly after release. She'll work on getting those people to launch suits. I already have that list."

"How many are there?"

"Forty-seven people died within ten days of being released from Carlane County Jail in the last two years. Some of them may have been on addiction medicine prior to being incarcerated."

"Shit. I hope you don't have any more *information to consider*."

"It is not a legal point, but you know that going to trial could be damaging, politically."

"Indeed I do. I anticipated we'd be discussing that. The guy you saw in my waiting room is my campaign advisor. If you agree, I'd like him to join this meeting."

"That would be good. Of course, once he joins, we will no longer be under attorney-client privilege."

Peter motioned through the window to his assistant to bring in the man.

"John, this is Stefan Larson." John and Stefan shook hands.

Peter looked at Stefan. "How much campaign risk is there in having this trial?"

"Well, it won't be a private trial, but people are generally apathetic, and some are even disdainful toward drug addicts. I don't think people will care too much one way or the other," said Stefan.

John leaned forward. "Gentlemen, I would have said the same thing a week ago. However, I've learned that the opioid epidemic is the leading cause of death for people aged twenty to fifty. Most people know someone who died recently or who is afflicted. That may start to affect the way they vote."

"Are you saying that going soft on drugs will win me votes?

Because I don't believe that," said Peter.

"No, going hard on the damage drugs do to our citizens may win votes. Those three young people did die of an overdose within days of being released. They had survived with their addiction before jail. These are facts. Facts that Angela will pound home to the media," responded John.

Peter looked at the clock. "Alright, we can talk about philosophies all day. We need to make progress. I want to keep being sheriff. I will not agree that we did anything wrong, and I won't use our limited budget to pay out people who sue us. And, by the way, contrary to what those families may think, I don't want people to die. I became a police officer to serve and protect, and that is why I'm in this job. That's why my police are in their jobs. Any goddamn one of them would risk their own life to save someone." He paused. "John, what's your advice?"

"I know I still owe you an answer to that. Just one more item to share with you first."

Peter remained quiet, but looked at John as if to say, "Spill it out, fast. I'm getting tired of this."

"I had a survey completed – a quick and dirty opinion poll. We asked five hundred people if they supported allowing addicted inmates to continue receiving doctor-prescribed medicine. The majority – sixty-eight percent – supported it." Peter had a look on his face like he found that information interesting and useful. John continued. "Stefan, I know this survey does not have the depth and sophistication of an opinion poll that your firm would conduct. However, the results are useful nonetheless."

"Indeed, for reliable results, we'd need to conduct a proper poll," said Stefan with some attitude.

John placed his palms on the table and looked at Peter. He had given Peter everything he had to set the stage for his recommendation. Now was the time to push for the close. “Here is my advice: Don’t pay damages, don’t admit wrongdoing, but do change the policy. Let inmates have their medicine, just like any other sick person. Angela and her clients will agree to drop the compensatory damages if we agree to change the policy and lift the media restriction. In my opinion, it’s a good settlement that you should accept.”

The room was silent for several seconds. Then, Peter asked, “Would changing the policy cost me anything?”

John was ready. “This would be medicine that the inmates bring with them or pay for directly or through their insurance. The jail administers other medicines now, so it wouldn’t cost anything.”

“What do other jails do?”

“There are 5,100 county jails and prisons in the country. Fewer than fifty allow inmates to continue taking Buprenorphine or Methadone if the inmate is on it when they arrive. However, a few jails offer the medicine even if the inmate isn’t already on it when they arrive. They have found that the post-incarceration death rate dropped by over sixty percent.”

Peter leaned back in his chair to command attention. He gave a pensive look to John and Stefan, then spoke. “I’m not a fan of giving in. On the other hand, I don’t like the potential political damage from a trial, especially a trial that we may not win and for a case that could grow. Stefan, what do you think?”

“I’m afraid I’m not as studied on this addiction topic as John. I do have a nephew who does heroin or something. And a family on our block lost a daughter about six months ago. It seems this is indeed becoming an issue that could sway votes. I generally like more certainty though. I can have our polling firm take a few days to conduct a more dependable poll on whether or not people support a policy change."

John refused to allow a delay that a poll would cause. He effused, "Gentlemen, with respect, we don't have a few more days. We would just be giving our opposition time to become stronger. And they will. Believe me."

Stefan looked offended. Peter stood. "Alright. Let's wrap up. John's points are persuasive."

Stefan swallowed and nodded in compliance.

Peter pointed at John. "Tell Parker we'll change the policy if they drop the compensatory."

"Remember, she also wants to lift the gag order, if we settle."

"Stefan, what do you think?" asked Peter.

"I think that should be okay. If John's inclination is right, publicity surrounding the policy change could be good. People might see you as tough *and* progressive"

"Okay," said Peter. He looked back at John. "John, thanks for your advice. You're earning your fees today."

John gave a crisp nod and felt his chest lighten. He'd done it. Lives would be saved.

CHAPTER SIXTY-TWO

John dialed Jackie on speakerphone before pulling out of his parking spot.

"John, I presume you're on your way to the office, so you can tell me how the meeting went?"

"No, I have a personal matter to take care of. Then I'm in court this afternoon with the pro bono case. I won't make it there today."

"Oh."

"I can give you a summary of the meeting as I drive."

There was a short silence, then with a tone that indicated she was not happy, she said, "Okaay …"

"Well, I know that Peter often calls you after I meet with him. Did he call you?"

"So now you're on a first name basis with him?"

"Yes." John waited for her answer.

"No, he didn't call."

"The meeting went well. Over the weekend, I got Angela and her clients to agree to drop the compensatory damages if the sheriff would agree to change the policy and lift the publicity restriction. I proposed that to Peter. I told him that based on my research, he'd probably win votes, not lose them."

"You don't know that. You should've stuck to legal advice, not political. I hope you didn't create an even bigger mess."

John was tired of her comments that were just jabs and added no value. "Jackie, do you remember what you said to me when you described this case?"

"Yes, I said, you better get it settled."

"Or I'd be asked to leave the firm," John added.

"Well, I said we'd have to discuss your future, but, yes, basically."

"Okay. If I don't settle the case, the partnership can ask me to leave. Until then, these daggers you throw out are not useful to anyone. In fact, they're against our code of ethics and may be of interest to the partner ethics committee. You may be office managing partner, but you and I are partners and should be talking to each other like partners."

There was silence on the phone, and John was not about to fill it. Finally, Jackie said, "My comments have been to help you, not insult you."

Again, John let silence inflict its power.

"So where do things stand?" Jackie asked.

"Peter agreed with my proposal. We're done. Tomorrow, we'll submit an executed copy of the agreement to the judge for approval, so the case can be deemed resolved."

"Okay. Thanks. Good outcome."

"Thank you."

Over the last few days, John realized that while he still did not respect her legal aptitude and never planned to be her friend, he himself had been prone to prejudice, judging her for her privileged upbringing when he was providing the same type of life for his own children.

John arrived home. Velinda was at work, and he assumed Daniel was upstairs finishing packing for rehab.

"Daniel, are you ready to go?" John yelled from downstairs.

He didn't hear anything, so he walked upstairs to Daniel's bedroom. His suitcase was on the bed, packed, but still open. Daniel was sitting on a chair, eyes closed, his back slipping to the side and his head drooped down. John nudged his shoulder. "Daniel, you okay?"

Daniel cracked open his eyes slightly. "What?" he murmured.

"Are you ready to go to rehab?"

He straightened his head, but his back still remained tilted. He mumbled, his mouth barely moving and his words barely audible, "I don't think I should go ... they're not effective."

"Well, let's just get in the car and start driving. We can talk on the way." John closed Daniel's suitcase and carried it to the car while Daniel remained seated, leaning over. Back in Daniel's room, John grabbed his son's arm under his shoulder to guide him up. "C'mon. Let's go."

"I don't think I should go," Daniel mumbled again.

"For God's sake, you're out on bond, and you're high now. You've got to go." John wondered what Daniel's mind was like right now. When so high on heroin, how much of his brain was available to think and talk?

Fortunately, Daniel's actions were not matching his words of opposition. With John continuing to guide him by the arm, Daniel walked downstairs then toward the car. John got him into the car and got the seat belt around him. Daniel again mumbled, "I don't think I should go." John started the drive to Gateway. Adam had mentioned it was a good place during the conversation with John and Gabby the previous week.

After the one-hour drive, they walked to the front door, again with John helping Daniel walk, and Daniel still saying he didn't want to go. A counselor came out and took them to a room. She pulled out a form and started going through questions. Although John was present, the answers needed to come from Daniel. He seemed to be getting enough brain capacity back to understand and answer most of the questions. A financial records person came by, and she and John went to a separate room to confirm fees, payments, and insurance.

With Daniel and John still separated, the counselor came to John and said that Daniel would go to detox for three days, then join the program. Family members could visit on Sundays. The insurance would cover the twenty-eight days.

"Is that enough time?" John asked.

"To be honest, it's not enough. It never is. But it's all most insurance programs cover. If he needs more time, we can petition the insurance company near the end of the program. Sometimes we get a few more days."

John left and wondered what life would be like from then on. Would Daniel be charged with just a misdemeanor since this was his first offense? Would he ever make it back to MIT? Maybe he would beat this addiction, and life would be good, or maybe the family was in for years of battles, driving to court cases, rehabs, disruption, and perhaps, the same final outcome as Adam.

CHAPTER SIXTY-THREE

John drove to the Carlane County campus after getting Daniel checked in. He was scheduled to meet Gabby in court at three o'clock. He arrived twenty minutes early, so he found an empty bench outside the courthouse to sit and soak in the sun for a few minutes. He'd likely be coming here often with Daniel to deal with his charge. As he appreciated the warm air, he thought more about when to inform Gabby of Adam's passing.

He walked into the courthouse and proceeded to Courtroom Five. He went around back and saw Gabby in her orange jumpsuit accompanied by a police officer. She looked weak and frail, like she had been through hell.

"How are you doing?" asked John

"At this point, I've gone through the worst of the withdrawal. It was torturous." She rubbed her forehead with the palm of her hand. "At least I knew what I was in for, since Adam had warned me." She smiled and said, "You must remember my friend, Adam?"

John's heart was racing. He forced calm into his voice. "I do, yes." He said nothing more because Gabby needed to be in good shape to understand him and the judge. He explained, "You'll plead guilty to a Class A misdemeanor charge of drug possession, and you'll testify against Base and Ink. You'll be sentenced to thirty days in Carlane County Jail, less the four days that you already served. Following that, you'll have one year of probation which will include an outpatient rehab program, a monthly shot of Vivitrol, and random drug testing."

"Getting here for the drug tests will be arduous," Gabby said.

"I know. You'll need to get a job, so you have money for public transit to come here for testing when required."

"Okay."

"You *will* have a criminal record, a misdemeanor. After you're done with probation, and provided you have no violations, you'll be able to get your record sealed. That will allow you to apply for most jobs and to move on with your life. Do you understand everything I've said so far?"

"Yes. It sounds like a good deal. I'm happy to accept it. What's happening with Base and Ink?"

"The fingerprints on the baggie and gun did match the guy you know as Ink. He appeared before a judge late Saturday for his arraignment and was denied bail, so he is still in jail. He'll eventually have his case, likely be found guilty, and stay in jail for a long time."

"Okay."

"However, Base posted his bail this morning and was released."

Her face showed fear. "So he's out there?"

"Yes. We'll get a restraining order to keep him away from you. I'm advised by the assistant DA, though, that once things have gotten this far, where an informant is testifying, the bad guys tend to be reluctant to cause harm because they're less likely to get away with it. Once they're facing jail time, they want to avoid the risk of more time. As a further safety measure, though, when you're out, you should take up residence away from Terrace."

"I understand."

"This could be a new beginning for you."

"Yes. Thank you for giving me a second chance. Well, a third chance. Adam gave me my *second* chance."

John nodded.

"What happens now?" she asked.

Criminal proceedings were new territory for John, but he could give Gabby enough guidance to put her at ease. He also had a criminal defense attorney with him nearby, in case he needed to consult her.

"You'll wait back here until your case is called." He handed her a document. "Here is the plea agreement. Read through it because you'll need to sign it in front of the judge. When you're called, the police officer will guide you toward the table, and you'll stand by me. The prosecutor will tell the judge that we've reached an agreement. Then either the prosecutor or the judge will ask you some questions. Just pay attention to what they ask and answer truthfully. If you're unsure about anything, you can whisper in my ear and ask. Okay?"

"Okay. Someday, I'm going to write about all this."

John returned to the courtroom, and approached the woman sitting at the prosecutor's table. "Good afternoon. Are you Assistant DA, Cunningham?" he asked.

"Yes. Hello, John. Good to meet you in person," said Cunningham.

John went back to his place on the front row. Three loud knocks sounded from behind the judge's quarters.

"All rise," yelled the court officer. "The Honorable Judge Holloway presiding." A middle-aged woman with dark blonde hair walked into the courtroom wearing a long black robe and a subtle smile.

"Good morning, everyone. Please be seated," announced Judge Holloway as she took her seat at the highest point of the courtroom facing the counsel tables and the audience. Everyone sat down except the court officers and her clerk.

A few minutes later, the court clerk started calling cases, and one by one, attorneys and defendants approached the defense counsel's table to have their matters heard.

After a few cases, Cunningham came to John and said, "I'll ask the court officer to call us next."

"Case Number 21 on today's calendar: People versus Gabrielle Jones. Please step forward," said the court officer.

John stood up, and the police officer directed Gabby to her spot beside John. ADA Cunningham stood at the DA's table.

"Counselor, please state your appearance."

"John Tylor, of Harris Clark, appearing for the defendant, Gabrielle Jones. Good morning, your Honor."

"ADA Cunningham for the people, your Honor."

"Will the defendant please state her name for the record."

"Gabrielle Jones."

"I hear we have a plea agreement in this case?" said Judge Holloway looking up from her files.

"Yes we do, your Honor," said Cunningham. "Before we take the plea, may we approach the bench briefly?"

"Yes. Approach."

Cunningham said, "Your Honor, this is a straight-forward plea agreement, but we have a situation regarding the safety of this defendant. She has been cooperating with my office to identify two drug dealers, one of whom already tried to kill her. That person has been remanded without bail, but the other was released on bail last night. So Mr. Tylor and I would like to request that your Honor not only take this defendant's plea but also sentence her today so she can return to jail immediately."

"What is she pleading guilty to?" asked the judge.

Cunningham gave her the details, and John confirmed his agreement.

"Okay, then I will order the sentence," said the judge.

After they stepped back, the judge said, "Officer, please swear in the defendant."

"Gabrielle Jones, do you swear to tell the truth, the whole truth, and nothing but the truth, so help you God?"

"I do."

The judge stated the charge and Gabby confirmed that she was pleading guilty.

"So do you now freely and voluntarily admit that on or about August 30, 2016, you were in possession of a quantity of heroin which did not exceed fifteen grams?"

"Yes, I do."

"Are you now under the influence of any drugs or alcohol which would prevent you from understanding what is happening here today?"

"No, I've been detoxing in our fine county jail, your Honor."

The judge looked unpleased. "If I ask you a yes or no question, just respond with yes or no."

"Yes, your Honor."

"By pleading guilty, you waive the right to a trial by jury. Do you understand that?"

"Yes, I do."

The judge read her a number of rights and asked if she understood. She said she did.

"For the charge you are pleading guilty to, I could sentence you to up to a year in jail and direct that you pay a fine of no more than fifty thousand dollars. Do you understand that those are the possible consequences?"

Gabby looked at John with surprise and concern. The criminal attorney who had been working with John had warned him that the judge would say that, but that it is rare for a judge to issue a different sentence from what the attorneys agreed to. John nodded to Gabby that it was okay.

"Yes, your Honor."

The judge confirmed that the plea was acceptable to the DA, accepted it, and Gabby and John both signed three copies of the agreement. John kept one and gave the other two to the court officer. The judge asked Gabby if she was ready to be sentenced, then read terms that were consistent with what John had told her.

The police officer who had been accompanying Gabby walked her out of the courtroom and into the hallway to begin the walk back to the jail. The officer held her there for a minute for a final discussion with John.

As John reached Gabby, she appeared dazed from how fast this had all transpired. "You did well," John said.

"This is a different world for me," said Gabby.

"You're on a new journey now. You'll be thirty days clean when you get out."

"That's right, I've never achieved that since being an addict."

John anchored himself and looked at her. "Gabby, I'm afraid I have some bad news."

"What? The jail library has a poor selection?"

"No. Really, it's very bad news about one of your friends."

Gabby looked like she had shrunk about a foot. "Adam or Camille?" she asked.

"Adam … He passed away … overdose."

Tears came immediately. "No," she muttered as her legs buckled. John and the police officer both grabbed her before she hit the ground.

She took deep breaths. "He saved my life, then he lost his. No. Where's the justice?"

John rubbed the side of his head. "I've learned that with this disease, there is none, Gabby."

"Why did God let me live and not him? Adam had his whole life ahead of him. It's not fair. Why?" John handed her a tissue. She cried for several minutes while the police officer waited patiently. She gathered enough strength to say, "I will honor his life by changing mine."

CHAPTER SIXTY-FOUR

Camille met Jerry outside Judge Castle's courtroom on Tuesday afternoon a few minutes before the four o'clock hearing. Jerry had obtained a copy of the audio that had been recorded by Rosalie's app. It revealed Camille's ex-husband yelling at Rosalie, then striking her leg three times. Child Services had also reported that there were new bruises on her leg.

Camille was worried about the girls being in foster care, but she was relieved to know they were away from Robert. She wondered if this trauma might make *them* prone to drug use one day.

She adjusted her clothes with steady hands. "What do you think will happen in court today?" she asked Jerry. "Is there any chance the judge will allow the girls to come live with me?"

"Things have definitely turned around since we were last here, but don't get your hopes up, girl. A bad father does not make the mother better in the judge's eyes. Giving custody to a recovering heroin addict is still a long shot, even for someone with as much success as you've had staying clean."

"I suppose," said Camille

Robert and his attorney showed up a few minutes later. All four waited outside the courtroom in silence. Robert's attorney used the time to file his fingernails. The court officer called them inside. Judge Castle was already at his place, looking down on all of them as they took their places at the counsel tables. The attorney for the girls, Lori Flores, was also inside the courtroom. She smiled at Camille as they walked in.

"Please call the case, officer. We are all here," said Judge Castle.

The court officer spoke. "These are case numbers DR01821 and DR04592 in the matter of the Cauchon children. All counsel, please state your appearances for the record."

All three attorneys stated their appearances, followed by Camille and Robert being placed under oath. Once they all sat back down, Judge Castle spoke. "Ms. Flores, have you had a chance to meet with your clients?"

She stood. "Yes, your Honor. I met with them twice. Once before they were removed and then again last night at their current foster home. They're nervous in their new environment, but they appear to be doing well, considering everything they've been through. They say they miss their mother. They asked about her and why they can't stay with her."

"What are the girls' thoughts regarding their father?"

"They're currently afraid of their father and would rather not see him," said Ms. Flores.

"Mr. Cauchon, as I am sure you are aware of the restraining order pending against you and the criminal case that has been filed against you by the DA's office, I will not be asking any questions of you today," stated Judge Castle. He looked at Robert and paused.

Camille looked at Robert, daring him to say something.

"I'm aware of those allegations, your Honor, but I deny them," said Robert.

"I am sure you do. But since there is now an open criminal case against you as well as a Department of Child and Family Services investigation, you would do well to follow your attorney's advice and not make any statements here today. My job is to decide what will happen with your daughters while those investigations are underway. Those open cases may take a couple of months to conclude, so I need to issue a final judgment regarding your prior open petition for a change in custody and issue an order of custody regarding your daughters, considering these more recent events. Despite my advice, do you have anything to say before I make my ruling?" asked the judge.

"I sure do, I …"

His attorney bumped him and signaled to him to shut up. "No, your Honor. My client has nothing to say and will not be making any statements at this time."

"Good," said the judge. He turned and spoke to Camille directly. "Ms. Simard, I have before me the results of your drug test and the home inspection report. I am glad there were no surprises here."

Camille smiled and felt grateful to Laticia Rivers for updating the inspection report. She was appreciative of Gabby pushing her to resolve the door and inspection report issue.

The judge continued. "Your lawyer has also informed me that your employment at Academy Theatre continues and that, in fact, you will have equity interest in and lead a new program that Academy is launching."

"Yes, your Honor."

"Congratulations. Beyond that, I am aware that it was thanks to you that the abuse of Rosalie was uncovered and documented."

"I just gave Rosalie the tool. She was a brave little girl to use it, your Honor."

"Nevertheless, before I can grant you custody …"

Camille gasped. He's *saying I might one day get custody?*

The judge paused at Camille's gasp then continued. "… I need to see two things happen. First, I need you to continue to submit to random drug tests a little longer and perhaps one or two additional surprise home visits. That will give Ms. Flores and me the assurances we need that they'll be safe with you. Second, I need you to complete a drug awareness program and find a sponsor who will be willing to submit monthly reports to this court. Do you understand these requirements?"

"I do, your Honor," Camille answered, trying to contain her smile.

"I am issuing an order today denying Mr. Cauchon's pending petition under case number DR01821. That docket will now be closed. And I am issuing the following relief under case number DR04592. The children shall remain in foster care for a period of three months, at which time we shall reconvene and reassess the situation. If the mother has passed all her random drug tests and home inspections, she shall be allowed to file for physical custody of the children, and I will entertain the petition at that point. In the meantime, the mother shall be allowed to have unsupervised visitation with the children three times per week starting immediately. Those visits shall be arranged through Ms. Flores with the cooperation of the foster parents."

I can apply for custody in three months!

The judge continued. "Starting one month from now and provided there are no issues with the random drug tests or home inspections, the mother shall be allowed to have the children for a weekend overnight visit, Friday to Sunday. During the following month, two weekend overnight visits, and then we shall reconvene during the third month."

Camille held her mouth closed to prevent a shriek of exuberance from exiting. These were far more generous terms than she expected. Jerry noticed her reaction, smiled at her, and tapped her back.

"In regard to Mr. Cauchon," the judge went on, "these girls are to have no contact with him until we reconvene. I am ordering Mr. Cauchon to complete a twelve-week anger management program and a parenting seminar and bring the completion certificates to me when we meet again in three months. If for any reason, the girls say they want to talk to their father, Ms. Flores and Ms. Simard, I want you to allow it. But only telephone contact, and only if they request it. No contact shall be initiated by the father. Understood?" The judge looked at all three tables in turn, and all three attorneys gave their assent. "That is my final order."

"Thank you, your Honor," said Jerry and Camille.

"I will see you all in three months. My clerk will contact the attorneys to set up a date that is convenient for all parties. We are done for today. You are all dismissed." Judge Castle stood up and left the courtroom through the back door.

Camille and Jerry walked out of the courtroom together. Camille thanked Ms. Flores for her work and asked if she could call her directly to arrange the visits with her daughters. Ms. Flores gave her a kind smile and said it was not a problem as long as Jerry agreed. He did, and Ms. Flores gave Camille her business card.

"Email or text messages usually work best as I may be in court and unable to answer. And please, call me Lori," said Ms. Flores as she shook Camille's and Jerry's hands.

Robert and his attorney had already walked away from the

courtroom, but Camille could see them down the hall. Lund was applying Chapstick, and Robert was yelling at him.

"Thank you. You've given my girls and me a new life," said Camille to Jerry.

"I just showed up for the court stuff. You're the one who did all the work. You should be proud, girl."

Camille and Jerry parted ways once they exited the building. Camille reached her car and looked at her phone, noticing there was an unheard voicemail. "Camille, this is Doctor Singh's office. Doctor Singh has had a couple of cancellations tomorrow. She can fit you in at ten to do your assessment and arrange a prescription. Please call back to confirm."

She thought about Adam and the role he had quietly played in her life – telling her about the addiction medicine, showing her the app that called police, helping her get a job back at Academy, and consequently the successful outcome she had just received in court. She wondered how many other people Adam had impacted in his short life. She felt honored to have had him as a friend.

ONE YEAR LATER

CHAPTER SIXTY-FIVE

David and Sharon had suggested that everybody meet at their place prior to heading out to the event. *Messages in Art – Tributes to Our Loved Ones* was part of the annual International Overdose Awareness Day. It was an opportunity for amateur musicians, singers, and writers to gather in an outdoor park and perform songs or poems they had written on the topic of addiction, its devastation, and what could be done about it.

Carter was still home before returning to school for his third year. He was sitting in the family room strumming his guitar. His face was expressionless, as were Meghan's and Eric's while they sat holding hands, listening to Carter's music.

Brooke arrived. She and Sharon had occasionally texted and visited each other over the year since Adam's passing.

While David was at the front door welcoming Brooke, he saw Camille and Rodrigo getting out of Camille's car. A few weeks after Camille had asked Rodrigo for help fixing her front door, he returned and asked her to dinner. They'd been dating ever since, and Rodrigo had been able to get a work visa for another year.

The back doors of Camille's Fusion popped open and Rosalie and Mia shot out, both girls an inch or so taller than the last time David had seen them. Camille had physical and legal custody of them. When Camille reached the front door, David spotted her eighteen-month-sober keychain and congratulated her. He introduced all four to Brooke, and they walked toward the kitchen and family room. As they passed the piano, David pointed to the uncovered keys and told Camille to feel free to play. He noticed all of the guests looking at the family pictures that included Adam as they walked down the hall.

Mia and Rosalie both had temporary tattoos on their arms. They were starting to wear off, but David could tell that they were a contour of a heart surrounding the words "Je t'aime." Eager to show hers off, Mia said, "Gra-mère gave us these. We went on an airplane to visit her in Quebec." Once everyone saw it, she added, "Mommy says we're gonna go there more often."

Although the event they were going to was melancholic, David and Sharon were looking forward to it. In the first months following Adam's death, they had gone to different bereaved parent groups, and they had even become close friends with a few couples in the same situation. They found that they needed to go to groups where the cause of death was specifically overdose. In other grievance groups, they felt a little out of place.

After some low-volume conversation, everyone left the house to drive to the event. Mia and Rosalie had taken an immediate liking to Brooke and wanted her to drive with them, so she went in Camille's car, and David and the family went in Sharon's SUV.

They arrived about a half an hour prior to the scheduled start time of six o'clock. All performers had been advised to arrive early. The park had plenty of open space with green grass. Brooke offered to watch Mia and Rosalie.

Camille and Rodrigo spotted the stage at one end of the field. It was a homemade twelve-by-twelve platform about two feet off the ground. It had a back wall that rose about eight feet. A large extension cord ran from the stage to a building nearby that provided the electricity. There were about two hundred chairs set up on the grass.

Onstage, someone was testing two microphones and a keyboard. Camille and Rodrigo walked onto the stage. Rodrigo took his acoustic guitar out of its case and leaned it against the back wall next to another one owned by someone else while Camille tested the feel of the keyboard.

David and Sharon walked around slowly, surveying the growing crowd. There were about fifty people present, and more were streaming in. Walking toward David was a young father holding a toddler. The man happened to kiss the boy on the cheek as David passed. It reminded him of many similar moments he had had with Adam, and how he hadn't sufficiently appreciated those moments at the time. Triggers like that tended to bring the pain of loss and guilt to the surface.

"Are you okay?" Sharon asked. They had learned to recognize the signs that one of them was struggling. David's giveaways were crossing his arms and pressing them into his stomach or covering much of his face with his hand to hide the crying. This time, it was the latter.

He nodded. After walking a few more steps, he took out a tissue, blew his nose, and composed himself. He was looking forward to meeting up with a few people at the event.

Somewhere nearby, he heard a voice that sounded like Gabby's, saying, "Let's go, Eight." David had gotten to know Gabby over the last year. Shortly after Adam died, David decided to reduce his work hours to have time to do something to help address the epidemic. He had taken courses on writing song lyrics. Camille had introduced David to Gabby, since she was a master with words and an experienced songwriter. Gabby helped polish the lyrics for two of his songs, and Camille put music to them. Camille and Rodrigo would be performing one of them at the event.

David saw Gabby struggling to hold a leash connected to a large German Shepherd wanting to walk faster than her. She still looked a little worn, but her clothes were clean, and she seemed content and healthy.

When she had gotten out of jail, Gabby had landed a job teaching English as a second language. She had also started a blog called *Surviving the Dragon*. She posted captivating stories about her time as an active user and how she survived on the streets. The site had also become a platform for addicts and families to share their own stories and offer their own tips on how to survive. Members made recommendations on topics like where to find clean needles, getting a reliable source, and how and where to take the first steps toward recovery. Gabby's ability to write well, her real-world experience, and the fact that the topic had struck a nerve, had made the blog a phenomenon, with close to a million subscribers. Advertisers provided a moderate income stream for her.

She had also found a new hospital where she resumed reading stories to terminally ill teenage girls. In fact, with the popularity of her blog, she had achieved small-time celebrity status in the hospital, and the staff were always happy to see her. With the teaching income and the advertising revenue, she was able to rent a small house about ten miles west of Terrace with a large yard for her dog.

Gabby had stayed mostly clean. She was on Methadone treatment, but would still lose the battle occasionally, skip her Methadone and relapse. She kept working on her recovery though, and the time periods between relapses kept getting longer.

"Is the dog yours?" asked Sharon.

Gabby scratched the dog behind the ears with both hands, and said, "Yes, she's my big old girl, aren't you?" The dog wagged her big tail and licked Gabby's face.

"What made you decide to get a dog?" asked Sharon.

"Well, her name is Eight – short for Step Eight."

"Is that the one where you make a list of people you harmed and make amends?" asked Sharon.

"Yes. It's a long story, but a few months ago, I met with a guy who provides guard dogs to protect vacant buildings. I asked him what happens to the dogs when they get older. He told me he tries to find homes for them, but most people are afraid to have a former guard dog as a pet, so he usually has to put them down. Well, I gave this old girl a new lease on life." She scratched Eight's long back. "I also blog about her and post lots of pictures. She's a celebrity. Apparently, taking former guard dogs as pets has become cool."

"She looks healthy," said David.

"Oh, she is. Also, she's still capable of protecting *me*. I can tell you that. Someone with my background never knows, you know."

"I'm going to go catch up with Brooke and the girls," said Sharon.

"John Tylor is coming today," said Gabby to David. "He's the lawyer who helped get me out of a mess a year ago. I've kept in touch with him."

"I remember him – the lawyer who got the sheriff to stop withholding addiction medicine from inmates. He came to our home the day after Adam died."

"Yes. That medicine topic became an issue during the sheriff election last year. Sheriff Mason ended up winning."

"I recall."

"Anyway, John and his wife and son are coming. Also, a friend of John's is coming."

"I look forward to seeing them," said David.

Gabby continued updating David, now at a lower volume. "John's son, Daniel, had addiction issues too. It seems like he's able to manage it, at least for now. He's been in recovery for a year and starts back at school next week," said Gabby.

Her eyes widened as she looked over David's shoulder. "John!" Gabby yelled in her unmistakable, feisty voice. It pierced David's ears at such close proximity, but he didn't care.

John came over with his group. "Gabby, nice to see you."

"You too. You may remember David Lambert."

"Of course. Good to see you, David. This is my wife, Velinda, our son, Daniel, and our friend, Angela Parker."

"Hello, everyone," said David. He pointed an index finger at each of John and Angela, "Weren't you two on opposing sides of that sheriff case?"

"Indeed we were," said Angela. "Since then, though, we've teamed up. Our organization helped sponsor this event. I'll be describing what we're doing in a short talk on stage. Very short because I know people want to get to the music and poetry."

"I look forward to hearing about it. If your work saves one life, it's worth it," said David.

"Absolutely. My condolences on Adam." David thanked her. She spotted activity on the stage and said, "Well, it looks like the host is about to kick this off."

CHAPTER SIXTY-SIX

David, his family, and their friends found chairs, sat down, and looked at the stage. The host for the event introduced herself and welcomed everybody. She told the audience that she was a bereaved parent and had lost her daughter to fentanyl. She looked to be about fifty years old, with blonde hair that didn't quite reach her shoulders.

By now, the crowd was close to two hundred people. The host described what was planned for the next ninety minutes or so. Then she said, "This event is a tribute to the following people who lost their lives in this national epidemic." She began reading a list of names in alphabetical order – names that had been submitted by the event attendees.

After a few minutes, she reached surnames beginning with "H." Adam's name would be soon. David and Sharon put their arms around each other and listened.

"… Patrick Henderson … Maria Jimenez … Tomesha Kelley … Adam Lambert …"

His name hit them hard. Sharon gasped, and David tightened his mouth and eyelids to keep his pain inside.

The names finally stopped, and the host introduced Angela. She adjusted the height of the microphone to fit her five-foot-two frame. She made some comments about the severity of the epidemic and what we do to people with the disease – arresting them, incarcerating them, and giving them criminal records, which marginalizes them further.

"We've had a policy of maximizing harm to these people. Why? For any other disease, we try to cure it, and we try to minimize the harm. Why is it different for this disease?"

The audience cheered to indicate their agreement. She continued. "I know each of you has a horrible story. However, we need to not only cry about this situation, but we need to yell. Yes, we should feel sad. But dammit, we should also feel angry. This crisis has to be addressed. Talk to your members of Congress, talk to your county sheriffs, talk to anyone who will listen. Hell, talk to people who won't listen. Tell them that your sons, daughters, parents, friends, and loved ones weren't bad people. They had a bad disorder, and that we need to save them, not jail them! We need to treat them for their sickness, not arrest them!" The audience cheered more.

"I will say, though, that our country is making progress. Many states have passed Good Samaritan laws, so people can dial 911 in a medical emergency and not fear being arrested or getting the person for whom they're calling arrested." More applause.

"John Tylor and I have a mission to pass national legislation to force jails to stop discriminating. If a person suffers from substance use disorder and takes doctor-prescribed medicine for their disease, they must be allowed to receive that medicine while incarcerated – just like any other person. Two hundred jails have now agreed. That's better than a year ago, but it's less than four percent of the nation's jails. Our objective is to get that to one hundred percent. If we do, thousands of lives will be saved. We will get there." More applause.

"Anyway, you're not here to listen to me. You're here to listen to the heartfelt music and poetry that these lovely people have created. Thank you." Angela gave the microphone back to the host.

"Alright. It's time to hear from our performers!" said the host. "These are songs and poems that people wrote from their hearts and from the depths of their despair about this horrible epidemic. Remember, most of these people are not professional musicians or poets. They're people who had normal lives that were shattered. They're people who had normal loved ones who got sick. Some of them have the disease themselves. Tonight is about feelings. You'll hear mostly love, but also grief, guilt, perhaps some anger, and some hope."

She introduced the first performer – a boy about sixteen. He told the crowd that his older sister suffers from opioid use disorder. He said she was not at the event, and he hoped she would be alive when they got home. The song was about the fear the boy had of losing her, the torment the family was experiencing, and a plea for her to get better.

The second performer was an older woman who lost her fifteen-year-old grandson when he tried painkillers for the first time. Her poem was about the permanence of death and the pervasiveness of grief.

The host then introduced Camille. She walked on stage and sat at the keyboard facing the crowd. She spoke into the microphone, "Hello, I'm a recovering heroin addict."

The crowd applauded, showing appreciation for her courage to announce her affliction.

"I have two daughters. I wrote this song for them about a year ago. I sing it every day when I wake up." Camille performed the *Higher Power* song. Mia and Rosalie ran from their seats to Camille and hugged her tightly. She kissed them, and they returned, the happiest kids in the audience. The music was beautiful, and the audience was beholden.

"Thank you. I love you, Mia and Rosalie," she said over the microphone. She continued. "I lost a dear friend a year ago. Adam Lambert. Adam was close to many people. His father, David, has worked on putting his feelings into lyrics. My dear friend, Gabby Jones, helped him polish the words, and I put music to them."

The crowd applauded, probably at the prospect of hearing more music composed by Camille.

"David is not a singer, so Rodrigo and I will handle that. David, please step up and introduce the song."

David and Rodrigo walked to the stage. Rodrigo strapped his guitar around his shoulder, and David stepped in front of the microphone.

"We live near Terrace, and there is a busy road there called Granville Street. It's a beautiful street with nice clothing stores, fancy restaurants, and well-off people. But there are also addicts there trying to survive. Gabby herself almost died on Granville Street. My son called 911, even though, at the time, we didn't have Good Samaritan laws, and he was on probation. I wrote lyrics that I thought Adam might have written about the incident and about the state of this problem and the progress we're making. Here it is."

David stepped off the stage but stood close by to watch. Camille and Rodrigo played some opening chords then Camille sang.

"I took a summer walk
Down Granville Street last night
People shopping, people singing
People feeling quite alright
Most of them

Oh, the life on Granville Street
Many sides to Granville Street

I saw a woman walking
With a handbag and cool clothes
I saw a woman sitting
In a familiar unconscious pose
People saw her, and walked right past her
Years ago, I would have too
But not this time,
It's someone's life

Oh, the life on Granville Street
Many sides to Granville Street

Soon, the sirens came
To Granville Street last night
They came to save her, not to jail her
Seems this town has got it right
They saved a life
A precious life

Oh, the life on Granville Street
Many sides to every street"

The crowd applauded. David, Camille, and Rodrigo returned to the audience to rejoin their families and friends, most of whom were wiping tears.

David took his seat beside Sharon. She had brought a framed 8 x 10 picture of Adam. In it, Adam was sitting on the dock at the lake house. He was in his element and at peace. She and David held it together. They watched the remaining performances, appreciating the love of each other, their living children, and the people who had been closest to Adam.

DISCUSSION TOPICS

Enjoy discussing the following questions in your book club or study group. Add "Why?" at the end of each question.

1. Which character do you believe changes the most over the course of the book?
2. Do you believe it is appropriate to refer to addiction as a disease?
3. Do you believe people who suffer from substance use disorder face substantial prejudice?
4. What main ideas or themes did you take from the book?
5. Has the novel changed you in some way?
6. The scenes at Adam's lake house contain symbolism and metaphors for addiction. Did you spot them? Which was your favorite?
7. How realistic were the characters and the problems they faced?
8. Was the setting appropriate for the story, and does it reflect today's world?
9. Which passages or quotes did you enjoy the most?
10. What questions do you have for the author? Post them on www.louislamoureux.com, and he will answer them.

ABOUT THE AUTHOR

Louis Lamoureux, BMath, MBA, balances his time between his work as a software entrepreneur and his passion for writing. He knows the ravages of the opioid epidemic firsthand, having helped a loved one deal with an opioid addiction for several years before a fatal overdose. Louis immigrated to the USA from Canada in 1999 and lives in the Chicago suburbs with his family.

Connect with Louis on social media:
www.facebook.com/louisDlamoureux
www.twitter.com/louisDlamoureux

Or via his website:
www.louislamoureux.com